PEN(

MURDERER

A dizzying journey through a world of incompetence.

MIKE NAIVE

Copyright © 2021 Mike Naive

All rights reserved.

Cover photograph by
Hans-Jurgen Mager on Unsplash

ISBN: 9798712571567

This story and all names, characters and incidents portrayed are fictitious.

No penguins were harmed in the writing of this book.

Not even for research purposes.

Prologue	1
PART ONE - GOING THERE	2
A few mistakes	3
A naval tradition	17
There will be a next time	28
You are all my guests	38
Was Helen of Troy Greek?	49
Judge, jury and executioner	60
She's not imaginary	71
The American bird	83
What if she's me?	94
A proper bear hug	106
We're all penguin murderers	116
The best wig I've ever seen	128
PART TWO - COMING BACK?	138
I'll no-platform her	139
Two left thumbs	153
The size of a satsuma	165
Red all over	176
He's a big fan of genocide	188
It didn't mean anything	201
Awooga	213
One heavily armed lady	225
I'm going to name it after you	237
Happy days	249
Today, I don't care	259
Let's do this	270
Epilogue	280

Prologue

This story takes place in the very near future, on a world much like our own.

On this world, the surface is predominantly made up of water, polluted by plastics, with rising sea levels and shrinking polar ice caps. The last remaining animal species fight for space, driven closer by the expansion of cities and the destruction of their environment. Food can only be produced with the use of harmful pesticides and hormones which further pollutes the water supply.

Mental illness increases throughout the population due to environmental, social and economic factors. Diseases and infections spread uncontrolled, through densely concentrated populations, unaffected by outdated medicines. Experts and science are ignored and the truth no longer matters. In the shadow of all these things, some terrible decisions led to a terrible mistake and one woman took the blame.

This book has been written as a suicide note from all of us. I hope that wasn't too presumptuous?

PART ONE - GOING THERE

A few mistakes

Courtney Woodbeard was struggling to walk the short distance along the gangplank to board the polar research vessel, Somali Pirate Ship II. It was late evening, dark, and unseasonably cold, she had a heavy rucksack on her back and the wooden slats beneath her feet were frozen and slippery. She couldn't gain any traction, her feet slipped several times as she tried to advance, she was stuck half way along, clinging to the handrails to stop herself from sliding backwards. Everything was covered in a thin layer of ice and tiny icicles had formed beneath the handrails, icicles that snapped off and tumbled into the sea each time Courtney tried to move.

Courtney was well wrapped up against the cold, she had thick gloves on, they were warm, a bit too warm, her hands were clammy and sweaty. The scarf around her neck was pulled up to cover her mouth and her nose but that caused her glasses to mist up. Her eyes watered from the wind and the cold, tears ran down her cheeks, she was struggling to see, struggling to breathe, struggling to move, and it looked like she was crying.

Courtney was infamous, everyone in the world knew who she was, and if they didn't know her as Courtney Woodbeard then they knew her as The Penguin Murderer. A short while ago, Courtney was part of a well-intentioned expedition, put together to save the last few remaining polar bears on the planet, but things didn't exactly go to plan. There were some unintended consequences, some repercussions, and Courtney took most of the blame.

Courtney wondered whether boarding the ship was actually worth the effort, the physical and mental effort. She didn't want to be here, she didn't want to be on board this ship, she wanted to be at home, she wanted to wave a magic wand and make the last two years of her life disappear, she wanted to press a reset button and return to how it was before, she wanted to hide away and never speak to anyone, ever again. She was absolutely sure that no good would come from her boarding this ship. Part of her reluctance, her current anxiety, was due to the fact that she didn't know anyone else on board, and yet they all knew her and they all had reason to hate her.

Courtney's only contact with anyone from the UN team had been a couple of short telephone calls, one to persuade her that she had to be on this ship and one to confirm her travel arrangements. Courtney had flown from England alone, alone with her thoughts and her worries. She had spent twenty-seven hours in a blur of taxis, planes, airports, shuttle buses, more planes, more airports, more taxis, and every hour had been spent trying to think of a way to avoid getting on this ship. A feigned illness was top of her list of excuses but was dismissed due to the latest global pandemic. It wasn't a good idea to visit a hospital right now. A sudden family emergency was an option but she had no family. What if she just disappeared, what if she went missing for long enough that the ship left without her? A fake kidnapping, people get kidnapped all the time in South America, she told herself, even though it wasn't true. People would believe it, of course they would, just turn up after a few days, hide in a local hotel and say that her taxi was hijacked, or that she got lost, or maybe fake a robbery, she could hide all her things and come back for them later. She was definitely not thinking straight.

Courtney looked down at the gangplank and slowly inched her way towards the ship, she could just about see the white of the waves below her feet, as the black sea lapped against the ship's hull, not that she could see much of anything through the tears, or through the mist and the rain on her glasses. Maybe I should just jump in, she thought, maybe it's time to put an end to this, but, before she could throw herself into he sea, she was snapped back to reality by the sound of a voice up ahead.

"Welcome," someone shouted, "you made it?"

Stupid question, thought Courtney, as she looked up to see who was talking, she could see boots and legs, clad in green corduroy trousers, hardly ideal for these conditions. They were sturdy, the boots, not the legs. She struggled to see anything above knee height so she hauled herself up the last few metres until she stood at the end of the gangplank, level with where the voice had come from. In front of her stood a man who had obviously just come out into the cold to greet her. He was slightly taller than Courtney and older, mid to late fifties. His hood was pulled up over his head, although his jacket wasn't zipped up, the fleece around the hood was being buffeted by the wind and obscured most of his face. He stepped forward and wrapped his arms around Courtney, holding her tightly, his head next to hers, the hoods of their jackets pressed close together and he spoke to her in a soft, warm voice, barely audible above the wind and the icy rain.

"It's so good to see you again," he said.

Alain Govenor released Courtney and stepped back, he tried to remove his hood with a flick of his head but it wouldn't budge so he moved it with his hands, revealing his face to Courtney. He was light skinned, although his cheeks and face were flushed red from the exposure to the cold and the wind. He had a rugged face, craggy and worn, the face of an explorer, an adventurer, a man who spent every minute of his life clinging to a mountain side, sailing the Atlantic, or hacking at undergrowth with a machete. He was clean shaven, although a beard or a moustache, or a combination of the two, wouldn't have looked out of place. His hands were gloved against the cold, but, if you could have seen his hands, you would have realised that Alain was no action man, he was no daredevil explorer, he had the hands of an administrator, an academic, a desk jockey, perfect nails and skin, save for the odd paper cut. These weren't the hands of a swashbuckler, these were the hands of a man who paid someone else to mow his lawn. No euphemism intended.

It took Courtney a split second to register who it was. It couldn't be, she thought, not after all this time. Alain's face was familiar, although older, much older, and some of the sparkle had gone from his eyes, he looked tired and sad, but he looked pleased to see her, at least that was a good thing.

"What the fuck are you doing here?" Courtney asked bluntly, in response to Alain's warm, friendly welcome.

"Come inside, come on, we'll talk in here," said Alain, as he turned to lead Courtney through the door and into the corridor, "it's been a long time, how are you?"

Courtney stepped inside, out of the wind and the rain, and she noticed how much quieter it was once, she was in the shelter of the ship. She removed her hood, revealing her blondish hair, her dark roots and the first sign of some premature grey. She pulled the scarf from her face and looked at her old university lecturer, Alain Govenor, standing in front of her with a grin plastered across his face. He'd always looked smug, he had the resting face of a man who thought himself superior, but Courtney had never seen him looking quite this pleased with himself. The last time they had seen each other was shortly after Courtney graduated from the University of Middle England. They had a brief relationship in her second year at university, although Alain seemed to have had a brief relationship with most of the young women he taught.

"What on earth are you doing here, Alain?" she asked him again.

"I bet you didn't expect to see me, did you?" asked Alain. "I came to see you, I thought you could use some moral support, it's really great to see you again, Courtney, you look fantastic."

He was lying of course. She looked tired, emotional and exhausted. She looked like she had been crying for two days, she looked like she had been forced to fly halfway round the world, against her will, and against her better judgement.

"Come on," said Alain, "I'll show you round, you're in a cabin along here, next door to mine."

Alain turned and walked along the corridor, steadying himself to cope with the uneven floor, caused by the ship listing slightly to one side. The walls of the corridor were light grey and the rust and rivets, that were holding the ship together, were coated in layer upon layer of paint but you could still make out the rust and you could still make out the rivets, through the paint. Courtney followed closely behind Alain, trying to work out why he was there. He was the last person she expected to see when she arrived, well, maybe not the last person, but in the top ten at least.

They rounded another corner and Courtney could clearly see which cabin was hers. It wasn't like all the other cabins, they didn't have the words, 'Penguin Murderrer,' crudely painted across the door and the wall in foot high, dark red letters. It had been painted in haste and was misspelt. The excess paint had run and dried as it dripped down the wall and spots of paint speckled the door handle and the floor. If Alain or Courtney had looked up, and looked closely enough, they would have seen more paint on the ceiling where it splattered off the brush as the enthusiastic artist raced to finish. There was an odour of fresh paint in the corridor, whoever had done it had known that Courtney was arriving today and they wanted to welcome her on board.

Courtney felt sick, she put her left hand up on the wall for support. There was an ache in the pit of her stomach that had been there, on and off, since finding out she was going to Antarctica and it flared up again. She felt cold, she shivered, she was giddy, her legs were about to give way beneath her. She forced herself to stand up straight, she shut her eyes and took a deep breath.

"Shall we go in?" asked Alain as he pushed open the door. "I promise you, it looks much better from inside."

Alain smiled and looked at Courtney, she looked pale, like she'd seen a ghost. He was worried about her and keen to get her away from the graffiti, that seemed to be having such a negative affect on her, so he placed his hand on her back and half guided, half pushed her into the cabin.

"I'll speak to the ship's Captain about getting that cleaned off, don't worry about it, it'll be gone in the morning," said Alain, "I'll see to it. Trust me. Sit down on the bed, I'll get you a glass of water."

Alain tried to stay calm and remember his first aid training. What to do if someone faints? Don't panic, he thought, don't panic. Lie her down, check her breathing and loosen her clothing.

Courtney dropped her rucksack onto the floor and then she sat on the edge of the bed and took in her surroundings. Her cabin looked and smelt clean, although it was a bit spartan. There was a light above the bed and a single ceiling light illuminating the room, the walls were painted the same shade of grey as the corridor outside. There was a bed and a small table, both of which appeared to be fixed to the wall. The bed was topped by a blue and red blanket that looked scratchy and rough and there was one pillow on the bed, encased in a white pillow case that had seen better days. There was some built-in storage and a small dressing table, positioned beneath a wall mounted mirror, Courtney glanced at the mirror just long enough to establish that it was firmly fixed to the wall and couldn't be removed. Even in the roughest of seas it looked like nothing would move, except maybe the chair and Courtney herself. There was another door in the cabin, that Courtney correctly assumed would lead to the bathroom, and a pair of porthole style windows that were currently closed and bolted against the elements.

Alain was very excited and very pleased to see Courtney. It had been fifteen or sixteen years since they had last met. He had followed her career from afar, much as he had done with all his former students, former conquests. He had cut out and kept the newspaper front page, featuring a photograph of Courtney in full arctic gear, wearing a white, hooded jacket and mirrored goggles, with a few strands of her blonde hair peeking out between her pale face and the hood. The photograph captured Courtney stood with one foot on top of a sedated polar bear, in the style of a victorian explorer, rifle in hand. She hadn't fired the shot that took down the bear, nor was she the only person to have their photograph taken that day, in that pose, but it was her photograph that they published, her face that they used, her name that they vilified. Alain had folded over the top of the newspaper, to hide the, 'Penguin Murderer,' headline, and pinned it to the wall of his home office.

The picture was taken almost two years ago, towards the end of Operation Polar Saviour, an attempt by the Senior Director for Climate Action at the United Nations to save the last few remaining polar bears by capturing, sedating, and transporting them from what remained of the Arctic to what remained of the Antarctic. The move was widely supported by the Arctic nations, especially Canada and Russia, who were only too happy to provide the funding to rid themselves of what had become an expensive problem.

There were many video recordings available of polar bears in populated areas, rummaging through bins for food, but a photograph by acclaimed wildlife photographer, Matteo Kwesi, caught the world's attention and went viral. It was first published in Italy, and showed an emaciated polar bear clinging to a piece of ice that was too small to climb on to but just large enough to keep the bear afloat. There were three other people on the small boat that day, when the photograph was taken, and the whole scene was filmed on a mobile phone, Italian voices could be heard in the background, their frustrations clear as they passionately argued about whether to continue filming, whether they should throw a rope for the bear to grab onto, or whether they should shoot the bear to end its suffering. The photographs and the mobile phone footage captured the world's attention and accelerated calls for action. It wasn't the plight of the polar bear that caused the most distress, it was the sound of people watching and arguing about whether they should step in and help, while a once strong animal desperately tried to save its own life.

There were estimated to be fewer than three hundred polar bears at the time the UN announced Operation Polar Saviour. A team of climate scientists, biologists, animal welfare experts, special forces, air transport teams, vets and many more was assembled and despatched to round up and deport the bears from what remained of the Arctic ice and from the remote northern towns they had sought to occupy. In the end, the expedition team found fewer than one hundred bears.

Courtney was a valued member of Operation Polar Saviour, she was, after all, an expert in her field, having spent over five years as Head of Polar Operations at an international wildlife charity, but her role in Operation Polar Saviour wasn't an important one, she wasn't leading, or managing the project, she was just there to take part, to do her bit to help. Despite this lack of importance, Courtney had been summoned to travel to Antarctica again to investigate satellite images that appeared to show a penguin massacre at the hands, and teeth, of the relocated polar bears.

Alain put a glass of water on the table next to the bed and he noted that the colour had started to return to Courtney's face. She was in the process of removing all her outer garments, waterproof over trousers, gloves, hood, coat, scarf, snood, boots, jumper, another jumper and finally she began to look, and feel, slightly better. She was still confused by Alain's presence. What was he doing here? She took a sip of water and looked up at Alain. What did I used to see in him? she wondered to herself, it's so long ago I can barely remember anymore. He used to be attentive and paid me compliments, he was always handing out little gifts, or loving words. Whatever I saw in him all those years ago, it's not there anymore, she thought as she stared at the sad old man stood in front of her.

"Seriously, what the fuck are you doing here, Alain?" Courtney asked again, her frustration clear in the tone of her voice.

Alain looked round for somewhere to sit before he pulled a wooden chair away from its position against the wall. He dragged it towards the middle of the room and sat down facing Courtney. He had briefly considered spinning the chair round and sitting Christine Keeler style, with his arms resting on the back of the chair but he knew it would play havoc with his hips. Sitting with his legs so far apart had become painfully uncomfortable in recent years, so he chose to sit down in a sensible manner.

Hearing Courtney swear at him brought back fond memories of their time together. He could remember how she looked when she was at university, he could remember how she felt in his arms, the smell of her hair, the taste of her lips, but he had forgotten the swearing, the constant swearing, until this moment in time, and it made him smile.

Alain had always found young people attractive, not too young mind. He had treated it as a perk of the job as a university lecturer, one of few perks. He often wondered if it was a substitute for his own, sorely missed, youth, he felt younger around young people, their enthusiasm, their ideas, their liveliness, seemed to rub off on him, although now, these days, he was starting to feel old around young people. He suspected that he found young people attractive simply because they were young, he told himself that looks didn't matter but they did really.

"You want to know why I'm here?" Alain asked. "Well, I'm the ship's doctor."

He said it much louder than he had intended, as if it was a boast, something to be proud of, something to be shouted from the rooftops. He laughed as if he was sharing the funniest thing in the world with someone. Me, the ship's doctor, who'd have thunk it?

"But you're not a doctor, not a medical one," said Courtney, "at least you weren't when I knew you."

"I know, it's crazy, right?" said Alain, who was unable to wipe the grin off his face. "I heard you were going to be part of this mission, this project, this, er, whatever it is, so I spoke to Graham Murky, you remember Graham, the University Chancellor, or maybe he was there after you left, anyway, he knew a friend of the ship's owner and he put me in touch with them and told them that I'd like to get on board. He wrote a letter of recommendation and that's how I ended up here. I'll admit that there might have been a smidge of confusion on their part, I was a bit surprised when I found out I was to be the ship's doctor and I did think of saying something, but..."

"But you're not a doctor. How can you be the ship's doctor?" protested Courtney. "What's your doctorate in, Alain, climate studies or something?"

"Don't worry. It's not what you know, it's who you know," said Alain with confidence, "I've done some first aid training, it was a few years ago I'll admit, but I've got a medical app on my phone to help with diagnostics, I've got a cupboard full of pills and I'm sure there will be another doctor on the ship as part of the expedition team, so everything's okay, no need for you to worry about me. I've been here over a day already and I've treated two patients and they're both still alive."

Courtney's head was spinning. She had been preparing herself for worst case scenarios, going over and over in her head all the things that could go wrong but she hadn't come close to imagining this.

"Why are you even here, why are you not at the university?" she asked.

"Well, it's long story," said Alain, his mouth suddenly dry and his smile gone. He swallowed and stared down at his feet, unable to look Courtney in the eye.

"I was let go by the university, there were a few complaints and an official investigation and it was decided I should take early retirement. I'm pretty sure I won't work at another university after all the publicity, it was only the local papers, thank God, not the nationals but, still, most employers are going to look me up and there it is, top of the page, my shame. A twenty-five year career ruined by a few mistakes."

"A few mistakes?" snapped Courtney. Alain was starting to irritate her and she'd only been in his company a few minutes. "A few mistakes? You made a few mistakes with the girls on my course when I was there, including me. Spread that out over twenty-five years and it's more than a few, it's more like hundreds. Did your wife find out? I assume she left you, did she? Or did she stand by you, then sneak out the door a few months later on her own terms?"

Alain still couldn't look Courtney in the eye. He thought that, of all people, she'd understand, or maybe even sympathise. He felt foolish, why would she understand, why would she sympathise, why would she be any different from everyone else? They hadn't seen each other for years. He had stared at her picture, on his office wall, for so long that he'd convinced himself that she was the only one who understood him, that she'd tell him it was going to be all right, she'd stroke his hair, pat his cheek and tell him it was all okay, like she used to do when they were together.

"She left me years ago," said Alain as he unsuccessfully tried to squeeze out a tear or two for sympathy. He raised his head to look at Courtney, who was sat just a few feet in front of him. She looked seriously unhappy with him. It looked like he would have to work hard to gain back her trust and respect.

"She found out well before the university did," said Alain, "she left me and took Colin with her, we're divorced now."

"Colin, your son?" asked Courtney.

"No, Colin was our dachshund," said Alain, by way of clarification, "Charlie had already moved out by then to go to university. I took a long hard look at myself, at what I was doing, hanging around with girls half my age, I was an idiot, so I stopped. I started dating women my own age."

Alain laughed out loud at the thought of dating women his own age, at how absurd it was, to him at least.

"I hadn't dated a student for years when they started investigating me, the complaints were from ages ago. Did you get a letter?" asked Alain.

Courtney didn't respond and Alain barely paused before continuing.

"They wrote to all my old students. Anyway, I've changed, I even went to a self help group once, for sex addicts. I made a mistake, a lot of mistakes, I'm not asking for anything from you, I'm not asking for forgiveness. I just thought it would be nice to see you again, I thought you were the one person who didn't hate me but I'm not so sure now."

"This isn't how normal people behave," said Courtney, "normal people don't get in touch with someone they haven't seen for years by getting a job as a fake doctor on a research vessel going to Antarctica."

"Please don't hate me," said Alain, who was getting concerned that this wasn't quite going to plan, although it wasn't much of a plan. No thought had been given to how Courtney would react when she saw him, he had assumed that she would be delighted. He wasn't exactly sure what had driven him to come here in the first place, it wasn't to rekindle old flames, heaven forbid, it was more about seeking out someone who was there the last time he was happy. It was a long time since he'd been happy.

"I don't hate you," said Courtney, and she didn't. She also didn't pity him either. "It's me everyone hates," said Courtney, "I don't know about all the people on this ship but at least one of them hates me enough to paint, 'penguin murderer,' on the wall of my cabin. Do you think I could swap cabins with someone? Do you know the captain, could you ask for me?"

"I'll speak to her but who in their right mind would want to swap into a cabin with, 'penguin murderer,' painted outside?" asked Alain, trying unsuccessfully to lighten the mood. "Don't worry. I'll speak to the captain and get it cleaned off, or painted over. I'll sort it," said Alain as he stood up to leave, "you must be exhausted, I'll speak to you tomorrow. Shall I see you in the morning? I'll come and take you to breakfast and show you around the ship."

"I'm sorry by the way," added Alain as an afterthought.

"Sorry about what?" queried Courtney.

"About how you've been treated by people, in the papers and whatnot. It's not your fault. I know you were there but it doesn't make it your fault. It doesn't make you responsible. I just wanted you to know that I don't hold you responsible."

"Thank you, Alain," said Courtney, "it's nice to see you again."

She meant it, although she was still confused as to how or why he was on the ship.

After he left, Courtney stood up and walked over to the door and locked it. She removed an old newspaper from her rucksack along with some scissors and tape. She cut the newspaper to the approximate size she wanted and picked up the tape. She spent several minutes trying to find the end of the tape, turning it round in her hand, then, once she had found the end, she pulled off a long strip and cut it into four pieces and attached a piece of tape to each corner of the newspaper. She walked across the room to the mirror on the wall and then, without looking at the mirror, which is easier said than done, she placed the newspaper over it, covering the glass completely and she pressed the tape against the wall, running her finger across the tape to smooth it down and make sure it stuck.

Next, she opened the door to the bathroom and glanced inside, it was small but adequate, it had a shower, toilet and sink, probably small enough to use all three at the same time. Having caught a glimpse of the mirror above the sink, she returned to her rucksack and repeated the process, cutting a newspaper to the approximate size, taping the corners and returning to the bathroom to secure it over the mirror. After smoothing down the tape at the corners, she cut four more pieces of tape and reinforced the sides.

"And relax," said Courtney, out loud, as she threw the scissors and tape onto the bed. Let's go explore, she thought, rubbing her hands together like an excited child.

Courtney quickly put her boots back on and pulled a jumper on over her head before she opened the cabin door and made her way out into the corridor.

A naval tradition

Somali Pirate Ship II had originally been a Soviet ice breaking ship and was designed, primarily, to keep shipping lanes free of Arctic sea ice. It was not designed to carry passengers. It was refurbished for the first time about thirty years ago when it was converted for use as a polar research vessel and then, more recently, it was refurbished again when it entered private hands, after being sold at auction. The interior layout had undergone considerable changes over the years and now featured a passenger deck of small cabins connected by endless corridors.

The cabins on the outside received some natural light through the small porthole style windows but the interior cabins were lit only by artificial light and the lack of fresh air, or any sort of view, led them to be considered second class accommodation, especially the ones set up for four to six people, sleeping in bunk beds. Courtney was in first class but, having not seen any other cabins, she wouldn't have known it, and, from the basic nature of the room, I doubt whether anyone would have described it as first class, especially someone as indifferent as Courtney Woodbeard.

Despite Alain's offer to show Courtney round the ship in the morning, she intended to spend some time wandering the ship now, just to get her bearings and to find out where all the mirrors were. Courtney was tired but she had slept on and off all the way here, snatching whatever sleep she could get along the way, and she was sure she could manage to stay awake for another hour or so.

Courtney looked at the graffiti painted across the door of her cabin. Someone on this ship really hates me, she thought, before she turned her back on the problem and decided which direction to go in. From her cabin she went towards the bow of the ship, although the corridor didn't go far before it turned to the right. There was no natural light in the corridor that ran between the inner and outer cabins and the electric lights were dimmed slightly, due to the late hour, giving the corridor a more closed in and claustrophobic feel. The ship was silent and Courtney looked up and down the corridor, listening to see if anyone else was around.

She walked past closed cabin doors and wondered, who was inside? Were they even occupied? She thought about pressing her ear to one of the cabin doors to see if she could hear anything. Surely everyone would be asleep at this time of night? She reached out her arms and ran her fingertips along the walls as she walked, she was easily able to touch both walls at the same time. The walls felt cold and, if the air in the corridor had been just a few degrees colder, she would have been able to see her own breath. She shivered but wasn't sure what had caused it, it wasn't the cold, it wasn't that kind of shiver. Courtney stopped and looked behind her, there was no one there, she waited a second, still no one coming, a few seconds more, she listened hard, still no one there. Reassured, she continued along the corridor.

Courtney was being followed. As she wandered the ship, she was being watched by someone, always out of sight, always watching, although she couldn't possible be aware of it, unless she had a sixth sense, which she didn't. She didn't even believe in the notion of a sixth sense and, even though she had personal experience of the supernatural and the unexplained, she firmly rejected the idea. She was in the skeptic camp when it came to ghosts, pixies or angels. Or unicorns for that matter. All her movements were being scrutinised by an unseen watcher, someone else unable to sleep, although not for the same reason as Courtney.

Courtney was walking as quietly as she possibly could, not wanting to be discovered, she took careful, light steps, testing the floor beneath her feet before shifting her weight. Although she was doing nothing wrong, she didn't want to bump into someone. It doesn't create the best first impression if you meet someone while silently creeping around at night, whatever your motives. She felt on edge. It was so quiet, her heart raced at the slightest nose, the slightest creak from the ship's hull. She kept having to remind herself to breathe.

The next corridor led to another corridor that was full of closed doors. There were a few exterior doors along the way, at regular intervals, leading out onto the deck, clearly marked by exit signs in both English and what Courtney assumed was Mandarin. This whole deck appeared to be just passenger accommodation, she would have to go up or down to explore further. She found the stairs to the deck above, they were steep, wooden and worn and each tread creaked loudly under her weight. The noise from the stairs broke the tension, she breathed and relaxed. There was no way she could climb the stairs silently so she made her way up as quickly as she could.

She was still being watched.

On the next floor, the rooms all appeared to have a more practical purpose, signs on the doors indicated their use, or warned about their contents. Yellow and black warning triangles. Red circles cautioning against entry. Warnings about dangerous contents. Flammable. Poisonous.

The corridors were similar to those downstairs although painted a slightly different colour, more green than grey. There was a slight humming noise from further along the corridor, back towards the stern of the ship. An electrical hum, along with a change in the light in the corridor. Courtney walked towards the light and turned the corner. She was faced with more corridors and more doors. What did she expect?

One door was slightly open and there was a low humming noise and a bright light coming through the crack in the door, lighting up the otherwise silent, dim corridor. The sign on the door read, 'Communications,' and it seemed to contain the only other living person on the ship.

Courtney knocked on the door and opened it, all in one movement. Inside was sat a young man with his back to her, in front of him on a large desk was an array of electrical equipment and monitors, several keyboards and mice, a soldering iron and various other tools that Courtney didn't recognise.

"Hello," said Courtney.

The man at the desk swivelled his chair round to face her and responded with a simple, "Hello," of his own, although, to Courtney's ears, it sounded less like a hello and more like a who are you, what are you doing here?

"I was just passing and I saw your light on," Courtney replied, although the questioned had never been asked, "you seem to be the only person still up and I couldn't sleep."

"Come in," he said, flashing his best smile, turning on the charm, "I'm always glad of the company."

His accent sounded North American to Courtney, either American or Canadian, she wasn't quite sure which. She took a good look at him as she sat down, he was in his mid twenties, quite good looking, closely cropped hair, dark brown skin, brown eyes, long eyelashes. He's got a very nice smile, thought Courtney.

"Do you want a drink?" he asked, as he leaned backwards and reached into the desk drawer. He pulled out a half-full spirit bottle and two glasses and put them on the desk between them. He poured a small amount into each glass and handed one to Courtney.

"What is it?" she asked.

"Dark rum. We get given a bottle a day to drink. It's a naval tradition."

"Really?" she asked, before she realised that he was making fun of her

"No, not really. I got it at the airport on the way here," he said, smiling at his own joke.

He's got a nice smile, nice eyes, where's he been all my life, thought Courtney.

"What do you do?" she asked. "Why are you the only person awake?"

"Well, firstly, I doubt I'm the only one awake and secondly, as it says on the door, this is the Communications Room and that's what I do. I communicate."

"And what are you doing at the moment?"

"Communicating with you."

"But what are you, I mean, what do you do? What's your job title?"

"I work for Hanad Said, he owns this ship. I'm his Communication Manager, it's not a real management job, not like a suit and tie thing. I keep all his personal communications equipment in order as he needs constant communication. That's his thing, constant communication. Constant communication."

He banged his right fist into his left palm as he said it again.

"Constant Communication. I do other stuff as well, I fly the drones, I sit up late at night drinking. It's not my real job though. None of this is my real job. My real job is much more exciting, I just can't talk about it."

Courtney chose to ignore the hint about an exciting secret life. He seemed very keen that she ask him about it and, for that reason, it that was the last thing she was going to do.

"So you're not part of the ship then, not part of the crew?" asked Courtney.

"No, I'm part of Mr Said's personal team, there's only a few of us so we double up as bodyguards, drivers, that sort of thing. The ship has it's own communications equipment, obviously, but I'm here as a sort of back up for Mr Said's personal use. Most of the technology we use is way more advanced than what's already on the ship."

As he was talking to Courtney, something triggered a thought, a memory, a lightbulb came on and suddenly he remembered who she was, who he was talking to.

"I know you, don't I?" he asked. "You're the penguin lady?"

"I prefer Courtney, Courtney Woodbeard, and you are?"

"Lester, Lester Cherry-Stone," he said, mimicking her, "it's hyphenated you know, not one word."

"What is?"

"Cherry-Stone. It's like two words with a hyphen, not like the stone you get in a cherry. My parents couldn't agree on anything, my dad wanted his name first, so I could have been Lester Stone-Cherry, but my mom made him see sense, eventually."

"Mmm, okay," said Courtney, impressed by his easy charm, although he did seem quite drunk. Had he been drinking before she arrived?

The rum warmed Courtney's mouth and throat. Given a choice, she'd rather not be drinking it neat but there was no sign of any mixers anywhere in the room, or any ice, or lime, or mint, all the things that would have helped to take the edge off. She would just have to drink it through gritted teeth, if that was even possible.

Lester had no problem drinking it neat, he'd got used to it a long time ago and he didn't really function very well without a certain amount of alcohol in his system. He drank for many reasons, some more serious than others. Tonight he was drinking because that's what he does. He drinks.

Lester knew Courtney was going to be on the ship, everyone did, but it was still a surprise to meet her, to be sat so close to her like this. She seemed almost normal, not the monster he had imagined. She didn't look like a penguin murderer, but what does a penguin murderer look like? She looked quite average, fairly attractive, around forty years old, with collar length, dyed blond hair, a straight fringe, and glasses. Lester thought that she came across as too serious, humourless perhaps, but not evil.

He was still a little disappointed that she hadn't asked him about his secret job, his job as a spy. He was desperate to tell someone about it, he kept dropping hints but no one questioned him about it. Only he wasn't a spy, not really. He was more like an asset, an informant, an amateur. He didn't really know who he was working for, they told him they were Americans but he had his doubts.

They definitely weren't Americans.

He supplied them with information about his employer, Hanad Said. Where he went, who he met, what he was doing, and he received irregular payment in cash, no questions answered.

He knew of Courtney Woodbeard from the news, everyone did. She was one of the people famous for the ill-fated, polar bear rescue mission.

Lester no longer remembered that public opinion had been strongly in favour of some kind of intervention, that something drastic had to be done. Slowly, public opinion changed, nothing specific, no single event that swung opinion one way or the other, just a slow drift, until people started to suggest that maybe, just maybe, it was too much. Too much interference, we were meddling with something we didn't fully understand. We told ourselves that we didn't know what the consequences would be, but people did understand the consequences, people had been studying the ethics, the methodology and the outcomes of interfering with nature for years. The scientists who studied it, they ran simulations, they observed species in their natural habitat, but their opinions were largely ignored, their voices unheard outside their echo chamber of scientific journals and papers.

Now, the only thing the public remembered was that it was a bad idea, badly executed, and someone had to take the blame.

"You killed all the penguins then?" asked Lester, instantly regretting his bluntness when he saw the distress in Courtney's face. "Sorry, I didn't mean to..."

"It's okay," replied Courtney, "yes, I killed them all. With my bare hands. Bear hands. Do you see?" she asked, holding her hands up like bear claws, but Lester didn't get it.

"Is it true?" he asked. "Are they all dead?"

"We don't know, that's why we're going there, to have a closer look, to see what really happened. The satellite images suggest there's been a problem, I mean, they're detailed enough to enable us to count the number of penguins in a colony but we can't tell from satellite images if they're alive or dead. The reddish colour of the ice is a worrying sign but we won't know until we get there. It's not my fault you know. I tried to talk them out of it but they wouldn't listen."

She held her empty glass out for a refill and Lester obliged, pouring himself a much larger top up at the same time.

"This is nice, thank you," she said, and she meant it, not about the drink, but about the warm welcome.

Courtney was familiar with hostility from strangers, it had become the norm, she wasn't used to people talking to her in a friendly way, offering her drinks, joking with her. If he calls me a penguin murderer under his breath, when I get up to leave, then I'm going to cry, she thought, almost welling up at the thought of it.

"Where have you been all my life?" she asked, rhetorically, not expecting an answer.

"Military academy, special forces, Iraq, Syria, Libya, got injured, got PTSD, got dismissed, got some close protection work with the help of a veterans charity and now this. I doubt our paths would have crossed before now," he said, giving her far too much information. If only she would ask me about my real job, he thought. He willed her to ask him about being a spy but she wouldn't play the game.

"Oh," said Courtney, "my father was in the army as well. He was in the Falklands, have you heard of it?"

"I heard of it. So you're not the first person in your family to kill a penguin then?" asked Lester, teasing her some more.

"Sheep."

"What?" asked Lester, confused.

"Sheep. They killed sheep in the Falklands. Not penguins. For the meat."

"Well, I didn't think they killed them for the wool."

They both laughed.

"Do you know when we sail?" Courtney asked.

"It'll be a few hours yet. I think we're still waiting for a couple of people, but they're on their way from the airport now so we should be on schedule. Should take us a couple of days to get there, depending on the weather, the sea ice, although the ice shouldn't be too much of a problem this time of year."

"You sound like an expert?" said Courtney, half flattering, half teasing him.

"Oh, I do a security assessment for Mr Said before he goes anywhere, so I've done my research. You've been there before, obviously."

"Oh yeah. You don't get to kill penguins without going to Antarctica a few times," she joked, "unless you can get access to them in a zoo, which I can't, and I haven't tried to either. Not that they'd let me."

Courtney finished her drink in one swig and instantly regretted it. It took two gulps to get it down and it left her throat on fire but the heat soon faded.

"What else is there for me to explore on board?" asked Courtney.

"Well, there's the cabins below, but I guess you've already seen those, there's a galley and a mess, a canteen on this deck and the bridge is upstairs at the front. You should get some sleep though. It's much easier to get to sleep when we're not moving."

"Will do," said Courtney as she stood up to leave, "you ain't seen me right," she added, jokingly, as she walked towards the door.

"Right," said Lester, but he was unsure what Courtney meant. If she wants me to pretend I've never met her, the next time we meet, then I can do that, he thought, I can use some of my spy craft.

Courtney was glad to get out of the Communications Room. All the equipment in the room made it very hot and she had to remove her jumper to cool down, once she was back in the corridor. Her glasses got caught up in the jumper as she pulled it over her head and they came off her face but, after a bit of a struggle, Courtney managed to retrieve her glasses from inside the jumper and put them back on her nose. She carried the jumper in one hand as she continued to explore the ship.

Whoever was watching Courtney, before she got to the Communications Room, was still watching her now. Out of sight, following her, constantly watching.

The rest of the deck was pretty much as Lester had described, there were lights in the galley and, up close, Courtney could hear voices and the sound of food being prepared. The canteen was in darkness and she couldn't find a light switch. She could make out the shapes of tables and chairs in the dim light but not much else.

She assumed that there were mirrors in the toilets on each deck, but she didn't check. She knew they weren't called toilets on a ship but she couldn't remember, at this precise moment, what they were actually called, not that it mattered. Like any normal person, she had always thought that the toilets on a ship were on the poop deck. It's a common misassumption among most people, like thinking that Billericay is in Ireland, or that Skegness is in Scotland.

She thought she would put off visiting the bridge until she had a reason to go there, leave the outside deck until daylight, and avoid the lower decks and engine room altogether. She couldn't shake the feeling that she was being watched and she knew that no good would come from going down a few decks to poke about in the dark.

A combination of the rum and the hours spent travelling were beginning to take their toll on Courtney, she was feeling very tired all of a sudden so she made her way back down to her cabin.

Courtney didn't see, or hear, anyone else on the way back, although Emily was only ever a short distance away, watching and listening, always just out of sight.

There will be a next time

Alain Govenor woke early, in a cabin almost identical to Courtney's. He had been on the ship for about thirty-six hours now, long enough to attach a handwritten sign to the door of the doctor's surgery that read, 'Open 10am - 12pm.' That gave him enough time for a lie in before breakfast, if he was being lazy, and enough time to get to the canteen for lunch. He planned to call on Courtney later and show her around the ship, he had already got to know most of the crew and some of the expedition team, the last of which had arrived very late the previous evening. The ship was due to sail any time now so he knew the captain would be on the bridge, or in her cabin, so it was a good time to go and see her, to see if he could help Courtney by getting the graffiti painted over.

Alain liked Courtney and wanted to do this for her, he also knew it might soften her attitude towards him and maybe help her forget his numerous indiscretions.

Alain had packed clothes that he thought a doctor might wear, because he wanted to look the part, including a tweed suit, some brightly coloured braces and a bow tie but today didn't seem like a bow tie sort of day. In hindsight, in the cold light of day, Alain realised that the bow tie was a waste of money as he would never wear it. I should throw it away, he thought, maybe I should just open the porthole right now and throw it out. Every time I look at it, it will taunt me and remind me of the thirty quid I'll never get back, it's just a yellow and pink reminder of my own stupidity.

He was being harsh on himself. It wasn't a bad bow tie but, having gone fifty years without wearing one except for very special occasions, it was a bit late in life for such a dramatic, sartorial make over.

Alain pushed the bow tie right down to the bottom of his bag, a bag that still contained most of his clothes. The thought of unpacking had never even crossed his mind. I'll throw it away some other time, he thought and then he decided he would dress up as Doctor Alain a little later, after breakfast maybe, no need to do it just yet. He picked up the clothes he had worn yesterday, from where he had thrown them, and he quickly put them on and left his cabin. He was still pulling on the sleeves, straightening his trousers and doing up his fly as he walked along the corridor. Every now and then he would pass a ceiling light that had either failed completely, or was flickering, shouting it's last screams of light before dying.

Alain walked towards the bow of the ship and climbed two flights of wooden stairs to the bridge. They were steep stairs, the treads were noisy and worn and he needed to hold the handrails and pull with his arms as he made his way up, so he was slightly out of breath when he got to the top. The view from the bridge was spectacular, as would be expected. The large, wide windows gave an almost one hundred and eighty degree view out towards, and beyond, the bow of the ship, and off to port and starboard. I wonder which side is which, thought Alain.

"Good Morning, Doctor," said Sander Alexanderson, Chief Officer of the Somali Pirate Ship II, "everything okay?"

Sander was about five feet, six inches tall, Scandinavian looking, early twenties, stubbly beard, balding but with blonde hair, tufted and pulled up from his scalp, designed to give the impression that he was a bit mad, a bit eccentric, but that was far from being the case. Alain had found Sander to be extremely helpful since he arrived on the ship and he gave no impression of tiring at Alain's constant questions. So far, he had been Alain's only contact with senior crew, Alain hadn't had the opportunity to meet the captain until now. Several other crew members were making themselves look busy on the bridge, although it appeared that someone had just made everyone tea, as they all had mugs in front of them, still piping hot, still giving off steam. One of them's drinking fruit tea, thought Alain, as he caught the scent of red berries over the background smell of diesel fuel.

"Sander, my friend," began Alain, "I have a favour to ask, it's to do with the graffiti on Miss Woodbeard's cabin door, she's an old friend of mine and..."

"Look, I'll stop you there," interrupted Sander, "I would like to help you but you need to speak to the captain about this. I don't want to get involved. She's in her cabin back there," he said, gesturing to a door at the rear of the bridge, "I've not seen her since yesterday morning so I don't know what state she's in but you can knock and see if she'll talk to you. Do you want my advice though?"

"Always, Sander, always," replied Alain.

"Don't knock on that door. Don't go into that cabin. And most importantly," he said, as he paused for effect, "don't mention the graffiti to her because I know what her reaction is going to be."

"Do you think she knows who did it?" asked Alain.

"Oh, she knows," came the confident reply.

"Thank you, Sander," said Alain. He took a deep breath. It was now or never, don't stop and think about it or you'll never do it. What would I say to Courtney if I didn't do this one small thing for her? he thought. I have to find out who painted the graffiti and I'm sure the captain knows who it was. I have to get the graffiti cleaned off, for Courtney, and the captain is my best hope to get that done.

Alain started to move towards the cabin door and, in just a few steps, his hand was raised and he was knocking on the door. He stepped back to wait for a response.

"I warned you," said Sander.

Alain turned to look at Sander and silently mouthed the words, "I'll be okay." He reinforced the message with a thumbs up.

"Come in," shouted a voice from behind the door.

Alain turned the handle and opened the door, he'd expected a scene of debauchery, for some unknown reason, but the cabin was clean and tidy, except for a full ashtray and a cloudy, water-spotted, empty glass on a side table and a few clothes on the floor, where they'd fallen off the back of a chair. The cabin was smaller than Alain and Courtney's but had a bright and airy feel that theirs didn't have.

The captain was stood next to the bunk that she'd been reclining on, just a few seconds earlier. She was wearing no shoes but she had blue trousers on and a faded, navy-blue sweatshirt that had seen better days, the logo on the left breast was unreadable, parts of it having peeled off in the wash over time.

Mikaela Larson had been captain of the Somali Pirate Ship II for twelve years, although it hadn't always been called Somali Pirate Ship II, it was once named RV Morten Harket, before it was sold to a private buyer. There was no Somali Pirate Ship I as far as she knew. Mikaela was slightly taller than her First Officer, Sander, maybe five feet, eight inches, with dark, shoulder length hair, brown with plenty of grey, tied up in a bun. Her face was cheerful and round and her eyes were lined by age, by exposure to the wind and sea, and by yesterday's mascara.

"Doctor. Good to see you at last, I heard you were on board, no medical emergencies yet, I hope? Have you seen my hat?" she asked.

"Your hat?" replied Alain, looking round the cabin.

"Ah, here it is, I was lying on it," said the captain, while punching the hat from the inside to try to get some shape back into it before putting it back on. Unlike Alain, she didn't believe in looking the part, and the hat was her only concession to any kind of uniform. Without it you wouldn't have known she was the captain.

She seemed a bit disorientated, as if she had just woken up, but there was a steaming cup of something brown on the table that suggested someone had been in to see her recently, unless they'd crept in quietly to leave the cup without waking her.

"What can I do for you?" she asked. "Sander has been helping you settle in, yes?"

"Yes, everything is perfect," said Alain, who was suddenly nervous about what he was about to say. He put off saying it by exchanging small talk with the captain for a while. Drink was offered and declined, the talk was professional, about the ship, about the voyage, about the work of a ship's doctor. When do we sail? Do you have all the medicine and equipment you need? That sort of thing. A mutual respect between them that shattered as soon as Alain asked the question that he had come to ask, in a roundabout sort of way.

"Are you aware of the graffiti on Miss Woodbeard's cabin?"

"Of course I'm aware of it," snapped Mikaela, suddenly not so friendly after all, "I might have been drunk when I did it but of course I'm aware of it."

She felt a sliver of guilt at having painted it but the best thing to do was to brazen it out. It's my ship, I can do what I want, she told herself, I don't have to answer to anyone, especially not some provincial English doctor. Actually, she thought, is he even English? He sounds English, he looks slightly Spanish and his name sounds French, I don't actually know anything about him, she thought, and she made a mental note to find out more. He was recommended to her and she hadn't asked any questions. I'll ask Sander later, she thought, he's spent more time with him than anyone else.

Alain was rather taken aback, he'd expected to be asking questions about finding the culprit before a follow-up question about getting it cleaned off. He rather fancied himself as a Hercule Poirot figure, wandering the ship, asking questions before gathering everyone together in one room and pointing the finger at someone for having paint on their hands. He had been looking forward to all the pats on the back, the congratulations, the handshakes, being carried aloft around the ship, but that seemed as fanciful as ever now. He felt disappointed, although the chances of him turning out to be a master detective were always slim to none. Actually, all he had ever intended to do was ask the captain and then tell Courtney he'd done everything he could.

"You?" was the only word he could muster when he did finally speak.

"Do you know how many penguins she's killed?" asked Mikaela, pointing her finger in Alain's direction.

"Well, no, no one does, it's not really her but, look, she's really upset about the graffiti and I appreciate now, very much, how upset you are about it as well, but I wanted to ask if you'd mind if I got someone to paint over it?" asked Alain, bracing himself for the response.

She waited four or five seconds before replying but it seemed like longer.

"Paint over it then," she said, "speak to Sander, he'll get it sorted but, I'll tell you now, don't be surprised if it gets painted again."

Emboldened by the unexpected progress he was making and mistaking their earlier professional cordiality for friendship, Alain chose this moment to bring up the spelling of the word, 'murderer.'

"You do realise that you spelt murderer incorrectly don't you?" he asked. "It's not murdererer, there were too many ers."

There was a long pause before Mikaela replied.

"I shall try to spell it right next time," she said. And there will be a next time, she thought.

Alain was acutely aware that this was the best result he was going to get, so he bowed slightly, which he instantly regretted, and started to back towards the door.

"Thank you, Captain, thank you very much," he said as he reached out for the door handle and then one more, "thank you," and he was back on the bridge, closing the door behind him.

"Well?" asked Sander.

"Paint over it," said Alain proudly, "she said paint over it. Make it so, number two," he barked at Sander, to the amusement of everyone else on the bridge.

Alain fairly flew down the stairs and along the corridor to Courtney's cabin. He knocked on the door, waited for Courtney to tell him to come in, then he made his entrance. Courtney was stood by the bathroom door, drying her face with a small towel.

"It's sorted," said Alain, joyfully, "they're going to paint over it."

The bringer of good news, an excellent role, he felt very pleased with himself, but then he saw the newspaper taped across the mirror and his mood changed from slightly smugger than normal to extremely concerned friend.

"Oh my God, Courtney, are you still doing that, are you still having the nightmares?" he asked.

"Afraid so," said Courtney, "I'm still having nightmares. I don't know if I'm talking in my sleep anymore, as it's been a while since I've shared a bed with anyone, but I still wake with a start, covered in sweat."

"But you've not seen her again in real life, in a mirror I mean?"

"No, I still can't, won't look in a mirror. You know how scared I was, I've told you before. I still see her in my dreams, I don't know who she is, whether it's me or not. She looks like me, just not quite right. Every night, or at least every time I have the dream, I ask her if she's me but she doesn't answer, she just keeps moving away from me or chasing me, I can't get close enough to catch her or talk to her, she's there then she's not there."

Alain knew all about the night terrors, he knew about the figure in the dreams and he knew that Courtney had seen the figure more than once in real life, in the reflection of a mirror. She was terrified of seeing herself, or what appeared to be herself, in the reflection. By the time she turned round to look there was no one there, but the fear of it still remained with her to this day.

Courtney had been fourteen the first time it happened. She saw someone in a mirror in her parent's bedroom, a figure behind her in the reflection, she froze as they approached. When they got closer she recognised the figure as herself. It appeared to be her, it looked just like her but something was off, something peculiar that she couldn't put her finger on. Still frozen, completely unable to move, she watched herself walk up, reach out and put a hand on her shoulder at which point she lost consciousness.

Some time after the incident, Courtney smashed every mirror in the house, terrified that it would happen again. She eventually allowed her parents to replace the mirror in their bedroom, and the one in their en suite bathroom, and she stayed out of their bedroom from that moment onwards.

"I did get help," said Courtney, "I had some CBT, still on the tablets, they help me sleep and I'm better with it, but she still haunts me, my spirit twin."

Courtney winced at the word, she didn't like it but she hadn't come up with a better way of explaining the version of herself that haunted her dreams and, on several occasions, haunted her real life too. It was difficult to live without mirrors, not impossible, but difficult, Courtney was always aware of the reflection in windows and went to great lengths to avoid looking at them, but there was always the sense that something might be there, just in the corner of her eye, just out of sight. Although Courtney had joked about it with Alain when they were together, to reassure him that it was just a minor inconvenience, it consumed her thoughts, every minute of every day. It was one of the reasons why she had been so reluctant to join the ship in the first place. At home, she had control, mirrors were covered and reflective surfaces were avoided but, here on this ship, she had no control, mirrors were uncovered, her spirit twin was out in the open. She was scared.

"I spoke to mother about it," said Courtney, "I asked her if I was a twin, if she had ever lost a child, she was horrified when I asked her. What sort of thing is that to ask your own mother out of the blue, did you lose a child? She wouldn't talk to me about it, I don't know if she was offended at being asked, or if she had something to hide. She just shut me down and we never spoke of it again. I went through all her old photographs but there was nothing, no pictures of me as a baby, nothing until I was about three years old. I don't know what I was hoping to find, a picture of two identical babies, I suppose."

"And your father?" asked Alain. "Was he able to help with any information?"

"I didn't get the chance to ask him," replied Courtney, "I left it too late."

"Is there anything I can do?" asked Alain. "Do you need anything to help you sleep, are you anxious? I've got a cupboard full of pills if there's anything you want. Half the ship is on anti depressants, you should see how many I've got, there's boxes and boxes of them. I've already changed mine to another brand to see if they're any better for me."

"That's very kind of you," said Courtney, "but I'm okay, Alain, really, I'm okay."

She had been living with this for what seemed like her whole life, it overwhelmed her thoughts and controlled her actions. She was constantly tired and found it hard enough to get through the day on her own, without having to worry about other people's concerns. Tell him you're okay and smile, she thought, reassure him, put his mind at ease.

"I'm okay," she said, smiling at Alain, "honestly, there's nothing for you to worry about."

Despite having had a good look around the ship the night before, Courtney didn't want to disappoint Alain, who was very keen to show her where everything was. It seemed like a good way to change the conversation so she picked a up cardigan from the chair, where she had left it last night, she slipped it on and she reminded Alain of his promise.

"Weren't you going to show me around, Alain? I thought you were taking me somewhere nice for breakfast."

"I'd love to," said Alain, "come on, I'll give you a quick tour of the ship ending at the canteen."

"Oh, did you find out who did the graffiti?" asked Courtney.

"No," said Alain, "but it won't happen again, I'll make sure of it."

You are all my guests

Courtney followed Alain out into the corridor and they passed a tall, young, Indian man carrying a pot of grey paint in one hand and an old, badly worn paint brush in the other. He stopped outside Courtney's cabin and put the paint pot onto the floor.

"That was quick," Alain said to Courtney.

As they walked around, it was obvious the ship was moving, the low rumble of the engines could be heard in the background, and Courtney felt slightly unsteady as the floor moved beneath her feet. They were still in relatively calm waters and it was easy for Courtney to adapt her movements to the slight sway and rock of the ship. Courtney put a hand on the wall, just to steady herself, reposition her feet, legs apart for balance and, after a few minutes, it became second nature. She had plenty of experience of being at sea and it quickly felt familiar. She could see Alain wasn't quite as comfortable, wait until it gets really bad, she told herself, if he struggles now, what will he be like when it gets rough? The thought triggered a memory and the smell of vomit reached her brain, she gulped and swallowed and was glad it was just her memory, for now.

"Morning, Lester," said Alain as he and Courtney stepped aside to let him pass.

"Morning, Doctor," said Lester, turning to face Courtney, "who's your friend, don't tell me, ah, do I call you Courtney, Miss Woodbeard or Penguin Murderer?" he asked, while smiling and laughing.

Such beautiful eyes, she thought as she looked up at his face.

"I think I'll call you Penguin Lady, is that okay?" he asked. He didn't wait for a response, he walked away from them, backwards along the corridor, waved his hand, turned and was gone.

"That was Lester Cherry-Stone, the ship's radio operator," said Alain, "at least I think that's what he does."

As they walked, it turned out that Lester wasn't the only crew member that Alain had acquainted himself with in the short time he'd been on the ship. Courtney was impressed with how he seemed to know everyone's name and what they did. It was a whirlwind of introductions to people whose names she instantly forgot, the only people he didn't introduce her to were those working in the noisy engine room, although he exchanged waves and nods with them as if they were old friends.

"Hungry?" asked Alain.

Courtney hadn't realised she was but the mention of food reminded her that she hadn't eaten since yesterday afternoon. Her stomach woke up and rumbled, just to remind her of its existence. She followed Alain toward the canteen and they were approached by a tall, young, red-headed man with a hipster beard, the moustache hair twirled and waxed to a point at both ends.

"Morning, Carter, this is Courtney Woodbeard," said Alain, formally, by way of introduction.

"Delighted to meet you, Miss," said Carter Cumbernauld in a broad Highland accent while offering his hand in greeting, "I'm looking forward to working with you."

My God, she thought, what massive hands. They swallowed hers up, enveloping her hand, squeezing slightly. They hadn't felt sweaty but he wiped his hand on his trousers, nonetheless. Maybe it's my hands, thought Courtney, maybe he's wiping my sweat off his hands, are my hands sweaty? Before she had time to worry about it further, he began to walk away from them along the corridor.

"How is your foot?" Alain called out to Carter.

"It's improving, thank you, Doctor," replied Carter as he left.

"What's wrong with his foot?" asked Courtney, when Carter was out of sight.

"Sorry, can't tell you," replied Alain, "doctor patient privilege."

"But you're not a doctor," she reminded him. Courtney was rather annoyed at Alain for keeping a secret from her.

"Oh, yes, sorry, I keep forgetting," said Alain, "Carter came to see me yesterday with a really bad blister on his heel that I drained for him. It went everywhere, you should have seen it. I almost gagged. Next time I'll cover it up so it doesn't squirt over everything. You live and learn don't you?"

Courtney wished she hadn't asked. They soon entered the canteen which was starting to empty as they'd missed the early rush. There were plenty of empty tables and small groups of people scattered around the room. Alain made his way across to the food and picked up a tray.

"Help yourself," he said to Courtney.

There was as good a selection of food as Courtney had ever seen. Some of the hotels she'd stayed in hadn't had a spread like this and it was way better than what had been served up on the ship during Polar Saviour. There were fruit juices, tea, coffee, four different milks, cereals, bread, pastries, eggs, hot and cold meats, yoghurts and fruit. Behind the counter, a giant of a man strode around replenishing food as quickly as it was taken while also exchanging small talk, he seemed to be everywhere, doing everything.

Courtney took a plate and filled it, if she had a plan it was to try a bit of everything and then come back tomorrow, or maybe in twenty minutes, and be a bit more selective. As she caught up with Alain he introduced her to the man behind the counter.

"Brian, this is Courtney, she's a good friend of mine, Courtney, this is Brian Unsafe, a man of many talents, including chef."

Brian must have been well over six foot tall and wore large, thick, black rimmed glasses and a pork pie hat. His face was tanned and clean shaven. He appeared to have 'love' and 'hate' tattooed on his knuckles but, on closer inspection, it was clear that he actually had 'love' and 'hats' tattooed atop his fingers. He didn't break stride, moving plates and food around while briefly acknowledging their presence.

"All right, love," was all he said as he gave Courtney a quick glance.

"The food looks amazing, Brian," said Courtney, "so much fresh food. It's wonderful."

"Yeah, all fresh," replied Brian, "I defrosted the bread meself this morning."

"Amazing guy," said Alain, who was somewhat in awe of Brian, "he's done everything, scaffolder, actor, chef, I'm sure he'll tell you about it some time. Let's get somewhere to sit, shall we?"

Courtney led the way to a large empty table in the centre of the room.

"Look at that, it's on the wonk," said Courtney pointing at the full glass of apple juice she had just set upon the table. The glass obviously wasn't sat on a level surface, the juice was higher on one side and lapped at the rim of the glass, threatening to spill over. On further inspection, it seemed that it wasn't just the glass and the table that were uneven. The whole room, indeed, the whole ship was listing very slightly to one side.

"Is it meant to do that?" asked Courtney, gesturing with her arms and looking round to indicate she meant the whole ship and not just the glass on the table.

"Oh, you get used to it," said Alain, dismissing her concerns.

They ate in silence for a while before Courtney spoke.

"Who did it, Alain? You know, don't you? I can tell."

"Did what?" replied Alain, although, as he said it, he remembered that he hadn't told Courtney about his discussion with the Captain, all he'd told her was that it would be cleaned off and he didn't know who did it.

"Oh yes, the graffiti, sorry, it was the Captain."

"The Captain?" replied Courtney. "What have I done to upset them?"

"I didn't really get into too much detail. I'm just pleased that she agreed it could be painted over. Couldn't wait to get out of there if I'm honest, she unsettled me somewhat."

"Well, I'm glad you're okay," said Courtney, sarcastically, but, before she could say any more on the subject, a man in a wheelchair propelled himself towards their table at a rate of knots. He looked about thirty years old with light brown skin and short, dark curly hair. He wore a burgundy polo neck and sandy coloured cargo pants, and Courtney's eye was drawn to the full plate he had balanced on his legs as he wheeled the chair with both hands.

"Kick that chair out of the way, Doctor," he said, with the authority of a man who was used to giving orders.

Alain put down his spoon and turned to his left to pull a chair out from under the table. He pushed it away to one side to make room, while still chewing a mouthful of cereal.

The man in the wheelchair wheeled himself forward until he was able to put his plate on the table, along with the glass of juice that he carried between his thin legs, then he wheeled himself quickly, backwards and forwards, until he fitted into the gap Alain had created for him.

"Hi, I'm Hanad Said," he said to Courtney, offering her his hand. She reached across the table as far as she could and they touched fingers, not a proper handshake, more like half a handshake, fingers only. He didn't wipe his hand on his trousers, which impressed Courtney very much. She was easily impressed.

"I hope you're enjoying yourself," he said to Courtney, "any problems, you let me know."

He turned to look at Alain before addressing him.

"Do you have everything you need, Doctor? It's got to be one of the best equipped surgeries you've every worked in isn't it?"

"It most certainly is," replied Alain.

Courtney watched Alain to see how well he lied, not very well was the answer. He seemed cold towards Hanad, unlike everyone else on the ship, who he seemed to go out of his way to be friendly to.

"Hanad owns this ship," Alain said to Courtney, "it's all his, every nut and bolt, including me."

"I've heard of you," said Courtney, thinking back to last night with Lester, "this is your ship? Really? It's amazing to think that you own all of this," she said, looking round the canteen.

"Why do you look so surprised? Is it because I'm in a wheelchair, you don't think that I could own a ship like this?" asked Hanad, looking for a reaction.

Courtneys mouth hung open, unable to think of what to say, she turned to look at Alain only to find him head down, concentrating on eating his cereal.

"Good God, no," said Courtney, who was most offended, "of course not."

She felt embarrassed at the accusation and could feel her cheeks blush.

"I'm teasing you. Don't be embarrassed. You're my guests, you're all my guests," he said while opening his arms out and looking round at all the other people in the room.

"YOU ARE ALL MY GUESTS," he bellowed, which was greeted by some bemused looks and general indifference from the rest of the room.

"How did you come to own a polar research ship?" asked Courtney. "At your age, I mean, what are you? Mid, late twenties?"

"Twenty-eight. I look younger don't I? I always loved snow, ice, penguins, polar bears, whales, explorers, I read all about them. It snowed every year where I lived and I loved it. When I came into money, I bought this ship and had it altered so I could get around it in a wheel chair, we changed some doors, put in a couple of elevators, re-named it Somali Pirate Ship II, and now we hire it out, or we lease it for expeditions, or research, or pleasure, and I get to tag along whenever I want. When I heard you were going to Antarctica to see polar bears kill penguins, I thought, I've got to see that. Two of my favourite animals, fighting, wow, I wouldn't miss it for the world. Do you like the food? There's a room full of chefs back there, you want anything special, I'll get them to put it on the menu."

He talked quickly and passionately about the ship and his enthusiasm was infectious, although Alain didn't seem too enthused, noted Courtney. She still wasn't sure why Alain had taken against Hanad, who seemed to her to be friendly enough. Maybe it was the employer, employee relationship or maybe a doctor, patient thing. She made a mental note to ask him about it later.

"And why the name?" asked Courtney. "Why Somali Pirate Ship II?"

"I'm half Somali," said Hanad, "half American, half Somali. My father was Somalian, a fisherman, it's a tribute to him, he would find it so funny."

"It must have cost you a fortune," said Alain, rather rudely, "how on earth did you get the money to afford a ship like this, if you don't mind me asking?"

"No, that's okay," said Hanad, "this is how."

He held up a lightweight virtual reality headset that was hanging from a strap around his neck.

"We made a fortune out of this, it combines AR and VR and we developed an app to give you the full communal dining experience. Like a conference call but with lunch," said Hanad, while holding up the VR headset, "this is my fortune and my curse. More a curse I think, but, I suppose when people hear about how much money I've made out of it, they think of it as a blessing. Not everything is about money though. Once you put the headset on and activate the app, it recognises your plate, your knife and fork and even the food you're eating and then it uses a combination of VR and AR, so you see what you're actually eating against the background of the virtual dining room where your friends could be. So if the three of us were sat in our separate cabins right now, having lunch, we could put on the headset, choose a dining room, pick a table together and we could be sat there having this conversation in a VR world. It doesn't have to be a dining room, it could be a boardroom or whatever."

"But why wouldn't we just come to the canteen and have dinner together?" asked Alain.

Hanad smiled. He'd heard this and many other stupid questions for years now and would love, one day, to say what he really thought but, for now, he just smiled and continued his story.

"Well, we could," said Hanad, "but what if we were thousands of miles apart and we wanted to get together over dinner and talk? Using this, we could be anywhere in the world and we could also be sat here having this conversation. It's important that people sit down and eat together, it's a social bonding thing. We crowdfunded it initially, while we were still in college but without much success, so we ended up offering the moon on a stick to people to get them to invest. We started with a few small investors and then it got a bit crazy, more and more money and then more lawyers and accountants got involved and people started wanting out and we had some problems with trying to get the initial investors to cut us some slack. Some of my friends, that I started it with, cashed out early but I stayed in as the value of the company skyrocketed and I sold a huge chunk of it, right at the top of the market. We never turned a profit, still haven't, but, as I'm the only original director of the company still left, I'm beholden to the promises we made to the original investors and one of the promises we made was that one of us would be in the virtual dining room every day, which didn't seem like too much of a problem as there were four of us and we'd use it every day anyway but, now there's only me, it's become a bit of a chore."

He leaned back in his wheelchair and stretched to try to relax his muscles. He had become hunched over and tense as he told the story, but, now that it was told, he relaxed his body, he sat back and rolled his shoulders and listened to the cracking noise as his joints moved.

"We tried talking to the initial investors, to get them to drop the clause, but their lawyers have worked out that they'll get more money suing me when I break the contract than they'd get from me paying them off, so they're just waiting for me to fail, so every day I check into the dining room just to avoid getting sued."

"Couldn't you just get someone else to log in for you and pretend to be you?" asked Courtney, who was unsure what she was talking about but it sounded like it was a sensible question and Hanad replied as if it was.

"We've thought of everything to get round it but, in the end, if I don't go there every day then I'm fucked, so every day I eat at least one meal in a virtual dining room, while talking to virtual people, while eating my real food in a real dining room, while surrounded by real people I can't talk to because I'm too busy talking to a virtual dining room full of people I hate. Well, I say full, it's not as popular as it was. In fact," said Hanad pausing for effect, "I went in there two weeks ago and I was the only person there, for a whole half hour, I was the only person logged in. Can you believe it? Fucking idiots. I was lucky, I got most of my money out of this shitstorm before it got real bad."

Hanad removed the VR headset from around his neck and put it down on the table in front of him then he looked at Courtney and Alain.

"Would you like to have a go?" he asked, offering the headset to Courtney.

"Go on then, I'll have a quick look," said Courtney, nervously, as she took the headset and prepared to put it on over her glasses. She was a bit apprehensive as she had heard that VR could make you ill with motion sickness and the volume of breakfast she had just consumed was a cause for concern.

She saw her arms and her left hand holding a spoon. In front of her was her plate but the table it rested on wasn't the table she was sat at. She appeared to be in a wood panelled dining room, at the head of a long banqueting table. There was someone, or at least a computer representation of someone, sat far away at the other end of the table who, from the jerky motion of their arms, appeared to be eating. As Courtney moved her arms in front of her body, she saw her virtual arms move in a similar way. She held her yoghurt pot in her right hand and peeled off the lid with her left hand, while still holding the spoon. She found it easier to feel with her hands rather than rely on what she could see.

"I suppose it gets easier the more you use it," she said.

"Oh yeah, you don't even notice it once you've been immersed for a few minutes," said Hanad.

Courtney put the spoon into the yoghurt pot and lifted what felt like a full spoon of yoghurt up to her mouth. Of course, she missed, not by much, but the spoon caught her lip and some yoghurt fell, unseen by Courtney, onto the table in front of her as she lunged her head forward to get the spoon into her mouth. It seemed easier to hold the spoon still and move her head.

Hanad and Alain were both laughing so she let go of the spoon with her hand, holding it in her teeth, as she lifted the headset away from her eyes and onto her forehead, catching her glasses in the process. Courtney found that Hanad and Alain weren't the only ones laughing, as several other people in the canteen had stopped to watch and were now pretending not to look. Courtney felt a wave of embarrassment at being the centre of attention.

"I don't think I'm any good at this," she said, through a yoghurty spoon mouth. She took the headset off and handed it back to Hanad and pulled the spoon from her mouth, licking the last of the yoghurt from it before wiping her mouth and chin with a white paper napkin.

"Did you enjoy that?" she asked Alain, as she wiped the last of the yoghurt off the table top.

Was Helen of Troy Greek?

Hanad put the VR glasses on and ate the rest of his breakfast, occasionally breaking his silence to say, "Hello," to someone in the virtual world. He didn't spill any food, or cut himself, or stab himself in the face with a fork, although Courtney kept a close eye on him, just in case she got the opportunity to laugh at his expense. He was an expert at it by now, his movements smooth, no lunging for the fork, hand to mouth not mouth to hand.

After a while, Courtney stopped watching him, he became invisible, just sat at the table half listening to Courtney and Alain but without joining in.

"I need to go," said Alain, pushing his plate away from him, "I've got to get changed for surgery, put my doctor's hat on, patients to see," he said, as he winked at Courtney.

"You've actually bought a doctor's hat?" asked Courtney. "What even is a doctor's hat?"

"It's just a saying, I haven't bought a doctor's hat, there's no such thing," protested Alain, "it's like a medical licence, it's just an expression, it's not a real thing."

"Are you sure you're not getting an artistic licence mixed up with a medical licence?" asked Courtney. "Because I think that medical licences do actually exist and I'm pretty sure you need one to work as a doctor."

"We'll see, shall we?" asked Alain, as he stood up to leave.

All a big joke to him, isn't it? thought Courtney.

Before he left, Alain quickly looked round the room and then he turned to Courtney and leaned in to speak.

"Have you met Heather, the expedition team leader?" he asked. "I'm sure I saw her in here earlier, you can't miss her, I've never seen anyone who looks more Greek in my entire life, except maybe Helen of Troy, although I've never met Helen of Troy and was she even Greek? I'm not sure now that I've said it, oh, there she is," he said, pointing over to his right at a woman sat alone at a table, hunched over a laptop.

Courtney looked across at an ample woman in her forties, with shoulder length hair, the colour of a muddy puddle and parted in the middle, wearing black rimmed glasses that framed her brown eyes. More Nana Mouskouri than Helen of Troy, thought Courtney.

"You'll like her. Heather Wożniak. She was Heather Christoyannopoulos, or something like that, before she got married. It's a lot easier now. Fluent in Polish and Greek I believe. Quite the linguist. You should introduce yourself, you'll like her."

Alain reached over to the table to pick up a glass and downed the last of his orange juice before putting the glass back down.

"I'll see you later," said Alain, "go and introduce yourself."

Courtney stood up and wondered whether she should say anything to Hanad. It seemed rude to walk off without saying goodbye but she couldn't just ignore him, however unsociable he was being. In the end, politeness got the better of her.

"Goodbye, Hanad, I'll see you later," she said.

He responded by lifting his right hand and he gave a short wave, at least she assumed it was a wave, he could have been trying to pick up his cup or been waving away a virtual fly in a wood panelled dining room somewhere. No, it was definitely a wave, he had definitely acknowledged her leaving, she was sure, fairly sure.

Courtney walked the short distance over to Heather's table and introduced herself.

"Good Morning, Heather, is it? I'm Courtney Woodbeard, I'm the reason we're all here, well, actually I'm not but we're here anyway," she waffled. Shut up Courtney, she said to herself.

Courtney sat down at Heather's table without waiting for an invite and she waited for Heather to speak. When she did speak, the welcome was a lot friendlier than Courtney was expecting. She almost seemed pleased that Courtney was there. Alain had made Courtney feel at home the previous day, even if she was still confused by his presence. The time and drinks she shared with Lester, last night, had restored her faith in humanity and now this, another warm welcome, from another stranger, someone who knew her through reputation alone but chose to give her the benefit of the doubt and accept her on face value. She had almost forgotten the graffiti that awaited her on arrival, she was feeling so positive, so at home.

"I hear Lester calls you the Penguin Lady," said Heather, with a slight accent, neither Greek nor Polish, maybe a mixture of both, "would you prefer it if I called you Courtney? It's really good to have you here, I was hoping we could talk about Polar Saviour sometime, I've read the reports but there's nothing like hearing it from someone who was actually there."

"I'd love to fill you in," said Courtney, who was unsure when Heather and Lester would have spoken together about her. Courtney realised, as she was speaking, that Heather's attention was elsewhere in the room. She seemed to be looking over Courtney's shoulder towards the door behind her. Courtney turned to look but there was no one there. Maybe she had missed them and they had just left. I wonder who it was, thought Courtney.

"Is that the only reason why I'm here?" Courtney asked, in an attempt to bring Heather's attention back to her.

"To fill me in on what happened? No," replied Heather, who was no longer distracted by events elsewhere, "you're here because I asked for you, I wanted your expertise, they said I could bring whoever I wanted and I wanted you. Well, if we're being honest with each other, I'd have liked Frank Jedro, or Professor Selmia Tajul, or even Koeda Tanburuu to be here but none of them were available. As I'm sure you're aware, getting hold of someone from Polar Saviour has turned out to be a bit tricky."

She wasn't joking. Of the core team of eighteen people involved in Polar Saviour, two years ago, Courtney Woodbeard was the only one currently available to travel to Antarctica. Four of the team had died during the original expedition, two of them from natural causes. One was in prison. Six had gone missing, one during the expedition and five since, three of them disappeared from public life on returning to their home countries. Three had died from minor infections that failed to respond to antibiotics and the remaining three were sick, two with the particularly severe virus that was sweeping the globe at present and one was too sick to travel due to bone spurs. As the last person standing, it was Courtney's job to represent team Polar Saviour.

"Who contacted you, was it Binkie?" asked Heather.

"Er, I'm not sure who it was, it was all a bit sudden. I'm not even sure I got her name, it could have been Binkie," said Courtney, "it could have been her. She was very insistent, she wasn't going to take no for an answer."

"That sounds like Binkie. How did she get you to agree to come?"

"Persistence."

"Really?"

"She wore me down. She threatened me, she offered to bribe me, she said I was still contractually obliged to the UN and I couldn't say no, she threatened to damage my career and hurt my family. Some of that might have worked, if she'd pushed hard enough, but, in the end, she just wore me down and I said yes."

"How long did it take before you said yes?"

"Not as long as you would think," said Courtney, who was rather embarrassed at the thought of how little resistance she had put up.

"How long?" asked Heather.

"I was already in a pretty low place, you have to understand that this whole penguin murderer thing has been quite difficult to deal with."

"How long? What did it take to wear you down, how many times did she phone you?"

"Just the one time."

Heather sat back in her chair and laughed, loud enough to get some funny looks from around the room.

"That was definitely Binkie," said Heather, while continuing to laugh, "look, I'm sorry, I shouldn't have laughed. I'm not laughing at you, if you knew Binkie, you'd be laughing too. It's impossible to say no to her, she's just impossible to get rid of. Half the people on this ship don't want to be here, they're only here, like you, because they couldn't say no to Binkie. Did she tell you what the plan was?"

"No, we just discussed more practical stuff like what to bring and where to go, when the car was picking me up, that kind of thing. She didn't really encourage me to ask questions," said Courtney.

"Well, one of the problems we have is that, unfortunately, the research station, nearest to where we think the, er, penguin problem took place, is currently unmanned as it was evacuated last winter due to safety concerns. One of the companies involved in the supply of parts for the construction of the research station was apparently mixed up in a scandal involving substandard materials and falsified test records. I've been told that it should be okay for us to use it, as long as we don't try to tow it somewhere else. The legs might give way if we do. It's health and safety gone mad, isn't it? We're going to get a team to the research station, as soon as we can, and get it back on line so we can use it as a base then we can head over to the ice field to take a look at your polar bears and see what they've been up to. It's a shame we couldn't just fly in but there's no one on the ground to clear a runway for us."

When Heather was assembling her team to travel to Antarctica to investigate the possible penguin massacre, probable penguin massacre, penguin problem, as it was being referred to, things were a little bit rushed, to say the least. Normally it would take years of meetings and planning to get a team together for an Antarctic expedition but, on this occasion, Heather Wožniak was suggested as a safe pair of hands and she was given less than a month to get a team together. Although Heather and Binkie did their best, it wasn't like a Hollywood movie where they get a gang together made up of the creme de la creme of good looking, smartly dressed people, each an expert in their field. What Heather and Binkie had assembled was a ragtag collection of mediocre people who were available to travel at short notice.

Their levels of experience varied wildly, from none to some. Heather Wozniak was chosen because of her experience, she had been to Antarctica many times, she had spent months living there in research stations, she had led an expedition or two and was considered reasonably competent by her peers. She wouldn't have been anyone's first choice but, on the list of possible names, she was the first one who didn't say no and Binkie did the rest.

Carter Cumbernauld was Heather's second in command and she was confident enough in his ability to do the job that she simply told him what was going to happen and let him get on with it. Between them, they led a small team of loose cannons, oddballs and inexperienced university students. What could go wrong?

"What are you looking at?" asked Courtney, noticing that Heather's attention seemed to have wandered again. Courtney looked over her shoulder and saw Hanad still sat at the table with his VR headset on and she wrongly assumed that he was the source of Heather's distraction.

"Have you met Hanad?" asked Courtney.

"Yes," replied Heather, "he's an interesting fellow isn't he? Wouldn't be here without him and his ship though. It was the only suitable research vessel available, although it's a bit smaller that what I'm used to."

"I don't really understand how he made so much money out of a company that didn't make any money," said Courtney, "my head hurts just thinking about it."

"I know," said Heather, still distracted by something the other side of the room, "anyway, you've heard we're a bit short staffed haven't you?" asked Heather.

Courtney hadn't heard. She was far too caught up in her own despair to take much notice of what was going on around her. Should she pretend that she knew what Heather was talking about? She didn't want to appear out of touch, that might make a bad impression, but she didn't want to lie about it. Best thing to do was admit it and feign interest.

"I hadn't heard," said Courtney, "how come?"

"You are aware of the latest pandemic?" asked Heather, rhetorically. "Well, several of the expedition team have got caught up in it. A couple of them got sick and ended up in hospital in L.A. They got treatment quickly enough and they're going to be all right but a lot of flights are being cancelled because they haven't got the staff. Doctors and Nurses are being recalled from leave, it's left us very short staffed. Even Doctor Kennedy didn't make it here so we're very pleased to have your friend, Alain, on board as he's the only doctor on the ship now. I don't know what we'd do without him. Have you known him long?"

Courtney didn't know what to say. Yes, she had known Alain for a long time, but that wasn't what she was thinking. Should she say something about Alain not being a doctor? He'd treated it all as a bit of a joke before but, now he's the only doctor on board, it's no longer a laughing matter. It's serious. I've got to say something, thought Courtney, with so many people getting sick, what if someone dies, what if they find out I knew he wasn't a doctor and I didn't say anything? I'd get into trouble. And she didn't like being in trouble. The guilt of knowing and not saying anything was already starting to weigh heavily on her conscience. She made a decision. I've got to say something.

"Yes, I've known him since I was at university," she finally said.

Heather looked across towards a table to her left and her mind seemed to be elsewhere again.

"Is everything okay?" asked Courtney.

"Oh yes, I'm sure everything will be fine, we've got enough people for what we need to do and, now we've got your doctor on board, we'll be fine."

"We won't. I mean, he isn't," said Courtney and she immediately felt better for saying it. The tightness in her chest disappeared the moment she spoke. Her muscles relaxed and she freed herself of guilt, but it didn't last long, barely long enough to enjoy it. What have I just done to Alain? she thought. Will he ever forgive me?

"Isn't what?" asked Heather.

"There isn't a doctor on board," said Courtney. In for a penny, she thought, too late to back out now, the damage is done. Phew.

"Alain isn't a doctor," continued Courtney, "well he is, but not a doctor of medicine. He blagged his way on board to see me, I think, to give me a bit of moral support. But if you're relying on him to treat sick people or deal with a medical emergency then you're going to be very disappointed."

"Well, of course he's a doctor, I saw him myself, only yesterday," said Heather, "of course he's a bloody doctor."

"He's not. Absolutely, definitely not. He's definitely not a doctor," said Courtney, who was unsure how she could spell it out any clearer, "I don't know what you went to see him for yesterday, but he is not a doctor. He's got an app on his phone he said he was going to use to diagnose symptoms. He's no more a doctor than you or I."

Heather went pale, pale enough for Courtney to think she was going to faint.

"He did use his phone when we were talking," said Heather, "he said it was the latest tool in the doctors' armoury, all the doctors are using them now. I thought nothing of it but, if what you're saying is true, then I need to speak to my team and decide what we're going to do next. We can't have him seeing any more patients."

"What did you go to see him about, if you don't mind me asking?" asked Courtney.

"Erm, I'd rather not say if that's all right with you," said Heather, "it's a personal matter."

As Heather spoke, her eyes seemed, to Courtney, to be tracking something as it moved across the room so Courtney turned to see who or what it was but, again, there was no one there, the canteen having mostly emptied in the last ten minutes. Brian Unsafe was still behind the counter, clearing up, while having a conversation, in a language Courtney didn't recognise, with someone stood in the doorway to the galley.

"I need to speak to Carter and the rest of the team about this," said Heather. The last thing she wanted was to call off the expedition and turn back but the safety of her team was her number one priority. It might be too risky to continue without medical support and she needed to speak to all the people affected. She decided she would call a meeting, get everyone together and decide what to do next.

"I've got to go but we'll speak later," she said to Courtney as she stood up. She folded her laptop shut and put it in her bag, that was on the chair next to her. She gathered up all her belongings and either put them in her bag or she held on to them. She threw the strap of the bag over her shoulder and began to walk away. As she left, she turned to look at Courtney.

"It was lovely to meet you, honestly," said Heather, "you've been vilified in the press and you're nothing like they've made out. I hope we can get together later and talk some more."

And, with a quick look around the room, she was gone, Courtney stayed at the table for a few minutes, thinking about what she had done. She had thrown Alain under a bus, that was obvious. She had to speak to him about it before anyone else did, to get her excuses in early.

"Have you finished with that?" asked Brian, as he came over and picked up Heather's bowl and cutlery from the table.

"Oh, they weren't mine," said Courtney, looking up at the man mountain towering over her.

"Brian," she said, "what would you do if you had stabbed a friend in the back? By accident I mean."

"I'd take the knife out," responded Brian, without hesitation, "and then I'd stab 'em again, and again, and again, and again."

He mimed the action of stabbing someone as he said it, stabbing harder each time.

"I'd stab 'em until they were dead," he said, "cos, if you stab a friend in the back, you've got an enemy for life so you better make sure you finish the job."

This wasn't the advice Courtney wanted, or needed, to hear.

"You got a problem you need sorting?" asked Brian, menacingly.

"No, no, God no, nothing that serious," replied Courtney as she saw the 'love' and 'hats' tattoos across Brian's knuckles, "I hope you don't mind me asking," she said, which he didn't, as he'd been asked it many times before, "but why have you got love and hats tattooed on your hands?"

"Cos I love hats," was all Brian said as he turned to take the dirty crockery and cutlery into the kitchen.

Judge, jury and executioner

Courtney returned to her cabin to brush her teeth and to think about what she could say to Alain. I've got to be the one to tell him, she thought. If it comes from me then I can control things. I can make it clear it was an accident, a slip of the tongue or, better still, that Heather forced me to say something and I was just confirming what she already suspected. Surely that would be better than saying I grassed you up, I couldn't keep your dirty secret any longer, I just had to tell someone that you're not a real doctor.

Once the confession was over, what then? She would be absolved of any guilt, again, and would feel much better, but what about Alain? How is he going to he react? Where will the conversation go after I confess? It was a worry. She didn't want Alain to hate her.

Courtney left her cabin and wandered the ship for a while, putting off talking to Alain for as long as possible. She knew she couldn't leave it too long, otherwise he would find out from Heather, but a little longer wouldn't hurt. She went outside onto the deck at one point but she wasn't dressed for the wind and the spray from the sea so she quickly went back inside, before she got too wet and too cold.

She knew Alain would be in the doctor's surgery and she knew where the doctor's surgery was but she still walked for quite some time, taking the longest route, putting off the inevitable. No one was sat on the two moulded plastic chairs outside the surgery, that acted as a makeshift waiting room. The door, with the brass plaque that simply said, 'Surgery,' was slightly ajar so Courtney entered without knocking.

Alain was stood in front of an open porthole window with his back to the door. He was leaning, with his face out of the window, with his elbows resting on top of some wooden shelving. He blew smoke out of the window before taking another drag on what looked, to Courtney, suspiciously like a joint.

"Alain," said Courtney, quietly, wanting to catch his attention but not make him jump.

Unsurprisingly she did both.

Alain threw the joint out of the window and span round to see who it was. He thought the door was shut and he wasn't expecting company. On seeing it was Courtney, he looked out of the window then back at the hand that, seconds before, had held the joint he was smoking and he looked crestfallen.

"Well, that was a waste," said Alain, "I wouldn't have tossed it if I'd known it was you. What are you doing here, creeping around?"

"I wanted to tell you something," said Courtney, "can we sit down?"

Courtney sat down at the desk, well aware of the mirror on the wall behind her, she keep her back to it and made a mental note of where it was, so she could avoid looking into it when she got up.

Alain sat in the doctor's chair behind the desk. In front of him on the desk was a stethoscope and a blood pressure cuff, along with various other medical tools that he didn't know how to operate. Alain had chosen the items on the desk carefully, to create the impression that he was an actual doctor, not an imposter. Appearances matter. In his later years at university he had utilised a similar trick, keeping piles of paperwork and stacks of books around to give the impression that he was busy, to keep people away and keep interruptions to a minimum.

Alain slipped easily into character, what he called doctor mode.

"What can I help you with today?" he asked Courtney.

"I'm not one of your patients," said Courtney while sat in the patient's chair, "I'm sorry, Alain, but I think I might have..."

She paused for a second whilst thinking of how best to word this.

"...dropped you in it while talking to Heather. I might have accidentally given her the impression that you might not be a doctor, at least not a medical one. It just slipped out, I'm sorry."

She watched him closely to see his reaction, he didn't seem too upset, although he looked disappointed in her, or was she just imagining it?

"What did she say, when you told her?" asked Alain, calmly. He was extremely disappointed in Courtney. He felt a rising mix of anger and fear, he could go to prison for this, but what have I really done wrong? he thought. I know I'm not a doctor but no one has been hurt, not yet anyway.

"She said she was going to talk to Carter and decide what to do, she'll probably come to see you later. I'm sorry, I know you were enjoying being a doctor, you seem like you're happy, and I don't remember you being happy before. Even when we were together you never seemed happy. You were caring, and loving, and attentive, but I don't remember you being happy. You smiled and laughed but I always worried about you."

"They're going to knock on that door later," said Alain. He was seething, barely managing to keep his anger in check. "There's going to be a mob of them, I wouldn't be surprised if they had burning torches and a noose. They're going to drag me in handcuffs to the brig and lock me up for this, and who's fault is that?"

He opened the top right-hand drawer in front of him, took out a padded envelope and slammed it down it on the desk. From the sound and weight of the package, it obviously contained something substantial. He tore at the envelope to reach inside and he pulled out a gun, not a modern gun but an old revolver with a short stubby barrel.

"I'm not going," he said, "we're at sea, maritime law, people are dying back home, normal rules don't apply."

It made perfect sense. To him at least.

Courtney was shocked. She'd never seen Alain like this, she'd never seen him with a gun before. Was she safe, was he going to shoot her?

"Where did you get that?" she asked. "Why have you got a gun Alain?"

"Dark web," he said, "same place I got the smoke from. Ordered them to be delivered to the ship in the name of the previous doctor, that way they would be here when I arrived and there would be no connection to me. I assumed that doctors get things delivered all the time, medicines, equipment, no one would notice a couple more packages. What did you think would happen when you told Heather? What were you thinking?"

"I didn't think. I didn't mean to tell her. It just came out in conversation, it was just a tiny slip of the tongue, she worked most of it out herself," said Courtney, lying through her teeth, "they're not going to put you in prison for pretending to be a doctor, but they might if you start shooting people. Please, Alain, put the gun away."

"They're coming for me," said Alain, still agitated. He was sat upright in his chair with his right hand on the gun, resting its weight on the desk. The fingers on his left hand seemed to have a life of their own, tapping away at an imaginary keyboard.

"Put the gun away, Alain," said Courtney, firmly, which seem to get his attention. His mood changed suddenly. He lifted the gun and put it back in the envelope then he threw it into the desk drawer and slammed it shut.

"Happy now?" he asked Courtney, who was very relieved. She felt like she had talked him away from the edge but she still had work to do to talk him down from the roof.

"There's not going to be a mob," said Courtney, "no flaming torches, no gun fight. This ship probably hasn't even got a brig to throw you in. I'm sure Heather will speak to you later, or she might send Carter to speak to you, but it's going to be all right."

"Carter," said Alain, virtually spitting out the name, "Carter, that massive handed, tiny headed twat. Do you really think I can just sit here and listen to his sanctimonious bullshit after what I've done for him and Heather? They've both been in to see me you know, as a doctor, I've treated them both. I'd only been here five minutes before they were knocking on the door wanting an appointment. An appointment? I'm not even a real doctor! Why would anyone book an appointment with a fake doctor? Fucking idiots. The both of them."

"That's enough, Alain," said Courtney, firmly, in an effort to calm him down, "I'll help you. We'll see them together and I'll speak up for you. When does your surgery finish? Have you got any more patients today?"

Alain shook his head to indicate no. He opened the drawer of his desk and pulled out a ready rolled joint and a cigarette lighter. He put the joint to his lips and lit it, the twisted paper at the end turned to ash and fell across the medical equipment on the desk.

"This isn't how I imagined things would end up," said Alain, in a disheartened tone of voice.

"Do you think we should wait in your cabin until they come to speak to you?" asked Courtney, who was relieved that his anger didn't seem to be directed solely towards her. "We could wait there together and when they turn up we can calmly talk it through. I'll be there to help you, to give you support."

So, having come up with a plan to do nothing, that was what they did. Alain smoked the joint as the two of them went to his cabin to wait. They passed a couple of people on the way, but Alain wasn't his usual sociable self and could barely raise a nod or a grunt in response to the amiable greetings directed towards him.

A chirpy, "Good morning, Doctor," was followed by, "What's wrong with him today?"

Once inside Alain's cabin, Courtney pulled up a chair and sat with her back to the mirror while Alain slouched and sulked on the bed. Courtney talked and, eventually, Alain joined in. They reminisced about old times and shared memories and, after a while, Alain calmed down, in fact, he calmed down so much that he nodded off into a light sleep.

Courtney closed her eyes but couldn't sleep. Thoughts raced through her mind, multiple scenarios of how this would turn out, some good, some bad, some shockingly bizarre. She couldn't switch off, couldn't stop thinking. She was about to stand up to stretch her legs when there was a knock on the door.

Although expected, the knock caught them both by surprise. Courtney stood up so quickly that she almost knocked the chair over. Alain opened his eyes, only half awake and a bit disorientated, he mumbled something unintelligible and hauled himself upright.

Courtney and Alain caught each others eye and shared a look that said, uh oh, here we go.

"Doctor," came the call from outside. A female voice, probably Heather's, they both assumed correctly.

Alain stepped past Courtney to open the door and found Heather and Carter waiting outside in the corridor. Alain took a long hard look at them both, without speaking. He couldn't gauge from their faces how this was going to play out. Either they weren't giving anything away, or they simply didn't know, or he was terrible at reading people's faces.

"What do you want?" demanded Alain, setting the tone for what lay ahead.

"We would like to talk to you, if that's possible," said Heather politely, "may we come in?"

Alain stepped back and held the door open for them to enter, he kept the door open for longer than seemed necessary and looked out into the corridor to see if anyone else was there.

"Are we all here?" he asked Heather, sarcastically.

"You know that's not necessary," said Heather, in her calmest, let's not make things any worse, voice.

Alain closed the door. Carter had taken a seat on the bed next to Heather, his hands clasped together on his lap in a giant, sweaty ball of fingers and thumbs.

Courtney stood up and offered her seat to Alain but he waved her away. "I'm sure this won't take long," said Alain, his comment directed at Heather, "I'll stand, if that's okay with everyone."

Courtney sat back down and waited, she was ready to defend Alain, up to a point, but she wanted to see how things played out first, see what Heather had to say and how Alain responded.

"Tell me Heather, is this the trial or the sentencing?" barked Alain defiantly, as he paced round. Courtney had wondered how he was going to react, well now she knew.

"Look, Alain," said Heather, "it's been brought to my attention that you're not a medical doctor, and so we've had a meeting of the team members and..."

"How come I wasn't invited?" asked Courtney. "I'm part of the team aren't I?"

"Well," said Carter, "I think we're all a bit confused by your status as both the whistleblower and the counsel for the defence and we weren't sure that you should be on the jury as well."

Carter laughed at his own cleverness, although no one else did. Courtney thought it was funny but, as the joke seemed to be at her expense, she maintained a straight face and held her tongue.

"Alain," said Heather, "there's no jury and you're not on trial. We got together to speak about what to do, now that there's no recognised doctor on board. We're not looking to punish anyone, we…"

But before she could continue, Alain stepped towards her, clearly agitated, and said, "We? We've spoken? We? So the three of you have got together and made a decision? Judge, jury and executioner. That's convenient isn't it?"

Courtney was shocked. I'm on his side, she told herself. Why would he think I'm part of this? Whatever conspiracy he has concocted in his mind, surely he doesn't think I'm involved?

"Don't include me in this, Alain," Courtney protested, "I'm not part of this. I'm not here to judge you, I'm here to support you, you know that."

"I wasn't talking about you," he said to Courtney and he put his hand on her shoulder to reassure her. "I was talking about Heather, Carter and Emily here."

"I assume she's here right now?" he asked Heather. "Where is she?" he demanded as he looked found the room.

"Who is Emily?" Courtney asked Alain. "There's only us three here. What's going on?"

"Where is she?" Alain asked Heather again.

"She's behind you," said Heather calmly, "but I'm not going to tell you exactly where she is as we don't want a repeat of last time."

"Why? What did I do last time?" asked Alain, before swiftly remembering how he'd waved his arms in the air where he thought Emily was standing, as a joke. It didn't go down very well.

"Oh, the arm thing," he said, sheepishly, "sorry about that."

He wasn't sorry. Sorry not sorry.

"Alain," said Carter in his broad Highland accent, Alain became Alun, almost reducing the name to just a grunt.

He had everyone's attention. He hadn't spoken much but now it was time to take control over the situation. This was Heather's plan and it was way beyond any of the bizarre scenarios that Courtney had managed to dream up earlier.

"Alain," he grunted again, "we've not come here to put you on trial, we're here to work out how we can keep this show on the road. None of us want to turn the ship round and go back. You might not be a doctor but you're the closest thing we've got right now so we need to find a way to work this out to everyone's satisfaction. I told Heather how you helped me, as a doctor, and we decided it didn't matter whether you were a real doctor or not, the end justifies the means, not the other way round. All that matters to me is whether you're prepared to continue working as a doctor, so we can continue."

Courtney couldn't believe what she was hearing. Were they really suggesting that they let Alain continue working as a doctor? She turned to look up at Alain, at the exact same moment that he turned to look down at her, and she couldn't help but notice a tear forming in his eye. He wiped it away with his sleeve before anyone else saw it and he took a deep breath, in through his nose.

"Well, I don't know what to say," said Alain, not quite speechless, but close, "what does everyone else think?"

"Everyone else thinks this is crazy," said Courtney, who was astonished that they were prepared to let someone, with no medical experience, work as a doctor on a ship, on a ship going to Antarctica.

"You can't do this," protested Courtney, "he's had a couple of hours playing at being a doctor and you're giving him the same responsibility, the same status as someone who's trained for years to do this. How is he even remotely qualified to do this? How can you put people's lives in his hands?"

"Listen," said Carter, "experience is overrated. You're going to have to tell people that you're not a real doctor, if they come to see you but, if they're happy with that, Alain, then we're happy to let you carry on. The expedition team are behind us on this. They're all fully aware of the situation. You've got a great bedside manner, Doctor, and we're glad to have you working with us."

He held out a giant hand towards Alain, who let it envelope his standard sized hand and they shook on it. Carter stood up and wiped his hand on his trousers.

"I think we're done here," said Carter.

Heather stood up from the bed and the two of them stepped around Courtney on their way to the door.

"Who is Emily?" asked Courtney. "What's going on? What just happened?"

Alain leaned back against the wall, staring blankly, mouth slightly open, not sure if he was dreaming. Did what just happened really happen? he asked himself.

The idea of pretending to be a ship's doctor had excited him, it put a spring in his step, it felt daring and risky. He held on to a fanciful safety net that involved declaring that it was all a joke, that he wasn't a real doctor and then everyone would laugh along with him, but now? Now, there was no safety net. He was expected to be a doctor by people who knew he wasn't. He felt the full weight of other peoples expectations. It wasn't a joke anymore, it was a real job, he was a real doctor, not a qualified one, or one with any experience, knowledge, or ability, but he was still a doctor. He needed a drink.

Courtney stood up to follow Heather and Carter, their work here was done, although she still had questions.

As Courtney closed Alain's door behind her, Heather stopped to speak to her.

"We need to talk," she said.

"Do you need me?" Carter asked.

"I think I've got this," replied Heather, as Carter sauntered off to his cabin.

"Shall we talk in your cabin?" asked Heather.

The graffiti on the wall of Courtney's cabin was painted over in a slightly different shade of grey to the rest of the wall so, instead of, 'penguin murdererer,' in red paint, it now read, 'penguin murdererer,' in grey paint on a greyer background.

Courtney opened the door to her cabin and Heather and Emily followed her inside.

She's not imaginary

Once they were inside her cabin, Courtney pulled a chair out, away from the wall, and positioned it in the centre of the room.

"Bed or chair?" she asked Heather.

"Which do you prefer?"

"I don't mind, you choose, you're my guest."

"I'll have the bed then," said Heather, as she sat down on the edge of Courtney's bed. She looked at Emily across the room, behind Courtney. She was pointing at the newspaper, that was taped to the mirror, with one hand and covering her wide open mouth with the other.

"What's going on?" asked Courtney, taking a seat on the chair. "Why are you letting an untrained man pretend to be a doctor and treat patients? Does the captain know? Do we not need doctors anymore, do years of medical training count for nothing? And Emily, who on earth is Emily?"

"Why have you got newspaper stuck to your mirror?" asked Heather in response.

"You first."

"The doctor or Emily?" asked Heather.

"Both."

"Well, the doctor, erm, it's simple, we need him. If there's a medical emergency, there's other ships in the area, other doctors, some of the team have quite advanced first aid training. I'm sure Alain can cope with the day to day job of a ship's doctor, he seems reasonably intelligent. It wasn't an easy decision to make but I stand by it. I know you're a bit shocked, I don't know what you expected me to do when you told me but, if you need to see a doctor while you're here, then he'll have to do. We're all in the same boat, quite literally."

This made no sense to Courtney. She still couldn't see how these two intelligent, professional people had come to such a decision. It had been the same on Polar Saviour, her's had been the sole voice of reason, in her opinion. She had objected to the whole enterprise right from the start and repeatedly said so. She kept a diary and recorded all the conversations she had, all the meetings she attended, and she noted down all the times she pointed out the madness of moving a whole animal species twelve thousand miles away from its natural habitat but she wasn't listened to. The decision had been made and had to be carried out. If she wasn't going to be a team player then they would put her on the next helicopter out of there, so she stayed, silent and in her place.

Courtney had never let go of the feeling that it was the wrong thing to do. The likelihood that the polar bears had begun to massacre large penguin populations made her even stronger in her convictions. She hoped that she was wrong and that the satellite images didn't show what they were all fearing. Anyway, they would find out for sure in a few days time.

Courtney felt the same about the decision to keep Alain as the ship's doctor, it was wrong and she wouldn't ever agree with it, but it seemed the decision had been made and she wasn't able to change it. Unless I speak to the ships captain, she thought. The ship's captain that hates me. What a mess.

"And Emily, who is Emily?" asked Courtney, keen to move on from Alain.

"Emily? Well, she's here now if you want to ask her. She saw you last night, apparently, when you went for a walk."

"Where is she?" asked Courtney. "I can't see anyone. There's no one there."

She looked around the room, half convinced that she was going insane. Why can't I see anyone?

"Oh, you won't be able to see her, only I can see her," said Heather, rather patronisingly.

"She's imaginary then?" asked Courtney. "An imaginary friend? Called Emily? That's what we're talking about here? That's why I can't see anyone?"

"She's not imaginary," Heather protested, "she's as real as you or I. It's just that I'm the only one who can see her."

"But how do you know she exists, that she's not a figment of your imagination, that you aren't just making her up?" asked Courtney.

"Well, she knows things that I couldn't know. She can go places I haven't been and tell me what's there. My imagination doesn't know what people are saying when I'm not in the room with them. My imagination can't tell me what is in a locked room, but Emily can."

"But surely that's exactly what your imagination is for," insisted Courtney, "to imagine what's in a locked room and to imagine what people are saying about you when you're not there? I don't see how you can know that she's not imaginary?"

"Why don't you say hello to her?" asked Heather. "She's right behind you."

Emily was leaning against the wall behind Courtney, feet slightly apart, arms folded across her chest. She was dressed for comfort in a light blue tracksuit and white trainers. The trainers had yellow laces and two dark blue stripes either side of a pale blue stripe. Her hair was a similar length to Heathers, although it was a lighter brown. They were the same age but Emily looked a few years younger than Heather, her skin was lighter, less tanned and the lines around her mouth and eyes were less visible. She also didn't need to wear glasses.

"Is she behind me? Is she though?" asked Courtney. "Is she really?"

"I'm behind you," said Emily.

"She says she's behind you," said Heather, "go on, say hello to her, I'm sure the two of you will be friends."

"Hello, Emily," said Courtney, reluctantly.

"Hello, Courtney," said Emily in a jaunty tone of voice. Not her normal voice but who would know? Apart from Heather, of course.

"She says hello," said Heather.

"What did Emily see me do last night?" asked Courtney. She asked partly as a way of testing whether Emily really existed but she also wanted to find out what Emily and Heather might know.

"She saw you leave your cabin, shortly after Alain, and then you walked round the ship. She saw you go into the Communications Room and speak to Lester and she saw you go back to your cabin afterwards. She said you were nervous and kept stopping and looking around, as if you were worried that you were being followed, which you were, I suppose."

"And was she in the room when I was speaking to Lester?"

Emily shook her head.

"No, she wasn't," lied Heather.

Emily didn't want people to think she was eavesdropping all the time. Last night, after following Courtney back to her cabin, Emily went straight to Heather and told her all that she could remember from Courtney and Lester's conversation. They actually said nothing of any interest, in fact she described the discussion as two people drinking and making boring small talk, while one of them flirted badly with the other one. She refused to tell Heather which one she thought was doing the flirting, and Heather declined to push her on the matter. Emily didn't like to tell Heather everything. She liked to keep back a few titbits and drop hints, to keep Heather guessing. She did it as a game, to entertain herself, to have some control, to feel superior to Heather.

"Look, anyone could know I had a walk around the ship last night and met Lester," said Courtney, "I mean, Lester could have told you earlier. You spoke to him this morning didn't you?"

"I did," said Heather, "you don't believe me do you? What can I do to prove that Emily is real?"

"Get her to tell me what's in the top, right-hand drawer of Alain's desk, in the doctor's surgery."

Emily rushed off, through the door.

"I can do," said Heather, "but it won't prove anything. I could get Emily to go and look and come back and tell you what's in the drawer, but it doesn't prove anything. I sat at that desk and I could have seen in the drawer or Alain could have told me what was in the drawer. It doesn't prove anything. You have to take a leap of faith and put your trust in me, you need to believe that what I'm telling you is the truth. I can't prove it anymore than you can disprove it. Whatever evidence I show you is never going to be enough to convince you, unless you want to believe it."

"It's a gun. A handgun in an envelope," said Emily as she burst back into the room, out of breath from running all the way.

"A gun," exclaimed Heather, "what on earth is he doing bringing a gun onto the ship. Where did he get it? You knew he had a gun and didn't say anything? I think we need to get Carter and have another discussion about Alain."

"Oh, please no," said Courtney, "not again. I can't take any more of this. You'll tell Alain that I told you about the gun, and then he'll think I've got it in for him, and then he'll get angry again, and then Carter will tell him that you've had a meeting and decided he can keep the gun, as long as he doesn't use it. What's the point of putting all of us through that again?"

"Why on earth has he brought a gun with him?" asked Emily.

"Why, indeed," responded Heather.

"Look," said Courtney, keen to steer the conversation away from Alain, "forget about him, forget about the gun. You're right. It doesn't prove anything. Tell me more about Emily, how long have you seen her? Known her, I mean, I think."

"Well, she's always been there, as far back as I can remember, and no one else has ever been able to see her. We grew up together. She's the same age as me, she looks like me, although she's not as attractive."

Emily pulled a funny face that Heather chose to ignore, pausing only for a second to roll her eyes at Emily.

"She was with me when I was at school, at university, at work, we go on holiday together, she was a bridesmaid at my wedding, she even helped choose my wife, Anna's, wedding dress. She's a godmother to my nephew, oh, and she can get my dog to sit. I don't know she does it but when she says, 'sit,' he sits down, it's so funny, you should see his little face when she does it. I think I'm closer to her than I am to my own sister, probably because we spend so much more time together. We're never apart, even when I'm sleeping she's there, I mean, we do spend some time apart, she will go off and do her own thing and, sometimes, I tell her I need some space, but we're never far apart and we're never apart for long. She's real, as real as you are. If you tell me that she isn't real then none of this is real."

Emily was bored. She was always bored. Bored of watching. Bored of listening. She still found it hard to be around a conversation and not be able to join in, especially one like this, one she had heard many times before. This kind of conversation didn't always end well. Emily had seen

Heather lose some very close friends after they had been introduced to her. Most people react more calmly than you would expect on being introduced to an imaginary friend. They sometimes laugh, either through amusement or embarrassment, they sometimes use words like mad or crazy, they sometimes get angry but, usually, they make their excuses and leave and don't come back.

Would it matter if I wasn't here? thought Emily. Courtney doesn't know if I'm here or not and I'm sure Heather could handle this without me. Do I need to be here for Heather to persuade Courtney that I exist? Does the presence in the room of an invisible, undetectable person make the possibility of an invisible undetectable person being in the room more or less believable? Heather's arguments will be the same if I'm here or not. Would she be any less believable, any less convincing, without my presence?

In fact, the only thing keeping Emily in the room was her own curiosity. She wasn't curious to find out whether Courtney believed in her, that didn't matter. She was curious about the mirror covered in newspaper. It intrigued Emily enough to persuade her to stay and push for an answer.

Emily walked over to the bathroom and looked through the door. She checked the bathroom mirror and she saw that it, too, was covered in newspaper. She returned to the main room and sat on the bed next to Heather and spoke to Courtney directly.

"Why is there newspaper on the mirrors?" she asked.

Initially, Heather ignored Emily while she continued to tell Courtney about their relationship and how it was symbiotic, how fulfilling it was having the constant support and reassurance, but she stopped talking when Emily asked the question again.

"Emily wants to ask you a question," said Heather to Courtney, "Emily wants to know, well, we both want to know, why is there newspaper covering the mirror?"

"In the bathroom as well," said Emily.

"Oh it's nothing, nothing to worry about," said Courtney.

What am I saying? thought Courtney. Instinct had kicked in, always deny everything, don't tell anyone, what will they think? Courtney's heart was racing, she put both her hands on her knees and gripped tight to try to prevent Heather from seeing her hands shaking. She was so used to keeping it a secret. Was she really going to throw away the chance to talk to someone about it, someone who might understand, someone who had just revealed their own secret, a grown up with their own real-life, imaginary friend? Surely Heather, of all people, would be sympathetic, but Courtney worried that she didn't have the words to tell her story. Just the thought of telling it made her anxious, she wasn't prepared but would she ever be? Is there ever a right time to tell someone that you can't look in a mirror in case you see something from your nightmares brought to life.

"You can tell us what the problem is," said Heather, who recognised Courtney's anxiety and her reluctance to talk, "I mean, I've just told you my biggest secret and you haven't called me crazy and you haven't stormed off and slammed the door. All the worst things that could have happened when I told you, well, none of them happened. None of them. If you want to tell us then we're both here and we're both listening but if you don't feel comfortable then you don't have to."

Heather's compassion and her words of encouragement were enough to bring a tear to Courtney's eye. She stood up and opened her arms. On seeing that Courtney was crying, Heather stood up and embraced her and the two of them hugged for so long that they both felt a little uncomfortable.

"Don't, you'll get me started," said Heather, breaking the hug and wiping her cheek.

"What I'm going to tell you is the truth," said Courtney, sitting back down, "I know that you might not believe me, I know that you might think I'm seeing things or making things up, but after what you've just told me about Emily, I hope you'll give me the benefit of the doubt."

"Of course I will," said Heather.

"When I was a teenager, I started having nightmares. They were all different, there was no one scenario, or setting, that kept cropping up, but they all involved me seeing myself but it wasn't me, it was a version of me, a version that wasn't quite right. I've never been able to work out what was wrong, it's subtle, but it's obvious at the same time, if that makes any sense, I mean, I know just by looking at them that something is wrong, I just can't tell what it is. In some of the nightmares I see her, myself, and I follow her but I'm never able to catch her, never able to get close enough to talk to her or get a really good look at her, she's always just out of reach, no matter how hard I try to chase her. In other nightmares, I'm running away from her and she's behind me but I can't see her well enough to get a good look and I can't stop running or she'll catch me. I can feel that she's getting closer and closer and I wake with a start and the sheets are all wet and clinging to me, or I'm out of my bed covered in sweat, lying on the floor or standing up, screaming or talking nonsense."

"Do you still have those nightmares?" asked Heather, while trying to imagine the horror and the fear that Courtney must go through every time it happened.

"Not every night, but it got worse about a year after the nightmares started. I was sitting at a dressing table in my parents' bedroom and I was brushing my hair when I saw my nightmare, my evil twin, behind me in the mirror. She was there in the reflection, stood about two metres behind me. I turned round to look but she wasn't there, there was no one there, but when I looked back at my reflection in the mirror, there she was, stood behind me. Then she walked towards me and I sat there watching her in the mirror as she got closer and closer, then she reached out her hand and I was frozen, I couldn't move, I couldn't break eye contact with her, with me. She looked just like me and she reached out her hand and placed it on my shoulder."

"And then what happened?" asked Heather.

"Nothing. I passed out, I must have banged my head on the end of the bed as I fell off the stool onto the floor. I had a big lump on the back of my head when I woke up. Mother heard a noise and came upstairs to see what I was doing and she found me unconscious on the floor. They got me into bed and called a doctor."

"What did the doctor say?"

"Nothing much. I had to go to the hospital a few weeks later for some tests but they didn't find anything and I think they must have thought I was arsing about and fell over and banged my head so they didn't really look into it any further. I didn't tell them about the nightmares, or about seeing her, or how I lost consciousness before I banged my head, so they didn't really have much to go on. Mother took me to see a doctor about the nightmares and I was sent to see a counsellor and we talked, but I didn't tell her about what I saw and she didn't help with the nightmares."

"Has it happened again, since then?"

"A few times, I've seen her in the reflection in shop windows, but when I look round she's gone, I can't go to the gym anymore after seeing her in the mirror there. Windows at night, they're a problem, I've got to remember to close the blinds before it gets dark outside, hairdressers are another issue."

"So who cuts your hair?" asked Heather, although she already knew the answer. Courtney's hair was cut at home with the kitchen scissors. It had been cut this way, and this badly, for so long that she was no longer self conscious about it, and yet she was still no good at it. Practice does not make perfect.

"I do, but it's really hard to cut your own hair when you can't look in the mirror," said Courtney, while laughing about it, "I've got a friend who insists on tidying it up every now and again, but he's not a real hairdresser and I'm not even sure he makes it any better."

"So you avoid mirrors completely, to shut her out, to protect yourself?" asked Heather.

"I try, but they're everywhere, it's not until you try to avoid them that you realise how many there are. I think mirror must be the most abundant element on the planet."

"I don't know how you do it," said Heather, "I mean, I look in the mirror about twenty times before I even leave the house in the morning. I need to look in the mirror to brush my teeth, do my hair, make up, everything, There's a mirror by my front door, just so I can make sure I look okay before I leave the house. Have you ever thought about confronting her in the real world rather than trying to shut her out?"

"Erm, no. Why would I want to do that?" asked Courtney. "She's terrifying. The dreams are terrifying. I don't think she's somehow misunderstood. She's not like a long lost relative that I need to sit down with and catch up on old times. This is something malign, something I need to keep away from. If you had seen her, if you had experienced the dreams that I've had, then you would know. You wouldn't be encouraging me to confront her."

"But sometimes we have to confront our fears, sometimes we have to face them head on. What if Emily could help?" asked Heather. "What if Emily could see her, or communicate with her, or find out what she wants from you? She must want something otherwise she wouldn't be here."

"I could try," said Emily as she wandered about the room, although she wasn't overly enthusiastic about the plan.

"We just have to get you in front of a mirror and wait," said Heather, starting to plan the whole process, working it out as she spoke, "I'll be there, Emily will be there. We see if she turns up and see if I can see her, we'll see if Emily can see her, maybe Emily can communicate with her. Maybe there's a connection between them somehow and, if Emily can't see her, then we won't let her harm you, we'll stop the whole thing before she touches you. You can tell us where she is, how close she is. I'll cover up the mirror before anything happens to you. Job's a good'un, as they say."

Emily could see the fear in Courtney's face, although Heather was too absorbed in formulating her plan to notice Courtney's anxiety. It's going to take more than this to persuade Courtney to sit in front of an uncovered mirror, thought Emily.

"I'll think about it," said Courtney. Which meant no. Not now, not later, not ever.

"You hungry?" Heather asked Courtney.

"Always," said Courtney, sounding keen.

The keenness didn't reflect the thought running through Courtney's head right now, which was, if she's going to try to force me to sit in front of a mirror, with her and Emily, then I need to get out of this friendship right now.

"Let's get something to eat and then make camp in my room," said Heather, "I've got vodka, polish vodka, and a large Toblerone. We can relax and have a drink and talk some more. I'm sure I can persuade you to do it. If not, I'll get Binkie to call you on Lester's satellite phone. I know she could talk you into it."

And that's how they ended up an hour later in Heather's cabin, with full stomachs and their first glasses of neat vodka of the evening.

The American bird

It wasn't long before Brian Unsafe knocked on the door to Heather's cabin. No euphemism intended. With a rare few hours off, he had been searching the ship looking for company. There was an impromptu party going on in Carter's cabin on the opposite side of the ship and most of the expedition team were there, squeezed into Carter's small cabin and flowing out into the corridor. Shots were being downed and the noise from the party could be heard on the deck above. Brian had popped down to investigate but he didn't fancy sitting outside in the corridor listening to what was going on in the cabin so he drifted away after a short while.

On passing Heather's cabin, he saw the open door and thought he would look inside and see what was going on. The sound of laughter from within, along with the clink of bottle on glass, gave him hope and he took a chance and knocked, although, once he looked inside, it appeared that he was a little early and, rather than joining a party, he might just be interrupting a private chat. At least he'd have somewhere to sit though.

"Having a party?" he asked, hopefully.

"Did you bring a bottle?" asked Heather.

"Of course, may I?" he asked as he entered the room.

Heather was quite pleased with the interruption. She had been discussing Operation Polar Saviour with Courtney for over an hour and had gained very little insight, over and above what was in the written reports. The only additional information she gleaned from Courtney was about how many times Courtney objected to what they were doing.

Not only did Brian bring a bottle, he also brought a glass and a plastic chair that he'd taken from outside the doctor's surgery. He seemed to take up most of the room until he sat down.

"So what do you do Brian?" asked Courtney. "Alain told me you've had an interesting life."

"Not interesting," replied Brian, "varied I'd call it and most of it was a long time ago. Not interesting at all really. I'm sure you don't want to hear all about me."

"Of course we do," said Heather, egging him on to tell his life story. What they eventually got out of him was more like a list of jobs that he'd had over the years, starting with his father's scaffolding company.

"Unsafe Scaffolding it was called," said Brian, "bit unfortunate really, but we went bust. It was my first job when I left school and I thought I'd be taking over the family firm when me dad got fed up but it turned out there was no business left. Me dad had been taking money out and fiddling the books and it turned out we owed money everywhere. I cared for my brother for a while when I wasn't working, he had Down syndrome. Then I ended up getting a place at catering college but I couldn't really afford it so I started doing odd jobs and a bit of acting, just extra stuff, you know, adverts and background characters. I must have played a bloke in a pub half a dozen times, if you watched a beer advert in England, twenty odd years ago, you'd have seen me in the background. I was always either at the bar, playing darts, or playing pool, or sat at a table pretending to drink. I did lots of sporting ones as well, usually as the big fat one in a football team or something. I did loads in costumes so you wouldn't know it was me. A few sofa adverts, you know, just sat with the wife and kids, pretending to change the television channel, or throw a cushion at each other, just the usual stuff. I had a showreel done of all my television appearances, it must have been over a minute long, but I've still never had a speaking part, and then I got a job on a ship and I've been on 'em, on or off, ever since."

"Who looks after your brother now?" asked Heather.

"He's not with us anymore but, when I wasn't there, me mum and me other brothers used to take care of him. It's nice to go back home and see them all when I'm on shore but I don't get home that much. Oh, I had a show at the Edinburgh Festival once, almost thirty years ago now, and I used to be a model as well, back in the day."

"A model?" asked Courtney, in astonishment.

"Yeah, a child model, when I was a kid. I did some modelling for knitting patterns and I was painted by this famous local artist once, round where I lived. The painting was up in a gallery in town and a bloke saw it and contacted me mum to say he was worried about me and that she should take me to see a doctor and get some tests done. He was convinced I had jaundice because of the colour of my skin so mum took me to hospital and they did a load of tests."

"And what was wrong with you?" asked Heather. "Did they find out?"

"Well, nothing was wrong. It turned out the guy who painted me wasn't very good and he'd made my skin look too yellow. He was famous because he was the only painter anyone knew round our way but he was never any good at it. Look, I'm surprised you're not at the other party," said Brian, which got Emily's attention.

"I'll go and have a look," she said to Heather.

"Where's this?" asked Courtney.

"Next corridor, it's your mate with the beard," he said to Heather and then he realised that probably didn't narrow it down enough so he tried to elaborate, "the one with the massive hands," he said, looking down, self consciously, at his own large, tattooed hands, covered in blue plasters to protect the cuts.

"Carter's having a party and I didn't get an invite?" said Heather, with mock disgust.

She was well aware of Carter's parties, they almost always ended with Carter being egged on to run around the deck of the ship, half naked, or sometimes completely naked. It had become Carter's thing. Get him drunk enough and you might be able to persuade him to run around naked. Everyone gets to go outside, full of warm liquor, to protect against the cold and the wind, and you get to see, well you get to see what you get to see. Although plenty of drink was required, to get Carter susceptible to the idea of a few naked laps of the ship, he was also a keen and willing participant. He believed it helped with team bonding, not just at the time, but the next day when everyone was talking about it, about him, and for days to come. And it worked, his colleagues rarely had a bad word to say about him, apart from the occasional complaint to Human Resources about indecent exposure.

Emily came back into the room and looked at Heather, she shook her head, they both knew what was going on and what was going to happen and they both spoke at the same time.

"He'll be naked in ten minutes."

"Sorry," said Courtney, "who's going to be naked?"

"Carter is, or will be soon," said Heather, "he gets drunk and then runs round the deck naked. If you miss it tonight then I'm sure you'll get to see it in the next few days. If we're lucky, he might even do a couple of laps indoors so we don't have to go outside," she said, laughing.

"That's gross," said Courtney.

There was no nudity on Polar Saviour, at least none that Courtney was aware of. She wasn't a prude but she was starting to worry about what kind of expedition she had come on.

"Doctor," said Brian and the three women looked up to see Alain Govenor's head appear round the door. The rest of him followed soon after and, like Brian, he had brought his own chair, also taken from outside the doctor's surgery.

"Snap," he said to Brian, who stood up and reached over to shake Alain's hand.

"May I come in?" asked Alain as he sat down.

"All right, Doctor," said Brian. He'd chosen to refer to Alain using his profession rather than his name, out of respect, although he wouldn't find it very respectful if someone did the same to him.

Heather looked at Courtney, on hearing Brian refer to Alain as Doctor, and they took a moment to decide which one of them was going to say something. Nothing verbal, just eye contact and facial expressions.

"He's not a doctor, Brian," said Courtney.

"Oh, come on," protested Alain, "I'm sure Brian doesn't want to hear all this, it's all technicalities and pedantry. Pour me a drink would you, Heather, let's talk about something else. I heard on the grapevine that it's all going to kick off later and there might be a bit of excitement."

"Do you mean Carter?" asked Heather.

"What about him?" asked Alain.

"We think, if history teaches us anything, that Carter is going to get naked and run around the deck of the ship. That's your excitement. That's what's arousing your interest," she said, with emphasis on the word, 'arousing.'

"Oh, well, that's a bit of a disappointment," said Alain, "might be worth watching though, it's slippery out there, nothing funnier than seeing a naked man fall over. Might film it. Do you still get two hundred and fifty pounds for sending in your clips?"

"You might not be a doctor, Doctor, but if he falls over and hurts himself, who do you think will be treating him?" asked Heather.

"Oh, shit. I hadn't thought of that. Do you think I should go and talk to him, persuade him not to do it?"

"Only if you're more persuasive than half a bottle of whiskey and half a dozen of his colleagues chanting, off, off, off."

Brian was confused, not about Carter and the naked deck run, he had seen that kind of thing many times before, but about Alain not being a doctor. He was dressed like a doctor, brown shoes, corduroy trousers, and Brian had even seen him with a stethoscope hanging around his neck and a thermometer in his shirt pocket. Yet, despite all his acting, all the times he'd pretended to be drinking at a bar, or pretended to be with his family on a sofa, Brian still couldn't see anything but a doctor when he looked at Alain. He certainly didn't see someone pretending to be a doctor.

"Alain," said Brian, "what do they mean when they say you're not a doctor?"

"Oh, I'm just pretending to be a doctor," said Alain, "but keep it under your hat, not everyone knows, and it's a well known fact that there's a strong placebo effect in thinking that I'm a real doctor so the less said the better. Don't want people's health put at risk by wild rumours. Loose lips sink..."

"But you agreed you weren't going to see patients without telling them," interrupted Courtney, "you agreed, just a few hours ago."

"Oh yes," said Alain, having genuinely forgotten, "sorry, forgot. Apologies, Brian. As these two ladies," or is it three, he wondered as he looked round the room, "anyway, as they have rightly said, I'm not a real doctor, Brian, but needs must."

"What have you been doing, Alain?" asked Courtney, somewhat accusingly. She thought she knew Alain quite well and she strongly suspected that he'd been treating patients without telling them about his complete and utter lack of medical training.

"Nothing, nothing," denied Alain, "I've not had a surgery since we last spoke so I couldn't have seen any patients, cross my heart."

"What have you been doing then, where have you been?" asked Courtney, the tone of her voice revealing an increasing frustration with her old tutor.

"I was playing darts with Lester and, since then, I've been with Seanne in her cabin, just talking," said Alain calmly, choosing to ignore the accusatory nature of the question.

"The American bird?" asked Brian.

"That's right, Brian," replied Alain, "the American bird."

Heather and Courtney looked at each other. They hadn't seen an American woman on the ship and they weren't sure whether to believe Alain's story or to question him further. As far as they were aware, there were no paying passengers on board.

"Ask him where she is and I'll go and have a look," Emily said to Heather.

Courtney had only known Heather for a short time but she could already tell when she was talking to Emily. She went quiet, her concentration was elsewhere, her eyes were looking at something no one else could see.

"Where is she now, what cabin is she in?" asked Heather.

"She was in her cabin, just two doors along from Carter's," said Alain, "but she might not be there now, she might have joined the party. Are you going to send your little spy to have a look?"

"I might just do that. What does she look like?"

"Oh," interrupted Brian, "she's beautiful. Golden hair, curly, beautiful hair. Bronzed skin, all shiny and shimmery, radiant, that's what she is. I only saw her a few times. She came to the canteen once. I take her a tray at meal times as she don't like coming out of her cabin much. I don't mind doing it. I'm not doing it for everyone though, so don't get any ideas, I'm not a delivery service," he said, laughing to himself.

Emily took off to have a look. As she passed Carter's cabin, a crowd of people, maybe eight or nine, were following Carter along the corridor to the stairs, laughing and giggling. Carter strode along at the front with his shirt off, stripped to the waist, his pale white, freckled skin and three nipples on display, for all to see.

Two doors along from Carter's could mean either of two cabins so Emily chose to start with the one towards the stern of the ship. Inside was a mess, there were clothes everywhere, giving the impression of a room full of soft furnishings, but really it was just a very untidy room with clothes strewn across the floor, the bed, the chair, and every other available surface. A young woman was sat on the bed, propped up by two pillows and reading a book, she looked exactly as Brian had described. She wore a loose, patterned, sleeveless dress that looked like it was homemade, out of many different materials, but what surprised Emily was that Seanne looked up from her book just as Emily entered the room. Emily froze. It might just have been coincidence but something had made Seanne stop and look.

She can see me, thought Emily. She can't see me, can she?

She had never felt this vulnerable before. Emily held her breath and stood as still as she could, too terrified to move, until Seanne finally looked away and continued to read her book. It can't have been more than four or five seconds, but it was a huge relief when Emily realised that she couldn't be seen. Emily stepped back out of the room and breathed heavily, she bent over and put her hands on her knees and tried to breathe normally. Eventually, she stood upright and walked back to Heather's cabin.

On the way back, Emily passed Mikaela Larson, the ship's captain, with a paint brush in one hand and a pot of red paint in the other. Mikaela stopped outside Courtney's cabin and began to repaint the graffiti from the previous night. The paint splattered as she quickly painted the words, 'penguin murdererer,' going over the letters still visible on the wall, deliberately misspelling it again. She looked left and right along the corridor as she painted, but no one came to interrupt her. The paint flew from the brush, specking her face and clothes, along with the floor and the ceiling. It didn't take her long and when she was done, she took the paint pot and balanced the brush across the top of the tin then she quickly headed back to the bridge, whistling while she walked. She stashed the tin of paint in the store room, ready for next time.

Emily returned to Heather's cabin to find Lester Cherry-Stone stood in the doorway, having agreeing to join them for a quick drink.

"I'm meant to be in the Comms Room," said Lester, "but a quick one won't do any harm."

Emily didn't wait for Lester to get out of the way and Heather looked up to see what she had to say as she entered the room. On seeing Heather's reaction, Courtney also looked, but she knew she would have to wait to hear the conversation second hand.

"She's there," said Heather to Courtney, passing on the message from Emily, "it's just as Brian described, the room's a right mess apparently."

"Who's there?" Lester asked Heather, while leaning across Alain to take a small coffee cup, half full of vodka, that Brian was offering to him.

"Seanne, the American bird," said Heather. She smiled at Brian, who knew she was mocking him, but he didn't mind. It made him feel welcome, he was part of the group now, so he smiled back.

"Oh yeah," said Lester, "she's, um, she's, um, interesting."

"She's on a journey," said Alain, in all seriousness.

Oh, give me strength, thought Courtney and Heather, although Heather only thought it, Courtney said it out loud.

"What sort of journey?" demanded Courtney. "We're all going on a bloody journey, that's what you do on a ship, what's so special about her journey?"

"I'm not the best person to explain it," said Alain, "she said she was going to Antarctica to find someone, to find something out. She was told to go there to speak to a shaman to find out whatever it is she's trying to find out. Probably a wild-goose chase, but who knows. I didn't ask her what it was that she was looking for, I didn't think to ask. She's very nice, you'd like her."

"I'll be the judge of that," said Courtney.

Outside the cabin, in the corridor, Carter was doing a lap of honour, wearing just a sock to cover his modesty. Lester pulled the door open to see where all the noise was coming from just as Carter passed the open doorway. He stopped and struck a bodybuilder pose and the crowd, following him, clapped and cheered and raised their glasses. Carter made a straining, grunting noise that somehow ended up with him howling like a wolf and then he ran off, along the corridor. He felt wild, exhilarated, alive and more than a little drunk.

Lester pushed the door to and said, "Wow, has he been outside like that? Man, that guy's crazy."

"You should go and see her," said Alain, to Heather and Courtney, "I'm serious, you'll like her, she's young and alive, full of life, I mean. She's travelled the world. Maybe she can help the two of you, maybe her shaman can help with Emily or your evil sister," he said, gesturing to them both in turn.

"I don't need any help with Emily, thank you very much," was Heather's response. Emily's rude gesture towards Alain was only seen by Heather.

"And when did you start calling her my evil sister?" asked Courtney, who was unsure when or where this new nickname had come into existence. "How long have you been calling her that?" she asked.

"Well," said Alain, who about to give Courtney the benefit of his wise thoughts and his wisdom on the subject, "she looks like you so she might be your sister, and you are scared of her, so it doesn't take a genius to work out that she's evil. Two plus two equals evil sister."

Brian stood up, downed his drink and said, "I think I'm done, I'm not even sure what any of you are talking about anymore."

"I'm with you, man," said Lester, finishing his drink in one. The two of them stood up to leave and return to work.

"You should go and visit her, is all I'm saying," said Alain, who picked up his own chair, along with Brian's, so that he could return them to the corridor outside the doctor's surgery.

"What do you think?" asked Heather, once she was alone with Courtney and Emily.

"I think we should pop in and see her tomorrow, it can't do any harm can it?"

"What do you think, Emily?" asked Heather, mainly for Courtney's benefit as she didn't need to speak to Emily to have a good idea of what she was thinking.

"I think you should go and speak to her," said Emily, "and I think you should tell Courtney that the graffiti is back on her cabin door, so that it's not too much of a shock for her when she sees it."

What if she's me?

The next day at breakfast, everyone was very quiet. Carter was sat at a table with two members of the expedition team while most of the others were still in their cabins. The waves had picked up overnight and everyone could feel the effect of the swell on the ship. An aroma of vomit wafted through the corridors.

Heather and Courtney ate breakfast together in silence. Courtney had seen the graffiti on returning to her cabin last night, she was upset at the time but had slept since and had forgotten all about it by the time she woke up. She saw it again on leaving her cabin and the injustice of it burned inside her. It wasn't fair that she was taking all the blame, it wasn't fair that she had become a scapegoat, it wasn't fair that people were targeting her, it wasn't fair, it wasn't fair.

"What are you going to do about it?" asked Heather, breaking the silence.

It was pretty easy for Heather to guess what Courtney was thinking, her facial expressions gave the game away, constantly switching between upset, worried and angry, her face muscles were working overtime to keep up with her thoughts.

"I'll tell you in a minute," said Courtney as she looked up to see Mikaela Larson walk into the canteen. She stood in the doorway, looking round, until she spotted Courtney and Heather, then she walked over towards their table, her shoes squeaking on the grey linoleum as she walked. She was still wearing the same scruffy uniform from yesterday, splattered with red paint, and she looked more like the captain of a small trawler that the captain of an ocean going research vessel.

Heather looked over her shoulder to see what the squeaking noise was and she spotted Mikaela walking towards them.

"Uh ho, here we go," said Heather, "stay calm, take a second to think before you say anything, don't say anything you'll regret," she advised Courtney.

"Good morning, may I join you," said Mikaela as she arrived at their table, it wasn't a question though, she was just giving them prior warning.

"Are you eating with us?" asked Heather, to be polite.

"No, I've already eaten," replied Mikaela in a matter of fact way, "but I might get myself a coffee. I'll be back in a minute."

"What does she want?" whispered Courtney. "What is she going to do now?"

"Don't worry about it," said Heather quietly, "she sought you out so, obviously, she's got something to say to you, just let her say it, see what she says before you do anything. She might even want to apologise."

"Oh, I'm not here to apologise," said Mikaela, arriving back at the table with her drink. She sat next to Heather, across the table from Courtney, so she could look her in the eye.

"I'm here to put a stop to this," said Mikaela, "I don't enjoy painting it. I get no pleasure from it. I've got better things to do and I'm sure you don't like getting up in the morning, wondering if I've been back. Agreed?"

"Agreed."

"So, we just leave it. We don't paint over it, because you can still read it anyway, so what's the point. And that way you don't get any more surprises and I don't have to get up in the night to do it again."

"You didn't have to paint it at all," protested Courtney.

"No, but it's done now, let's just leave it. Everyone knows it's there, what's done is done. People have taken their selfies with it, no one even notices it anymore."

"I notice it," said Courtney, not knowing whether to laugh or cry.

"It does make some sense, in a warped sort of way," said Heather, muddying Courtney's thoughts even further.

It doesn't make any sense, thought Courtney. But what can I do about it? I can't ask Alain to speak to her again. She's the captain of the ship so I don't really get a say in this. It's maritime law, as Alain would say, although I'm not sure that he even knows what it means.

Heather could see a wave of resignation sweep across Courtney's face and body. Her shoulders slumped and she sighed.

"Thank you," said Heather to Mikaela, taking control of the situation, "thank you for coming here and talking to Courtney about this, for taking the time to resolve this face to face. I'm sure Courtney appreciates it as much as I do, thank you for ending this. You do want this to end now, don't you, Courtney?"

"I suppose, yes," said Courtney, who was rather confused as to how or why she agreeing to something that failed to benefit her in any way.

"Good," said Mikaela, "did you see your friend over there, running around naked last night? Quite a sight, I hope you got a good look at it."

And that was that, end of discussion. For the rest of the voyage Courtney Woodbeard would be marked out as a penguin murderer. Her cabin, adulterated by foot high, badly painted, red letters spelling out the crime that she had been accused of, and found guilty of, by public opinion. It was there for all to see, and for all to take selfies with.

Courtney decided that she would ask Alain if he would swap cabins with her, next time they met.

"It shouldn't be too long now, you know," said Mikaela, taking a slurp of her hot coffee, "you ready to do your bit when we arrive?" she asked, directing the question to Heather with a glance.

"Well, by the look of most of my team at breakfast this morning, if we arrive today we're in trouble. They probably need a day or two to recover but I'm sure Carter's got everything under control. He's a darling, I just tell him what I want to happen and he gets on with it and it happens. I don't care how he does it, but he gets them to do the work and they still seem to like him. They're not the most experienced bunch, actually, they've got virtually no experience at all, they're mostly university students. We didn't have time to get who we wanted, they were either working, or they were sick, or..."

Heather's voice tailed off as she thought of her wife, left behind at home, and her friends and colleagues. She thought of the recent global pandemics, of the fires, the floods, the mass graves in public parks, all things that would have been shocking a few years before, but had now become commonplace, every year. She didn't even think twice when offered the chance to get away from it all, to travel to Antarctica and to escape from the death, and the stress, and the worry. She felt guilty about her wife, not guilty about leaving her behind, but guilty about how easy the decision was to leave her and come away.

"Captain," said Courtney, to get her attention, she only said Captain because she had forgotten Mikaela's name.

"Yes," replied Mikaela, who was about to suggest to Courtney that she called her Mikaela, rather than Captain, but she rejected the idea. Courtney seemed like a troublemaker and overfamiliarity could cause a problem at a later date. Being Captain allowed Mikaela to pull rank. Being Mikaela could end with her having to compromise to spare a friends feelings and we couldn't be having that.

"Why does the ship list to one side?" asked Courtney.

"It makes it quicker going round corners," said Mikaela with a straight face.

"No, I mean really?" asked Courtney. Even she wasn't going to fall for that one.

"It's heavier on one side of the ship, that's why it lists. It's not dangerous, it's within normal operating parameters. There's nothing to worry about, as long as you don't all go rushing to look out the windows on one side. We should be all right, fingers crossed."

"But why is it heavier on one side? Don't they normally balance out the weight with ballast or something?"

"Normally yes, but, when they installed Mr Hanad's elevator, they put it too far to one side so the weight unbalanced the ship and, no matter how we load the ship, we don't seem to be able to correct it. It's almost like the ship doesn't want to be upright, like an unseen hand is holding it in place and, whatever we do, we can't stop it."

I wish I hadn't asked, thought Courtney, who was unsure if Mikaela was telling the truth or teasing her again.

"Doctor," said Mikaela, looking up from her coffee as Alain Govenor approached their table with a stressed look on his face, "haven't you got any patients this morning?" she asked, knowing full well the answer to that question. "There's a bit of sickness going round I hear."

"They're queueing up. What am I going to do?" he whimpered. "I haven't got enough chairs."

"Come on, Doctor," said Mikaela, "this is what you took the oath for isn't it? Didn't you swear by the Greek Gods to care and protect those poor unfortunate hangover victims. It's what you live for, now go and play God with some people's lives. You might as well open up early, hadn't you, start dishing out some sickness pills and don't forget to tell people to drink plenty of water."

"But I haven't had my breakfast yet?"

"What's more important, Doctor? The wellbeing of the souls on my ship or your stomach?"

Alain could smell the coffee, he could see and smell the bacon, he could feel his stomach protesting. If only I could get my stomach to rumble really loudly they'd let me stay for breakfast, he thought. But it didn't rumble, at least not loud enough for anyone to hear, so he reluctantly turned to leave.

"Let's make some people better then, shall we," he said as he limply waved goodbye to Heather, Courtney and Mikaela.

"Right, I'm off as well," said Mikaela, putting her half-empty cup on the table and standing up, "the ship's not going to steer itself. Actually I've got Sander for that. Maybe I'll have a nightcap and a nap, been up all night. I'll see you chicks later."

And with that she was off, squeaking her way across the floor to the door.

"She's an odd one," said Emily, from her seat next to Courtney.

"She most certainly is," replied Heather.

"Sorry?" said Courtney, not realising, at first, that Heather was talking to Emily and she was only hearing part of the conversation.

"Sorry, Emily, I forgot you were there," said Courtney, to where she correctly thought Emily would be.

"You remember what we said yesterday?" asked Heather. "Well, Emily and I were talking last night and we really want to help you with your, er, I don't know what to call her, your dream woman, no that sounds wrong, makes her sound like your ideal woman. Your evil twin sister, was that what Alain called her? Anyway, I know you don't want to confront this but you'll be with friends in a safe environment. If you want, we could get Alain there with his gun and he could shoot the mirror if anything goes wrong. Not that anything is going to go wrong. That was a bad idea."

"My evil twin sister. You want to find out who she is?" asked Courtney. "But what if, what if she's me? What if it's all in my head? How do I deal with that? What if you don't see anything and I do? What if Emily doesn't see anything? How do we even know this will work?"

"We don't," replied Heather, "but if you don't try then you'll never know. Imagine if we can see her, and we can stop this, wouldn't you wish that you'd done something sooner? Wouldn't you rather try something, instead of doing what you're doing now which is just ignoring it and hoping it will go away?"

The anxiety gripped Courtney, her body became tense, her head and her heart had a race. No, she thought, no. I can't do it. We can't do it. I won't.

And then, for the second time since she'd sat down in the canteen, Courtney found herself agreeing to something she didn't want to do. It was the easier option, she had no fight left.

I know that Heather and Emily are trying to help, thought Courtney. Maybe we should just do it and see what happens. I don't want to think about what could go wrong. I won't have a better opportunity to face this. But what if?

The offer of help from friends, the peer pressure, just about won the day. Courtney agreed. She nodded to Heather but that wasn't enough. Heather wanted to hear her say it.

"Okay," said Courtney, "let's do it but we need to do it right now before I change my mind."

They left the table as it was, covered in dirty plates, bowls containing unfinished cereal, half-empty glasses, and scattered crumbs. The three of them headed to Heather's cabin as quickly as they could. Once there, they didn't waste any time, Courtney didn't want to think about what they were doing in case she had second thoughts.

"You stand in front of the mirror," said Heather, "where do you want me? Shall I stand next to the mirror ready to cover it up?"

"No," said Courtney, thinking on her feet, "the mirror isn't the problem, if she's going to appear then she'll be behind me and I'll see her in the reflection. If you cover the mirror she might still be there but we won't be able to see her. You're better off throwing something over my head so I can't see the mirror but you still can."

"What if I can't see her in the mirror?" asked Heather.

"Maybe Emily will be able to see her," said Courtney, "where should Emily stand? Should she be behind me or in front of me? She needs to be able to see in the reflection so she can see what I see but she needs to be able to get behind me to see if she can intercept her. Maybe she should be behind me but off to one side?"

"What are we trying to achieve here?" asked Emily. "This all seems a bit frantic and not very well thought out."

"Have you got something to throw over my head?" asked Courtney.

"I've got a fleece here, will that do?" asked Heather, holding up a large, red fleece with a United Nations logo stitched onto it.

"Why haven't I got one of those?" asked Courtney. "Has everyone on the team got one or is it just you?"

"Just me," lied Heather, "it'll do though, won't it? Do you want me to throw it over your head when I think it's time or do you want me to wait for a signal before I throw it?"

"What sort of signal? Just throw it before I start screaming. If I'm already screaming then you've left it too late."

"Stop, please," said Emily, "we need to think about what we're doing. Are we just trying to find out if we can see something in the reflection or are we trying to catch and kill whatever it is? I think we should just be taking little steps here, let's not get too far ahead of ourselves. We should just take a look and then we can stop and work out what we do next."

"You're right, yes, she's right," said Heather to Courtney, "Emily's right. We need to calm down and not get too far ahead of ourselves. We should just have a look and see if there's anything there, just a few minutes at a time. You tell us if you see her and, if you do, then we'll both look and then we'll quickly shut things down. Fleece on head then I'll rugby tackle you onto the bed before you scream. We don't want her to get anywhere near you."

"Shall we do this then?" asked Courtney, nervously.

"Where are we all standing?" asked Emily, in frustration.

"Let's do this," said Heather.

Courtney turned and stepped in front of the mirror and saw herself for the first time in a very, very long time.

"Oh my God, is that what I look like?" Courtney asked out loud as she stepped closer to the mirror to get a better look. I look so old, she thought, I don't remember having lines like that on my forehead, or around the eyes, they must be new. I wonder how long I've had them. My eyes look puffy and tired. Is this what people see when they look at me?

She stared at her reflection in the mirror for some time, occasionally touching her face, pushing or pulling at the skin, running her fingers through her roughly cut hair. The eyes are the same, she thought. I see myself in the eyes but I hardly recognise the face. I look like my mother. A decent haircut would help and is that a new mole on my face? I'm sure that wasn't there before, or was it? I'll need to look at some old photographs to find out. My hair is a complete mess, I look like someone who hasn't made any effort, and look how dirty my glasses are, there are finger marks all over them, I'm surprised I can see anything.

She took off her glasses to clean them on a distressed looking piece of tissue she took out of her trouser pocket.

"Do you see anything yet?" asked Heather.

"Hang on a second, I can't see anything without these on," said Courtney.

When she put her glasses back on, she focused her attention on the mirror, looking closely so see if there was anyone behind her. She swayed her whole body from left to right, one foot flat on the floor, the other up on tiptoes, then back the other way. She could see the whole room, one half at a time, except for a blind spot directly behind her. She was moving left and right, trying to see over her shoulder, to see if someone was timing their movements to coincide with hers to stay hidden but, while Courtney swayed from side to side, she failed to notice a figure stood in front of the bathroom door, off to one side.

"Can she see anything yet?" asked Emily, as she circled Courtney.

"Anything?" asked Heather.

"Wait," said Courtney, still swaying, "I think there's someone there. Over there by the bathroom, can you see them? It's her. It's me."

Heather looked and saw nothing, just the bathroom door. She stepped across in front of Courtney and looked at the bathroom in the reflection in the mirror. Still nothing. No one there.

The figure by the bathroom took a cautious step forward, towards Courtney, and raised their right arm. Courtney took a small step away, bumping into Heather, while keeping her eyes fixed on the mirror, fixed on the reflection of her evil twin sister.

"Emily," said Courtney, with a trembling voice, "can you see her?"

"I can't see her but I can't get to the mirror as you're both stood in the way," said Emily.

Heather moved across towards the bathroom, out of the way. She was aware that she was moving towards whatever it was that had appeared in the room. She hoped it wouldn't be able to harm her but, really, she had no idea. She gripped the fleece tightly, her fists clenched, and she prepared herself to wrestle Courtney away from the mirror.

"I can see her," said Emily, "I can see her coming towards us. I think she can see me too."

"She can see her," said Heather, "Emily can see her and she can see Emily."

Courtney almost collapsed on hearing that she wasn't the only one. Her legs went weak and she almost sobbed. She wasn't imagining it. There was something there. She wasn't going mad.

The figure took another step forward, she was close now, she could have reached out and touched Heather, if she hadn't been so focussed on Courtney.

"She really does look like you," said Emily, although, as Heather didn't pass the message on, it went unheard.

"Tell me when," said Heather, ready to pounce.

"Are you okay Courtney?" asked Emily. "Ask her if she's okay," she demanded of Heather.

"Are you okay?" asked Heather, but Courtney didn't look okay. She was frozen, watching as the figure approached her, unable to move, unable to speak. Another step closer, reaching out to touch her.

"She doesn't look okay," said Emily, just as Courtney was about to scream, just as Heather was about to lunge forward.

Heather threw the fleece over Courtney's head and, in one movement, she wrapped her arms around Courtney's shoulders and pushed all her weight forward. The two of them collapsed onto the bed with Heather on top, arms trapped beneath Courtney, legs stretched out, toes touching the floor.

The visual link between Courtney and her pursuer was broken. The plan had worked. They were all unscathed.

Heather managed to free one arm and roll herself to one side, taking her weight off Courtney, who started to struggle free from Heather's fleece.

"She's still there," said Emily, her voice full of fear, "she's still coming towards me," she said as she stepped back as far as she could go, until she was almost up against the wall.

The figure stepped forward, reached a hand out towards Emily and then Emily collapsed to the floor.

A proper bear hug

Alain Govenor was exhausted, not through hard work but through listening to people complain about how unwell they felt. He dished out rehydration treatments, painkillers and advice to drink plenty of fluids and then he moved on to the next patient. Same advice. Move on. Same advice. Move on.

If any of his patients were actually sick, with anything other than a hangover, then he didn't notice. Regardless of the symptoms, he treated them all for hangovers, even those that didn't have one.

After the last patient had been seen, Alain went out into the corridor and turned the sign on the door to, 'closed,' and then he went back in and locked the door. He took the gun out of the padded envelope in the drawer and put it on the desk in front of him. He had never fired a gun in his life but, since getting his hands on one, he had held it and played with it almost every day, turning it over in his hands, feeling the cold metal against his skin, loading and unloading the bullets, seemingly unaware of the potential damage it could do. He found it reassuring to hold and carry around with him, he convinced himself that it was for self defence, but from what, from whom? He didn't know the answer and it troubled him.

Alain took a pouch of tobacco out of his pocket and rolled himself a joint. He smoked it stood by the open porthole in the spray from the wind and sea outside. Due to listing, the surgery was on the lowest side of the ship and most of the view through the porthole consisted of grey sea reflecting the grey of the sky above. He stared out of the porthole long after he finished smoking, just staring at the sea. He thought he saw a whale at one point, a spray of water rose from the sea that he thought might be a whale exhaling air through its blowhole, so he stared at the same spot for an age hoping to see it again, but there was nothing there, no whale, just water, just spray, foam, waves and the occasional gull.

His stomach rumbled and distracted him from staring at the sea. If he had been hungry earlier at breakfast, then he was ravenous now. It would be too late to get breakfast, although he was sure that Brian would have sorted something out for him, after all, that's what friends do, but he didn't want to disturb him.

He unloaded the gun and put it away in the envelope, back in the drawer, and then he headed to where he knew there was a vending machine, near to Lester's radio shack. He assumed Lester would be working and he intended to pop in and say hello, maybe join him in a glass of spirits. He wondered when Lester found the time to sleep. He'd never mentioned having a cabin of his own but, surely, he couldn't sleep in the Communications Room, it was too bright and noisy in there, it was too warm. Maybe the heat and the hum of the equipment acted as a sleep trigger and he just slept at his desk, maybe he was a vampire and didn't need to sleep, maybe he should stop overthinking things.

The ship had become a hive of activity, Alain could hear Carter's voice, shouting instructions to someone along the corridor, out of sight. Preparations had ramped up as they neared their destination, there was equipment to be readied, items to be checked off a list, ready to be transported ashore after docking, although Alain wasn't sure when that might be.

Alain got a chocolate bar from the vending machine, ripped the packet open and ate it immediately. He looked enviously through the glass door at what he could have won. The biscuit and caramel was claggy in his mouth. He didn't like biscuit and caramel but he chewed and swallowed it anyway. It wasn't what he wanted from the vending machine but someone must have already pressed some of the buttons on the machine before he got there, so he ended up with the wrong thing, hence the disappointment.

Alain pushed open the door to the Communications Room, smiled broadly and asked Lester, "Don't you ever sleep?"

"Morning, Doctor," said Lester, looking up briefly from the monitor he was watching, "or is it afternoon already?"

"Seriously, Lester," said Alain, "you do sleep don't you?"

Alain wasn't sure if Lester thought he was a real doctor or not. He had lost track of who knew and who didn't. Some patients he told, some he didn't. Because of this uncertainty, he wasn't sure if Lester knew whether he was asking in his capacity as a healthcare professional or as a concerned friend.

"Yes, Doctor, I do sleep, I've got my own cabin and everything. There's a bed, it's even got pillows."

Alain still wasn't sure if Lester was sarcastically answering a medical question or if he was responding to a friendly enquiry. Only one way to find out, he thought.

"You do know I'm not a real doctor, don't you?"

"I think everyone on the ship knows that by now," said Lester, laughing to himself.

Lester turned away from the monitor to give Alain his full attention.

"Was there something you wanted or was this a social call, do you want a drink?" asked Lester, gesturing to a glass of spirits on the table in front of him.

"It's a bit early isn't it?" asked Alain, not wanting to seem too keen, but surprising himself with how prudish he sounded. He wasn't averse to the odd morning drink, a few pints with a full english or something stronger to perk himself up, mid morning, but he couldn't remember a time when he had spoken to Lester when Lester wasn't drinking.

"There's no such thing as early or late Doctor, especially when there's no night or day, especially when there's no windows and no light. I sleep when I'm not working and when I'm not sleeping, I drink."

Lester poured Alain a glass and then took a sip of his own drink.

"Cheers, Doctor," he said, raising his glass.

"Er, yes, cheers," said Alain, raising his glass and clinking it against Lester's.

"What are we drinking to?" asked Alain.

"Barely functioning alcoholics," replied Lester with a smile, "and all who sail in them."

"I can drink to that," said Alain.

He took a long look at Lester as he leaned forward to put his drink back on the desk. When they first met, Alain was enchanted by Lester, enchanted by a good looking, youthful man, eyes, sparkling and bright, surrounded by long eyelashes. Alain had been enchanted by Lester almost as much as Courtney Woodbeard had been. Was he really an alcoholic though? He didn't look like one. Maybe he had been lucky, or maybe he hasn't been an alcoholic for long enough, or maybe he was joking.

"Look," said Alain, "you've met Seanne haven't you, Lester?"

"Yes."

"And what did you think?"

"She's a little crazy, you know, she's got some strange ideas," replied Lester.

"Did she ask you to go with her?"

"No but, well, I'm not sure, I think she wanted to, she talked about us going and when we go but I assumed that was because she was going with other people, I didn't get that she meant me specifically. She didn't ask me outright. Did she ask you to go with her?"

"Yes," said Alain, "but it doesn't make any sense."

"But what if there's something there, what if she's telling the truth and there's someone out there who can help her, who could help all of us? What's the alternative? Not going and, well, what are we going back to after this?"

"Would you go if she asked you?"

"Oh, hell, I don't know," replied Lester, "what would you do if an attractive girl asked you to do something, eh?"

"Well, yes, exactly," said Alain, "I see your point. You know that Brian said he was thinking of going with her."

"That doesn't surprise me," said Lester, "he's infatuated with her, that's why she's the only person on this ship who gets room service. Even Hanad doesn't get room service. You know, I spoke with Brian yesterday and he apologised to me?"

"What for?" asked Alain, curious to know more.

"For being a racist."

"Wow," exclaimed Alain sitting back in his chair, a look of astonishment on his face, "what did he say to you?"

"Oh no, nothing like that, nothing racist. Last night, after a few drinks, he just said it, he said there was something he had to say to me, he said he wanted to apologise. I don't know why, but he did."

"What had he done? What was he apologising for?"

"He told me that he was in Edinburgh years ago, many years ago, they got a festival there or something? You know it?"

"Oh yes, the Edinburgh Festival, classical music, ballet and thousands of hippies laughing at left-wing comedians making right-on jokes," said Alain dismissively. He'd not been to the festival but he'd read about it in the papers.

"Well, he was doing a show on the fringe. A show with a couple of other white guys, he said, about Nelson Mandela and they called themselves the Three Nelson Mandelas and they wore black face and danced around and sang songs I think."

"Oh my God," said Alain, "and he apologised to you about it? For the blackface I assume?"

"He apologised to me."

"Well I never," said Alain, "and did you accept his apology, on behalf of black people everywhere?"

"No, I didn't accept the apology but I absolved him from the sins of his past. I said I was pleased that he'd chosen to repent and walk a righteous path to being a better man," said Lester, mockingly.

Alain wasn't sure exactly what Lester was mocking, was it Brian's apology or was there more to it than that?

"What did he say to that?" asked Alain.

"He hugged me real tight, a proper bear hug. I think he might have shed a tear, he was a bit drunk to be fair, a bit emotional."

Lester was trying to think of a subtle way to make the conversation about his secret job as a spy. He knew he wasn't meant to talk about it, so he was reluctant to bring the subject up but, surely, if someone were to ask him then it would be okay to tell them. Not tell them everything, just enough to tease them a little, maybe drop a few hints about what he did in the shadows, but no one asked. However big a hint he dropped, no one ever asked. He had tried suggesting that he had a secret life, that this wan't his real job, that he had something he couldn't tell anyone, he even told someone once that he was a spy, just came right out and said it. You know that I'm a spy don't you? Even that didn't work.

A walkie talkie on the desk cracked into life giving them both a start.

"Lester? Where are you? Over," said the walkie talkie.

Lester picked up the chunk of black plastic and pressed the button to talk.

"Hey, Hanad. I'm in the Comms Room with the Doctor, over."

"Come up. Bring the Doctor, over."

"You wanna see how the other half live?" asked Lester.

"Er...yes, that would be great, where are we going?" asked Alain, slightly reluctantly. He didn't like Hanad but he was unsure why and he felt slightly guilty about not liking him as he'd been so welcoming. Was he too welcoming? Was that the issue?

"He's up in his penthouse suite," said Lester, "top floor, behind the bridge and the Captain's quarters, he's got most of that deck to himself. It's only accessible through his private elevator, you know, the one that makes the ship list to one side. It should have been nearer to the middle of the ship but, apparently, the feng shui in Hanad's room would have been out of line with his chakras, or something, so they put it over to the side and never quite got the ship level again."

Alain wasn't sure whether to believe Lester or not, it sounded plausible, or did it?

Lester turned off the monitor on the desk and they both left the Communications Room and walked the short distance to the elevator. There was no button to call the elevator, just a single small keyhole to the right of the elevator doors. Lester took a small gold key from one of his many trouser pockets and inserted it into the keyhole and turned it. The sound of the elevator starting up was unmistakable. Lester removed the key and put it back in his pocket.

"You excited?" asked Lester, as they waited.

"Should I be?" asked Alain, who was already impatient and they'd only just called the elevator. It can't be going more than one floor thought Alain. How long is it going to take?

The elevator arrived and the doors opened with a swoosh to reveal a large, gold and glass elevator. They both stepped inside and turned round to face the door. There were no buttons inside the elevator, just a small panel with a single keyhole. The doors closed and they went up a short distance, stopped, and the doors opened again with the same swoosh. Hanad was in his wheelchair in the centre of the room waiting to greet them. He flung his arms wide open and warmly welcomed them.

"Doctor, so good to see you again, do you like it?" he asked, gesturing at the gaudy room around him.

It was ostentatiously decorated, five star luxury hidden away on top of a working research ship. It wouldn't have been out of place in the finest of cruise liners or the poshest of hotels. Plush furnishings, gold decoration, mahogany flooring, and elaborate table lamps, that appeared too fragile and top heavy for ocean going. A beautifully designed, bronze and cut glass chandelier defied gravity from the ceiling, almost directly above where Hanad was sat.

"Lester, help yourself to a drink and have a seat," said Hanad, "we need to talk about what we're going to do with the drone when we get there. Doctor, come with me, I want to quickly show you around."

Hanad wheeled himself away towards some doors on the far side of the room. The tour took in Hanad's wood panelled office, his bedroom, decorated in a similar style to the sitting room, a second bedroom, decorated in a much more reserved style, that Hanad explained belonged to his personal assistant, but they were nowhere to be seen.

"Do you get ashore much?" Alain asked Hanad. "With the wheelchair, I mean, it's not so good on the snow and ice I assume?"

"It's problematic, I'll admit that. I'll get up in the helicopter if the weather holds and I've got the drone so I'll get a good look at what's going on out there. Have you been before?"

"To Antarctica?" queried Alain, "God, no, it's my first time."

"You know there's an initiation ritual that you have to go through when you visit Antarctica for the first time, don't you? Rather painful and humiliating I seem to recall. I couldn't sit down for a week," joked Hanad from his wheelchair, doubling up with laughter.

Alain laughed along with him but he wasn't sure what Hanad was talking about.

"I'm looking forward to going ashore," said Alain, "it will be nice to feel the snow beneath my feet and I'd like to see a penguin, if there are any left."

"Oh, you won't be going ashore," said Hanad, "you're the ship's doctor. I don't mind lending you to the expedition team while they're on board, but you're my doctor, not theirs."

"But I was rather looking forward to it," said Alain, rather weakly.

Alain was starting to realise why he didn't like Hanad. He didn't like people telling him what he could and couldn't do.

"Anyway," said Alain, "you don't need me to stay on board, I'm not even a real…er, not a real…"

"A real what?" asked Hanad and Alain realised that he couldn't tell him. It would break his heart. It wouldn't. It really wouldn't. He just couldn't tell him. He still believes that I'm a doctor, thought Alain. He still believes in me.

"…a real fan of the cold," said Alain, "I'm not a real fan of the cold."

"You'll get to see it all though," said Hanad, as they wandered back to the seating area where Lester had helped himself to a drink, a large drink, somewhere between a treble and a quadruple.

"Is the drone ready to go, Lester?" asked Hanad.

"All systems go, Boss," replied Lester.

"What are you planning to do?" asked Alain, taking a seat at the opposite end of the sofa to Lester.

"We're going to get the drone up and fly to where they think the penguin massacre took place and we're going to see what happened before they get there," said Hanad, "we'll be the first to see it. Would you like that, Doctor? To be the first to see it? If there are dead penguins frozen on the ice, we'll see them. If there are bloodthirsty polar bears, their stomachs bloated with penguin meat then we'll see them first. Do you want to join us, maybe watch it with us?"

"Oh, I'd love to," said Alain, having got over his disappointment at not being allowed to go ashore. He was starting to warm to Hanad. He was part of their team. They were going to see what happened, together.

"When are we doing it?" asked Alain.

"Patience, my friend," said Hanad, "patience. We'll come and get you when we're all set up. It won't be too long, we'll be docked within the hour. Once people are ashore and things have died down a bit, we won't let you miss it, don't worry, we'll let you know when the drone is airborne and we'll watch it together. Lester will fetch the lift for you now as there are a few things I need to speak to him about. Thank you for coming, Doctor, it was a pleasure as usual."

Lester stood up and took out the golden key to call the elevator. He walked Alain over to the elevator door and it swooshed open as soon as Lester turned the key.

"We'll see you later, Doctor," said Lester, as the doors started to close.

As the doors shut, Alain caught a glimpse of Lester's face and he looked like a man who wanted help. A man who wanted to be asked if he was all right. He wasn't sure if he was doing the right thing in leaving him alone with Hanad, but the thought quickly passed, maybe it was nothing. He's always found it difficult to read people, to know if they were serious or joking, to know what they were thinking. He didn't even know what he was thinking half the time. He did know that he was still hungry though.

We're all penguin murderers

After Heather wriggled free from on top of Courtney, she saw Emily lying lifeless on the floor of the cabin and she called out her name. Emily stirred, opening her eyes and lifting her head to see where she was. She sat up and looked round the room. Heather was sat on the bed, misty-eyed.

"I though I'd lost you," said Heather.

"I'm okay," said Emily, "I'm okay, what happened? Where did she go? Is Courtney all right? That was quite a tumble, you didn't have to hit her so hard you know."

"Courtney's safe," said Heather, "we saved her. You saw her didn't you, in the mirror?"

"I did."

"What happened?"

"She touched me and then I blacked out. I don't know how long I was out for. I heard you calling my name."

"And did you find anything out?"

"Like what? I found out that if she touches you then you pass out but there wasn't a flash of light, we didn't link minds and learn everything about each other. I didn't see into her soul. Her life didn't flash before my eyes. I don't know any more about her now than I did this morning, apart from knowing that she's real and Courtney isn't making her up."

"What's going on?" asked Courtney, sitting upright, glasses askew and her hair a mess, not that you could tell.

"Emily saw her," said Heather, "but Emily passed out when they touched. She didn't learn anything that we didn't already know, but she is real. Emily saw her. You're not imagining her. She is real."

"Is Emily okay?" asked Courtney, remembering how she felt, all those years ago, when she blacked out.

"I'm okay, don't worry, just a bit of a headache, that's all," said Emily, to reassure them both, but she didn't feel okay, she felt badly shaken up.

"She's okay," said Heather, "so, what do we do now? Should we go and see Brian's American bird? Alain seems to think she has all the answers."

"I need to get out of here," said Courtney, "before I see her in that mirror again."

"Let's go and see Seanne then, shall we?"

The three of them walked the short distance across to the other side of the ship to Seanne's cabin. Courtney knocked on the door while Heather and Emily waited just behind her. Emily could have easily sneaked inside to see if anyone was home but she decided to wait to see if there was a response to Courtney's knock.

"Come in," came a high pitched voice from inside.

The three of them went into the room, it was pretty much as Emily remembered from her pervious visit, although the room was lit by the dull grey light coming in from outside this time. The room was untidy, Seanne was sat on the floor, on some cushions and a pillow, with a closed book in her hand. There was no bookmark or anything to indicate that she had been reading before they arrived, surely she hasn't just been sat there holding a book, waiting for us, thought Emily.

Seanne was as radiant and as beautiful as Brian had described, thought Courtney, as she looked down at Seanne, who was sat cross-legged in a yoga meditation position.

"You've come," said Seanne, making no effort to stand and greet them, "you must be Heather, and Courtney, and Emily, lovely to meet you, I've heard so much about you all."

"You know about Emily?" asked Heather, slightly concerned.

"Of course! I know everything about everything."

"Where are you from, Seanne?" asked Heather, recognising the American accent, but not being able to place it.

"Patience, California, originally, but I've taken a bit of a strange route to get here."

"And why are you here?" asked Courtney, abruptly, "I mean, what are you doing here? You're not part of the crew and you're not part of the expedition team, we were told there were no passengers on the ship so it just seems odd, you know, that you're here."

The bluntness of the question hung in the air. It sounded rude and impolite when she said it. She hadn't meant to phrase it like that. Should I try to rephrase it? Courtney thought, maybe ask it again, sugar the pill. Odd. Why had she said odd? No one likes to be called odd.

"It is odd isn't it," replied Seanne, without taking offence, "I couldn't have imagined a year ago that I'd be here now with you three, almost in Antarctica, but I'm destined to go there, I've always been destined to go there, I just didn't realise it until someone set me on the right path. I've been in South America for the last two months trying to get on a ship and, when I heard about your journey, I knew I had to join you."

"Can I just ask?" said Emily. "She can't see me can she?"

"Emily wants to know if you can see her," said Heather, passing on the message.

"Of course not," said Seanne, "don't be silly, you're the only one who can see her."

Seanne turned away from Heather and Courtney, who had both taken a seat on the edge of the bed, and she addressed Emily directly, where she mistakenly thought she would be standing.

"Hi Emily," she said, "I'm so glad you're here and I'd love to see you but no, I can't see you at the moment."

She made a heart shape with her hands as she said the word, 'love,' but the sincerity of the gesture was lost on Emily.

"Tell her I'm over here," said Emily, "tell her she's talking to a pile of dirty clothes."

"Emily says thank you, she's so glad to finally meet you," said Heather.

"Finally?" asked Seanne. "But I thought she was here the other night? Weren't you Emily?"

The question was again addressed to where she wrongly believed Emily to be.

"Well, she might have popped in for a quick look, I think, but how do you know she was here?" asked Heather.

"I know everything about everything," said Seanne, for the second time today.

"You don't though, do you?" asked Courtney, aggressively. "You don't know everything, otherwise you wouldn't be going on a journey. Is it a physical and a spiritual journey or is it just one or the other? Which is it? If you know everything, why would you be going on a journey to find something out?"

"You're right," said Seanne, calmly, picking up on the hostility coming from Courtney. She wanted to win her over so she was keen to keep things calm, polite, and friendly. "You're right," she repeated, "if I knew everything then I wouldn't be here now, I wouldn't be on this journey."

"And what is it, exactly, that you're looking for?" asked Heather.

"Well, firstly, my name is not Seanne Harris," said Seanne Harris, "Harris is just my parent's surname, it's not my name, it's just used to identify me as one of their unmarried daughters. And Seanne isn't my first name, it's just a name that my parents gave me when I was little, because that's what society told them they had to do. A child has to have a name. It's not my name, it's just what they called me, it was arbitrary, it was just the name of someone my mother saw on a television show about home improvements. She liked the name so she gave it to me and it's what my parents call me and what the Government and my bank call me, but it's not my name, it's just a random word that they use to identify me, to single me out from everyone else out there. They might as well have just given me a number."

Courtney and Heather sat silently, listening to what sounded very much like a stream of nonsense, but Seanne, or whatever her name was, spoke with enough passion and conviction that it almost sounded plausible. Courtney took off her glasses and breathed on the lenses before wiping them with a tissue from her pocket.

"I mean, that chair over there," continued Seanne, "it's not really a chair, that's just what we've chosen to call it. In other cultures, other languages it's not called a chair, none of us know why it's called a chair or what it's really called, but we use the word chair as a way of identifying that object when we talk to each other, so we know what we're talking about. Whether we're on a boat or a ship here is irrelevant as it's not a boat or a ship, they're just words that we use to describe something so people who use the same language as us know what we're talking about. I mean, who decided that we call that a chair, who decided that this is a book and that is a bed? Do you understand?"

Courtney opened her mouth to reply but made no sound. Heather took a deep breath, sat upright and blinked a few times, unable to think of the right thing to say or even anything to say. She brushed her hair back behind her ear and looked to Emily for some help.

"Tell her it's called a chair because it was invented by someone called Chair," said Emily, "tell her," but Heather declined the offer and remained silent.

"But surely your name is your name, isn't it? That's the point, your parents chose it for you," said Courtney, treating their discussion as if it was based on logic.

"I know your name," said Seanne to Courtney, "you're The Penguin Murderer, that's your name. That was the name given to you by the media, by the public. Do you just accept it? Do you shrug your shoulders and go along with it? You're the woman responsible for killing all those penguins. You moved the polar bears, you killed the penguins, it's almost like you did it with your own bare hands, that's why they call you The Penguin Murderer. Do you still think that a name is just a name? Do you still think that what people call you doesn't matter?"

"Well, no," protested Courtney, determined to fight her corner, "firstly, we don't even know that any penguins have died. The satellite photographs weren't conclusive. It could be anything that caused the reddening of the ice, it could be melting or algae, it could be anything. Even if a penguin has died, it's not my fault. I'm as much a passenger in this as you are. I didn't decide any of this. There's no blood on my hands."

"I didn't say there was," said Seanne, even though she had just said that, or words to that effect, "just because they call you Penguin Murderer, that doesn't mean that's your name and just because people call me Seanne Harris, that doesn't mean that's my name either. That's not how it works, people can't just make up words for things. I mean, we're all penguin murderers, we've all played our part in this, every one of us. It hasn't happened overnight, we've known for a long time that it was coming but we, as individuals, as people, as a species, we chose not to do anything about it until it was too late. We've all got blood on our hands, that's why everyone is so keen to point the finger at you and say it's your fault, because it deflects from their own guilt, their own complicity. We're all penguin murderers, come on say it with me, we're all penguin murderers."

She said it alone the first time.

"We're all penguin murderers."

Emily joined in enthusiastically the second time.

"We're all penguin murderers."

By the third time, it had become a rhythmic chant. Seanne was cross-legged on the floor, palms outstretched, eyes looking down at the floor while Emily jumped up and down, clapping and waving her arms above her head.

"Come on, join in," said Emily to Heather.

"We're all penguin murderers."

"We're all penguin murderers."

Heather spoke the words, not rhythmically like Seanne, not enthusiastically like Emily, but she said it, and then she said it again, then again, gradually picking up the rhythm of Seanne's voice.

"We're all penguin murderers."

"We're all penguin murderers."

"We're all penguin murderers."

Heather turned to look at Courtney who still hadn't joined it. There was a quick shake of the head from Courtney and Heather thought she caught something in Courtney's expression, in the brief moment their eyes met before they turned away from each other. Did she just look at me in contempt, or disgust? thought Heather. It was definitely one or the other, so, despite enjoying the chanting, after being a little reluctant to join in, Heather dropped the rhythm of the chant, spoke the words one more time and fell silent.

"We're all penguin murderers," chanted Seanne, one last time, "wasn't that good, do you feel better now?" she asked Courtney.

Seanne seemed oblivious to the fact that Courtney hadn't joined in, or maybe she wasn't meant to join in, maybe it was supposed to be supportive, we're all in this together. That wasn't how Courtney saw it. Courtney saw it through a thin veil of tears. She took off her glasses again to clean them, wiping away a tear as she put them back on, hoping that no one would notice.

Seanne paused as she shook her hair away from her face, tucking an unruly strand back in place, then she dramatically took an audible deep breath and she looked up to make sure she had their full attention.

"I'm going to find out what my name is," said Seanne, determinedly, "and there's a man out there on the ice somewhere who can tell me. A shaman, or whatever you want to call him. He knows everything, he's spiritual, in tune with the spirits, the planet, the universe. He knows my name and I'm going to see him and find out what it is. No one is going to stop me. He knows about you two. I know he does. He could help you both."

Heather and Courtney looked at each other in astonishment. I don't need anyone's help, thought Courtney whilst Heather looked over to Emily to see if she had any idea what Seanne was talking about.

"What do you mean by saying he could help us? Help us with what?" asked Heather.

"He could help you with Emily," said Seanne. Emily threw her arms up in frustration and turned away. She wanted to say something but she held back as she knew that anything she said to Seanne would go unheard and all she would end up doing was directing her anger and frustration towards Heather.

"I don't need help with Emily," said Heather, dismissively, "we're perfectly happy together," she said, directing her comment at Emily as much as at Seanne. They shared a look across the room and both smiled, the smile was a sign they were both thinking the same thing, an emotional confirmation bias, but their thoughts weren't quite as well aligned as they both imagined.

Heather was being honest when she said she didn't need help with Emily. She had normalised their lopsided relationship over the past forty odd years and she believed that Emily was happy with how things were. Heather always held the upper hand, the only one of them who could communicate with others, the only one who could express their opinions, her opinions. Emily had realised a long time ago that her opinions would never be heard, unless they aligned with Heather's. She loved Heather very much but she was giddy at the thought that there might be someone out there who could help her. Maybe it didn't have to be like this, maybe she didn't have to stay invisible, maybe she could touch things, feel things, taste things. Maybe she could talk to people, have opinions of her own, express her feelings, her thoughts, her emotions.

"But what if he really could help you, help you and Emily?" asked Seanne, again looking over to where she thought Emily would be standing. "What if he knows why no one else can see her or what if he knows how to change that? What if he could make everyone else see her, just like you can?"

"What if he could do that?" asked Emily. "What if I could be seen? Wouldn't that be amazing?"

"Would it?" asked Heather. She felt uncomfortable speaking directly to Emily while in the presence of other people. It was something that she had spent her whole life avoiding, almost all their conversations took place in private or in whispers, only very rarely did they speak openly in front of other people but Heather felt that this was important enough to make an exception. It was important to temper Emily's expectations.

"Of course it would," said Emily, "don't you agree?"

"We need to talk about this later," said Heather.

"What's wrong with now?"

"I think you know what's wrong with now," said Heather, keen to delay any further discussion until a more appropriate time, which, in her mind, was when they weren't with other people, but Emily had other ideas.

"If this shaman she's talking about can help, then why are we even discussing it? Even if there's only a small chance that he can help then it's got to be better than this."

"What's wrong with this?" asked Heather, using her hands to gesture between the two of them. She knew their relationship wasn't perfect but it had to be this way. It had been this way her entire life and she had never heard Emily complain before.

Emily's palms were sweating. She wiped them on her tracksuit bottoms and said, "I'm going with her."

"Oh no you're not," replied Heather.

"Stop me then."

"You can't go without me," said Heather, confident that was the case, that Emily couldn't exist without her presence.

That got Courtney and Seanne's attention. From the one side of the conversation they could hear, it appeared to be a discussion about having a discussion. Now it appeared that they were well past that stage and now they were having a discussion about joining Seanne on her journey. Seanne was pleased. If Emily could persuade Heather to go then that would make her job easier. Courtney was going to be tougher to persuade, thought Seanne, but she already knew she could count on Alain's help with that.

Courtney was stunned. Could Emily go without Heather? Why would she want to?

"Tell her that I'm going with her," said Emily.

"No."

"Tell her."

"No."

"Tell her."

"How do you think he could help me?" asked Courtney, as a way of interrupting Heather saying no, over and over again.

"He knows everything about you. He knows the reason for your visions and how to stop them. He knows you lost a twin sister and that she's trying to communicate with you. He knows how to communicate with her, you can find out how she died, find out what she is trying to tell you. She won't rest until she's spoken to you. You can't keep hiding from her, she's part of you, you're both connected."

"How can he know I had a twin sister? Even I don't know that I had a twin sister. The only person who thinks I did is Alain. Did Alain tell you to say this?"

"I've spoken with Alain," said Seanne, "we spoke about you and he told me what you're going through. He told me how you were still coming to terms with being adopted..."

"Adopted?" asked Courtney, incredulously.

"He told me..."

"And if Alain tells you something then it must be true? Is that it? Why would you believe anything Alain says? Alain's got his own theories about what's going on but that's all they are, just theories. He doesn't know any more about me than your shaman does. How could he?"

"We all think that we know ourselves but can we?" asked Seanne. "Can we truly know ourselves? Surely the people closest to us are in a better position to make judgements about us. How can you know yourself, you can't even look yourself in the mirror?"

Seanne regretted saying it as soon as the words left her mouth. She believed it was true, but it probably wasn't the best way to get Courtney on side. She hoped to persuade Courtney to come with her, to journey across the ice to see her shaman, but this wasn't working out how she had intended. Courtney was a lot more prickly than Alain had described. Seanne's hope, that Alain would be able to persuade Courtney, also seemed to be in tatters, his influence over Courtney seemed to have been rather exaggerated.

"Firstly, I'm not close to Alain, we hadn't seen each other for years until just a few days ago," began Courtney, "and secondly, I can look myself in the mirror. I've just done it and you know what I learnt from doing it? Do you? I don't need to look in a mirror to know who I am. What I see in a mirror doesn't represent me, it's just my physical body, that's all I see, that's all anyone sees when they look in a mirror. It doesn't reflect my thoughts or my emotions, you can't look at me and know what I'm thinking or what type of person I am."

"I'm sorry," said Seanne, "I didn't mean to upset you."

"I haven't finished yet," snapped Courtney, "thirdly, I, er, I've lost my train of thought. What was I going to say?"

They all fell silent as Courtney tried to think of a third point. Of course there wasn't a third point, there never was, she had just wanted to shut Seanne up. It had worked, but now she felt a little embarrassed.

Heather was still too angry with Emily to speak. Courtney was still trying to think of a third point, although surely, by now, it was too late. Seanne was waiting for things to calm down, she seemed to have Emily on side but the other two would take some persuading.

The best wig I've ever seen

"How did you find out about this shaman?" asked Courtney, eventually. "The one out on the ice?"

A sense of calm had finally filled Seanne's cabin after a short period of silence. Emily had stormed out of the room, although she didn't go too far, still close enough to hear what was being said. Heather had counted to ten and calmed her breathing. She clenched and unclenched her fists, feeling the sharpness of her nails as they dug into the skin of her palms, she focused on the pain until her heart stopped racing.

Courtney had found the penguin murderer chanting to be very unsettling, and not at all helpful, and it certainly didn't ease her latent hostility towards Seanne. She blamed the chanting for her bad mood but this was pretty much her default mood, snappy and short tempered. Every day she tried to start with positive thoughts, be nice to people and they'll be nice to you etc, but it never worked out that way.

"Who told you about him?" asked Courtney, drilling another question at Seanne. "How do you know he's even out there?"

"He's been there for years, out on the ice, frozen until now," began Seanne, "he's been there for hundreds of years, thousands of years, hundreds and thousands of years and now the ice has retreated enough to free him, to thaw him out."

"But how do you know this, who told you about him?" asked Courtney.

"Another shaman, that I met on my travels. Look, I don't know what you think of me, but I'm not some kind of rich girl travelling the world on daddy's money. I've worked hard to get here because I've been chasing this my entire life. I've always known that I would have to go to the ends of the earth to find out my name because I just have to know. It's an obsession, I know it is, but it's what drives me, what keeps me going. I didn't work every hour that I could, when I was at college, to spend it on clothes, or shoes, or whatever. I worked hard for that money so I could be here now. I've crossed five continents to get here, I've been starving, so hungry you wouldn't believe. I've slept on the floor, outside in the cold, so often that I can't sleep in a bed anymore, it feels unnatural."

Emily stifled a laugh, not that anyone would have heard. She was in the tiny bathroom, just off Seanne's cabin, squeezed between the sink, the toilet and the door, pressed up against the towel hanging from a single hook on the back of the door. The towel was still slightly damp and smelled of Seanne or, more accurately, it smelled of Seanne's body wash, as did Seanne.

"I'm not the only person in this world looking for their real name you know," said Seanne.

Heather was still thinking about Emily. Most of what Seanne was saying was just background noise, not loud enough to interfere with her thoughts. What if Emily could go without me? Should I go with her? Can she really go without me? They had never been apart, well, they had, but only ever for a short period of time, over a short distance, and it was always Emily who went off elsewhere. Maybe she could go off on her own, maybe she could travel anywhere in the world without me, thought Heather. But why has she never done so before? If she can go anywhere without me, anywhere in the world, why is she still here with me now? Why can I still hear her in the bathroom?

"There's a whole group of us, a community, on-line," said Seanne, enthusiastically, "there were lots of rumours about a shaman in Mongolia who was supposed to be able to help and then one of us went there to find them, to find the shaman, one of the community, agdab1234, although I don't think that was their real name."

Courtney laughed along with Seanne but Heather was still too distracted.

"Anyway, we lost them, they just stopped posting. One day, agdab1234 was in Mongolia and they were keeping us updated on their progress and then the next day, nothing. And that was it, we never heard from them again. So, I had to go to Mongolia myself. I had to. I quit my job, quit college, sold all my stuff, got a flight to Europe and then I crossed the world. Trains, ferries, buses, I hitchhiked, slept in ditches, stayed in strangers' homes, sometimes we didn't even speak the same language. I've eaten things and I don't even know what they were, I didn't want to know. I rode a yak. A yak! I didn't even know what a yak was before I left California. I didn't even know they existed and now I've ridden one."

"And it brought you here, this yak?" asked Courtney, hoping to shortcut the story and bring things back to the present.

"Well, no, not exactly, but it took me to Erhi's family and her uncle knew the shaman, he knew where the shaman lived so the uncle took me there but, when we got there, she refused to see me. So we went back the next day and took gifts for the shaman, but she refused to see me again. And again. And again. Day after day. And then Erhi found me a local family to stay with, nearer to the shaman, so I stayed with them for a while and I went every day to try to see the shaman, to leave gifts."

"How long did you stay with them?" interrupted Courtney.

"Days, weeks, months. They took me in and treated me like one of the family, they fed me, gave me somewhere to sleep, I even learnt a few words of their local language. I went to see the shaman every day. I knocked on her door at eight o'clock in the morning, every day for nearly three months, until she finally invited me in. We sat down in her tent, filled with incense and candle smoke, we drank some tea, she played a drum, rang some bells, and she told me that she knew the question that I wanted to ask and she had an answer for me. I didn't even have to tell her why I was there. She already knew."

"Could the family you were staying with have told her what you were looking for?" asked Courtney, always suspicious.

"Well, they could have, although they didn't speak English so when I told them what I was hoping to find I don't think they understood me. We had lots of conversations like that, when we were talking, but we had no way of understanding what the other was saying."

"Are you sure this shaman didn't just want to get rid of you?" asked Courtney. "I mean, that's what I would have done, if someone was calling at my house every morning and leaving presents for me, I'd have told them whatever they wanted to hear, to get them to go away."

"Wow," said Seanne, "you really do have issues, don't you? If you ask people for help, they'll help you, not everyone is out to get you, to do you wrong or exploit you. You can't live your life thinking the worst of people. This is a shaman, a spiritual leader, she wasn't thinking of me as some kind of deranged stalker, she was testing me, testing my endurance, my courage, my determination. She was waiting to see if I was worthy."

"And were you?" asked Courtney.

"Were I what?"

"Worthy. Were you worthy?"

"I must have been because she let me in didn't she?"

"Are you absolutely sure that she isn't sending you to the ends of the earth on a wild goose chase just to get rid of you?

I mean, I know I've said this before, but that is exactly what I would have done. And then, while you were off doing whatever stupid task I'd set you, I'd move house so you couldn't find me when you came back, if you came back. I mean, you could die out there wandering around looking for something that doesn't exist."

"Courtney," said Seanne, "please, please don't judge people by the standards you set yourself. I know how hard things have been for you, how you took the blame for something that you really had no control over. I know your faith in humanity has been tested and that many of us have let you down, but there are people out there who you can put your faith in. If you had met this shaman, you would know what sort of person she is. You would know that you could trust her. She is part of my spiritual journey and she is going to lead me to the answers I seek. I need to get out onto the ice and take the next steps on this journey."

Heather's attention had returned to what Seanne and Courtney were discussing. She wasn't quite as sceptical as Courtney and she wanted to know more about what they were getting in to.

"Do you know exactly where to find this shaman?" asked Heather. "Do you have GPS co-ordinates or anything like that?"

"It's not quite as simple as that," replied Seanne, who proceeded to lecture Heather about how spiritual journeys are not like car journeys, how the destination is decided by the route you choose to take, not by knowing where you want to go, how the shaman will steer us in the right direction, faith, belief, blah, blah, blah.

The sound of the ship's engine changed suddenly and they all looked at each other.

"Are we there?" asked Emily, stepping out from the bathroom.

Heather stood up and walked over with Emily to look outside, through the porthole.

"We've almost stopped," said Heather, "I really ought to show my face and make sure Carter has everything under control."

"Shall we go up on deck and have a look? Are you coming?" Courtney asked Seanne.

"Not yet," said Seanne, "I have some things I need to do and Brian should be here, any minute now, with some food for me but you two, you three, go and have a look. I'm sure we'll talk some more. You know that I'd like you to come and see the shaman with me. I know he can help all of you. I'm sure you've got plenty to think about. Speak to Emily, I'm sure you can work this out."

Seanne's last comment, which was addressed to Heather, caused Emily to roll her eyes. Heather and Emily both laughed. Heather was still a long way from agreeing to let Emily go and they would discuss it later.

The three of them left Seanne's cabin and proceeded upstairs to one of the small, upper deck areas.

"Is that her real hair?" asked Emily.

"Is it?" asked Heather.

"Is it what?" asked Courtney.

"Her real hair," said Heather, "Emily wanted to know if we think that's her real hair?"

"Seanne?"

"Yes."

"If it's not then it's the best wig I've ever seen."

They stepped outside and leaned on the handrail looking out over Antarctica. Rock and ice as far as the eye could see, rising up into the distance. There were a few small buildings near the shore line, next to which were parked a snowmobile and two larger snowcats. People could be seen walking towards the jetty where they were due to stop and unload.

It was unseasonably warm, about eight degrees centigrade and you could actually hear the ice melting.

"Emily wants to go," Heather said to Courtney, while looking out towards their destination.

"I thought as much," replied Courtney, "are you going with her?"

"How can I? It's madness."

"Aren't you curious?" asked Courtney.

"Yes, aren't you?" asked Emily.

"Curious about what? There's nothing there. She's walking to her death. She's got nothing, no equipment, no transport, no destination, no support team. If she just walks out there, not knowing where she's going, or for how long, then she's going to die and everyone with her is going to die."

"The only way to prove there's something out there is to go and find it," said Courtney.

"Don't tell me you want to go as well?"

"No, no, I'm not saying that, not really, but have you thought of the alternative? You were tested weren't you? Before you came here, we all were, none of us have caught it yet but people are dying. There's food shortages, riots, there might not be any planes flying to get us home and there might not be anyone there when we get back. This whole trip, just to see if some penguins are dead, is a complete waste of time and resources. Don't you feel guilty being here?"

"No," answered Heather, "this is an important scientific research expedition to study animals adaptation to enforced environmental change, that's valuable research. This isn't about guilt or blame, they're not scientific concepts. We're here for a few days to study what happened to the penguins and then we go home, home to our loved ones, home to whoever or whatever is waiting for us when we get back."

Emily hadn't said very much since her hissy fit. She wanted to go with Seanne but she knew she couldn't go without Heather. She would have to wear her down, get her to change her mind.

"You're a scientist aren't you?" asked Emily.

Heather turned her head to face Emily but she didn't reply. Courtney knew they were talking.

"You're a scientist aren't you? I can tell from the way you dress," said Emily, rather rudely. "you'll only go if you have proof that there's a shaman out there but you also know that the only way to get that proof is to go with Seanne and see for yourself. Well, aren't you curious to go, to find out, to prove that he exists."

"Do you believe in God?" asked Heather.

Courtney followed Heather's conversation with Emily, while unable to hear Emily's replies.

"Then why are you asking me to take a leap of faith?" asked Heather.

"You're asking me to believe in something when there's no evidence to prove that it exists," said Heather, in response to Emily.

"No, I don't. If we go out there then we will die," said Heather, with some exasperation in her voice.

"I meant you, you'll die," said Heather, "just because I said we, it doesn't mean that I'm going."

"We're not Antarctic explorers," insisted Heather, "Seanne doesn't have a scientific theory that there's a shaman living in Antarctica. She has some nonsense that she was told by someone who wanted her to go away. There's nothing to prove. Science can't prove it, nor can faith, the only thing that can hope to prove it is blind stupidity. Nothing can prove it. All that will happen is that you'll die trying."

"No, it's not better to have tried and failed," said Heather in response to Emily, "especially if you end up dead. And you're wrong, it wasn't Evel Knievel who said that."

From Courtney's perspective, that seemed to be the final word on the matter and, apart from a few petulant insults from Emily, it was, for now anyway. Heather stopped leaning on the handrail and stood upright.

"I really ought to show my face below decks," Heather said to Courtney, "and you should join me, after all, you're part of the team and we could do with everyone's help to unload the equipment and supplies."

"Do I get one of the UN fleeces that all the other team members have got?" asked Courtney, who was keen to fit in.

"I suppose so," said Heather, "although I think the only two sizes we have left are medium and extra large."

"Is it a small medium?" asked Courtney, hopefully.

"Not really."

"Will it look too big on me?"

"Yes," said Heather, honestly, "even if you put it on over several layers, I still think it'll be too big. The sleeves are quite long as well. Do you still want it?"

"Go on then," said Courtney, rather reluctantly, "maybe someone will feel sorry for me when they see me wearing it and they'll swap it for their small one."

"You've got no faith in people and yet you still think there's someone on board this ship who will take pity on you and swap their perfectly fitted fleece for your giant, saggy, long sleeved one?"

"Why not? Maybe I could persuade them to swap cabins as well, for the journey home," said Courtney, laughing.

Just the thought had cheered Courtney up. Maybe things were going to work out all right after all. People were starting to accept her as part of the team, not as an outcast to be avoided. Maybe she would get the right size fleece, and a cabin without any graffiti, and maybe the polar bears hadn't killed and eaten all the penguins. Maybe, by the time they arrive back home, she wouldn't be as hated as she was when she left. Small steps, just to be slightly less hated would be a start. Maybe she would stop having nightmares, maybe confronting her evil spirit, twin sister thing had scared her off for good. Things were looking up at last.

Courtney's optimism wasn't shared by Heather though, or by Emily for that matter. Heather wasn't entirely convinced that there was going to be a journey home, at least, not for all of them.

PART TWO - COMING BACK?

I'll no-platform her

Everyone worked late into the night unloading the ship. It wasn't just their own supplies that needed to be moved, they had also brought with them supplies to restock the research station in exchange for them being granted permission to use it. The Antarctic twilight supplied enough light to enable them to work until almost midnight when, on Heather's instruction, Carter announced that they were calling it a day and everyone should get some food, have a rest and come back in the morning.

After a good night's sleep, Heather and Courtney met up to eat breakfast together, as per their new routine. They were not exactly inseparable but they enjoyed each other's company and felt that they understood each other. How much one person can really, truly understand another, without being privy to their innermost thoughts, is a question for another day. They were both seeking answers, to different questions, but neither was inclined to take Seanne up on her offer. The thought of walking out onto the ice to look for a shaman, who may or may not exist, didn't appeal to either of them. It was clear that Brian was going and Emily was keen to go but, so far, Seanne had been unsuccessful in persuading any others to join her.

"What time did you finish last night?" asked Courtney, who had retired to bed early, due to a lack of interest in hard, physical work. She wanted to be seen as part of the team but, at the same time, she didn't really want to do that much to help.

"About midnight, I think," replied Heather, who had been promoted beyond the point that she had to manually labour with the rest of them. She still liked to help out, to give the impression that she could do it, that they were all in it together. I wouldn't ask you to do anything that I wouldn't do myself, she often said, untruthfully.

"I was getting tired just watching them move all that equipment around so I told Carter to break it up and send everyone to bed," said Heather, "if I'd left Carter in charge, they would have worked all night and it would be done by now. That's not a great look though, me asleep in bed and them working all night."

"I bet you made sure they knew it was you who wanted them to stop," said Courtney.

"Of course," said Heather, "I made sure they overheard me talking to Carter. This isn't about me seeming to be in charge. I am actually in charge you know."

"So, what's the plan for today, Boss?"

"Carter goes ahead to the research base and checks it out, gets it up and running. If it's okay, then the rest of us will follow and we'll set up a temporary base there and shuttle back and forth with equipment and supplies until it's fully stocked."

"Will you go with Carter?" asked Courtney.

"No need. He'll take a couple of the others with him and make sure it's still standing, get the generators running, then he'll radio us to follow on. I think I can handle it from this end without him. Just depends on what they find with the structural integrity of the place, it might have collapsed by now."

"Is that likely?"

"Probably not," replied Heather, hesitantly, "I think there's plans to strengthen the leg supports in a month or so, after the research team arrive back, but we should be okay in the meantime, it's still just within the required tolerances, I think."

"Can I go with Carter, to the research station?" asked Courtney, who was keen to avoid a day spent lugging boxes around.

"I don't see why not, check with him and see what he says. If he asks, tell him I said it was all right."

"Shall I ask him now?" asked Courtney.

"You don't need my permission," replied Heather, a smile lighting up her face. She was amused at Courtney's lack of confidence, her need for validation. Here was a well qualified, professional young woman with shattered confidence, seemingly unable to think for herself.

"I know," said Courtney, "but do you think he would mind me interrupting his breakfast to ask him?"

"What do you think?" asked Heather, keen not to make things too easy for Courtney.

Courtney didn't know. She struggled to make even the simplest of decision anymore. Should I ask him? she pondered. Will he mind? Why would he mind? Maybe I should ask him later, when he's not eating?

Just as Courtney started to push her chair back, to stand up, Heather took decisive action.

"CARTER!" she bellowed across the tables to get his attention. The shouting wasn't really necessary as Carter was sat within spitting distance of the two of them, but it got his attention, along with that of everyone else in the room.

"Can you take Courtney with you to the research station, please?" asked Heather, in her normal speaking voice.

"Aye, can do," replied Carter, without enthusiasm, "we leave in about thirty minutes, that okay with you?"

The question was directed to Courtney who was squatting above her chair, arse hovering, neither sitting or standing, stalled in between. She sat down with a bump and aimed a nod and a smile in Carter's direction. That seemed to answer the question to his satisfaction so he turned his attention back to his cooked breakfast.

Forty-five minutes later, Carter and Courtney were sat in a snowcat with one of the expeditions engineers, Ruan Chunwang, finally ready to leave. Ruan was a squat, balding, Chinese PhD student, with a broad Yorkshire accent. All trace of his original accent lost after many years spent in God's own country. He was wearing the brightest, fluorescent yellow, hooded jacket ever made, he could be seen from across the Pennines.

"It should be a fairly smooth flight but there might be a bit of turbulence along the way," said Shaggy, who Carter introduced as their driver for the day. Surely not his real name. What kind of parents would do that? Australian parents by the sound of his voice.

They threw up a dust of ice and other debris as they were driven towards the research station, leaving a trail behind them. The tracks of the snowcat dug into the icy surface to gain sufficient traction to haul one of the tracked box-trailers they had loaded the previous evening. The snowcat vibrated, and juddered, and hummed, continuously for the whole journey. Carter, who was sat in the front passenger seat, kept up a running conversation with Shaggy while Courtney and Ruan sat separately, and in silence, in the rear of the snowcat in between boxes and bags of who knows what.

In places, where the route to the research station was frozen hard and flat, they made good progress, but they slowed, every now and then, to navigate the less even terrain. It wasn't just pristine white ice that they encountered, there were bare patches of rock, melting ice, stained green by algae, and large pools of water to navigate around.

What might have seemed smooth and gentle to the driver, who could anticipate the movement of the snowcat, was a rough ride for his passengers. They either pushed hard, arms outstretched, against the seat back in front of them, or they were pushed back into their seats, waiting for the jolt as the snowcat levelled out at the top of an incline.

Courtney passed the time staring out of the window towards the horizon. She couldn't stop her thoughts racing. What if? What if? What if all the penguins are dead? What if Seanne is right? What if it's me in the mirror? She tried to focus her mind. She held her breath and closed her eyes. She opened them suddenly as they dropped what felt like a few feet after cresting a tiny bump. She counted, to distract herself from her thoughts. One to ten, then she keep going, but she was soon asking herself, what if? What if? When did I stop counting? What number had I got to? Should I start again?

Is Emily here? In the snow cat? Where did that idea come from? Why would she be here? Courtney looked round. Carter was still talking with the driver, she had caught the odd phrase during their non-stop conversation...last time I was here...it's beautiful that time of year...causes some ball shrinkage, I can tell you...but she heard nothing meaningful, nothing of interest. Ruan had earphones on and he had his head turned away from Courtney as he stared out of the window on the opposite side. Emily was here. Courtney was convinced. Where was she sat? Why had she come?

At least the presence of Emily stopped Courtney from worrying about anything else, but she was mistaken. At that moment in time, Emily was back on the ship with Heather, trying to persuade her to go with Seanne.

Courtney tried to think of a way to communicate with Emily, she could speak to her but Emily had no way to reply. She would have to wait until later, when she saw Heather, to find out why Emily was here with her.

After nearly an hour of arse numbing travel, they approached the research station. It towered up ahead of them, on stilted legs, in an architectural style that never really caught on. It looked old and dated and, to be honest, it looked exactly as you'd expect a research station to look after being abandoned for a long time. A thin layer of ice and snow covered everything, melting in the sun then freezing in the cold. Icicles hung from every vantage point and drifts of snow and ice piled up against the support legs and the outbuildings. The main structure was made up of a number of large pods, connected together in a long row, with steps at each end. The whole thing was held up in the air by slender legs that splayed out as they touched the ground, forming giant skis, allowing the structure to be towed anywhere, although no one knew if the structural integrity was sufficient to endure such stress, so here it remained.

Shaggy turned off the snowcat's engine and everything fell silent, the only noise was the rustle of clothing and the opening of doors followed by the sound of their boots as they stepped down onto the ice.

"Radio back and let them know we've arrived," Carter said to Shaggy, as he took charge of the situation, "Ruan, can you see if you can get the generators running? Courtney, come on, let's see what state they've left it inside."

Ruan went to find out whether the stand-by generator was still working while Carter and Courtney crunched across the ice towards the steps to the entrance.

I think my arse has gone to sleep, thought Courtney, as she struggled to walk normally. She stretched her legs and pointed her toes as she walked, to try to get some feeling back. She stayed behind Carter as she was worried it might look like she had shat herself.

"Have you been here before?" asked Carter, over his shoulder, in a deep Scottish burr, while absentmindedly squeezing ice crystals from the tips of his moustache.

"No, not here, I've been to one of the newer Chilean stations and one of the Uruguayan ones, I think, but they weren't like this. It looks quite old. Are we sure it's safe?"

"Would it make any difference?" asked Carter, pausing at the top of the steps.

"Well, I, erm, no, probably not," said Courtney, "it's not going to collapse though, is it?"

"From what I heard, some of the materials used were not up to scratch and that was why they temporarily abandoned it, but it was purely a precaution. There would normally be forty of fifty people here so I doubt that the three of us are going to make much difference. It's still standing now, isn't it?"

Kind of reassured, for now, Courtney climbed the last few steps and walked through the door that Carter was holding open for her. Always the gentleman.

Inside was pitch black so Carter wedged the door open with a fire extinguisher to give them some light. He pulled out a torch and shone it round the room, exploring every corner. They had both seen plenty of horror films and didn't want to take any chances so Carter did several more sweeps of the room before declaring it safe.

They both unzipped and removed some outer layers. It was cold inside but not quite as cold as outside.

Courtney had expected it to smell musty but it smelt fresh, the stand by generator must have been circulating air around the rooms while it was unoccupied.

"Where did you get the torch?" asked Courtney.

"Brought it with me," replied Carter, "did you not bring one?"

"No, I didn't realise," mumbled Courtney, "have we got another one?"

"I haven't."

"Can we turn the lights on?"

"Not on emergency power, but once Ruan gets the generators going they should come on automatically," said Carter, in an effort to reassure Courtney, "we'll need to open the shutters in each pod once the power is on. There's a switch by the entrance, like this one, just flick the switch and the shutters on the windows will retract and let daylight in."

Carter waved his hand towards the wall-mounted control panel to show Courtney what they needed to do.

"Can you make your way along the pods and open all the shutters while I see if I can get the computers online?" asked Carter.

"Can I have the torch?"

"You can but you won't need it," said Carter, who was reluctant to let go of his own personal property. A torch that he'd brought all the way here himself, all the way from Scotland. A torch with his name on it, written crudely on some tape around the handle. Why should anyone else get the benefit of his forward planning?

"You can only operate the shutters once the power is back on," explained Carter, "and, once the power is back on, the lights will be working. You still want it?"

"No, don't worry about it," said Courtney, feeling foolish.

As she spoke, the lights in the room flickered on and off, two or three times, and then they stayed on, illuminating every corner of the room. Carter walked over to the computer on the table, where a green cursor had begun to blink on screen. He sat down and turned to address Courtney.

"Off you go then, hen," said Carter, "do the shutters."

Courtney flicked the switch to open the shutters and then walked to the far end of the pod as daylight began to flood in and fight off the artificial light. She opened the door and walked through into a long corridor with several doors leading off to the right to, what appeared to be, the sleeping accommodation. Two large windows on the left ran the length of the corridor and were shuttered from the outside. Courtney located the switch panel on the wall and activated it.

The shutters whirred into life and started to lift. As Courtney looked along the corridor, in the mirrored reflection of the window she saw a figure looking back at her. She could see the figure, almost identical to herself, stood by the doorway at the far end, talking, lips moving, silently mouthing words that Courtney couldn't hear. The figure remained stationary and continued to talk as the shutters lifted, then the reflection disappeared, as the light filled the room.

She's here and she's trying to tell me something, thought Courtney. I'm trying to tell myself something but what? Is Emily still here, did she see it?

"Are you here, Emily?" she asked out loud, looking along the empty corridor. "Stay close, I might need your help. Can you tell what she's saying? Can you lip read her?"

Courtney walked to the door at the far end and opened it to find an identical corridor. She watched and waited and she decided not to press the switch to raise the shutters. There she was, at the end of the corridor, reflected in the window, still talking, still trying to communicate with Courtney.

"I can't tell what you're saying," said Courtney, taking a few steps closer. She turned to look at her own reflection, just to make sure it was still there, to reassure herself. Could she be in two places at the same time? She took a long look at her own reflection, moving closer to the window to see better. She ran her eyes over the reflection of her face and lips and she mouthed the words, 'help me,' to see what it looked like when she said it.

Courtney looked ahead, along the corridor towards her other reflection. One person with two reflections, in different places, doing different things. If it's not me, then who is she? Why does she look identical to me? At least she's not pursuing me, not trying to attack me. She's trying to communicate with me, to tell me something. What am I trying to tell myself?

"Emily, if you're still here, can you get closer and tell what she's saying?" she asked out loud, but Emily wasn't there to help, Courtney was on her own.

Courtney walked slowly, cautiously, towards the far end of the corridor, the second reflection moved away from her as she approached. About halfway along she paused. It was a long way back to the switch to operate the shutters. If she starts to chase me, will I make it back in time? thought Courtney. What will I do? I could run as fast as possible and go for the door or I could stand still and close my eyes. Would that even work? Were they the only two options? Fight or flight?

Of course, we all know that standing still and closing your eyes isn't putting up much of a fight, is it? But to Courtney it was. It was decisive action. If I can't see her then she doesn't exist. If she doesn't exist then she can't hurt me, went the logic. That's how I'll win the fight, I'll no-platform her.

Suddenly, emboldened by Emily's presence, Courtney took a few small, tentative steps forward then she started to walk briskly along the corridor, her second reflection retreating as she advanced. She stopped a few paces short, close enough to see the lips move and read the desperate expression on the face, but she still couldn't make sense of what she was trying to tell herself.

"Are you getting this, Emily?" asked Courtney, before addressing her reflection directly.

"Who are you?" she asked.

"What are you doing here?"

"I can't understand you, what are you trying to tell me?"

Courtney asked the questions out loud, to what Alain had previously suggested could be the ghost of a long dead sibling or a manifestation of her evil side, either way, she felt rather self conscious doing it, especially with Emily watching. Would it be any less embarrassing to find out later that Emily wasn't even there?

None of Courtney's questions were being answered and she was becoming frustrated. There didn't seem to be any way for Courtney to interact with her reflection. The mouth was moving and she was speaking but Courtney couldn't make out what she was saying. The fear that Courtney had felt her entire life, the nightmares, the sleepless nights, the cause of all this was in front of her, just feet away and, rather uncharacteristically, Courtney decided to do something she wouldn't normally have done.

Courtney raised her hand in front of her and positioned it carefully by looking at the reflection in the shuttered window. I can't believe I'm about to slap myself, she thought, just before she slapped herself, really hard.

Courtney's hand swept through the air, meeting no resistance, but the reflection told a different story. Her face in the reflection was enraged, the lips were no longer moving, the teeth were gritted, the mouth snarling. Courtney didn't wait to see what happened, she turned and ran. Fight or flight? She chose flight. She ran as fast as she could along the corridor to the door. She stumbled briefly and had to put a hand down to steady herself, the carpet felt rough against the skin of her palms as she pushed herself back up, one knee touched the ground, breaking the skin through her trousers, but she kept going. By the end of the corridor, she was back upright and she grabbed for the door handle with one hand while reaching out to hit the switch, to open the shutters, with her other hand. She pushed hard against the door and tumbled to the floor as it opened and her glasses flew off as she landed.

Courtney reached out to retrieve her glasses and she looked back to see if she had been pursued, but the shutters were going up and any remaining reflection in the window was disappearing into the light.

She took a few minutes to calm down. She lay on her back staring at the ceiling, breathing heavily, she thought she was going to have a heart attack and put both hands to her chest. Call a doctor! On second thoughts, maybe not. She propped herself up on her elbows, but the carpet was too rough to put too much weight on. Uncomfortable on the floor, she stood up and checked herself for damage. A slightly scuffed knee and a sore palm, but not too bad. It could have been worse.

She was far more apprehensive now than she was before, she'd enraged it, she's awakened the beast. She had survived but she took no confidence from it. All I've got to do now is open the shutters in the remaining pods, she told herself. What could go wrong?

She opened the remaining shutters by reaching through the doorway with her eyes closed and then fumbling for the control panel on the wall. Again, she thought, if the threat was in the reflection and she didn't see the reflection then she couldn't be harmed. That was the thinking, the logic, for what it was worth.

After more accommodation blocks, she opened the shutters in a large, two floored, communal living and dining area, and then she continued through two or three more pods, that appeared to be set up for scientific experiments. She flicked the switch in the last of these pods and waited for daylight to fill the room before walking towards the far end. As Courtney reached out to open the door, the handle turned and the door swung open, towards her.

Ruan pushed the door open and was surprised to find Courtney so close on the other side.

"Flippin' 'eck. I was just coming to find you," said Ruan, "kettle's on, You want a cup of tea, love? Do you think Carter would want one?"

"I'd love one. Milk, one sugar, but Carter hates tea," said Courtney, maliciously, just to save having to walk the length of the research station to find out how he takes his tea.

"Hates tea? How can you hate tea?" asked Ruan, incredulously. "I found some powdered milk, is that all right? I think what's in the fridge might have gone off."

"How did you get the lights on so quickly?" asked Courtney.

"Oh, it's a piece of piss, there's a standby generator running off solar power that keeps everything ticking over and, as long as the fuel hasn't frozen, it's straightforward, just flip a few switches and Bob's your uncle."

Courtney wrapped her hands around the warm mug and sipped the tea before it had a chance to cool down. Her heartbeat had almost returned to normal but her hands were still shaking. If she gripped the mug hard enough, no one could see her hands shaking, so she held on to it, tightly.

Ruan had taken off his yellow jacket and Courtney noticed he wasn't wearing his UN fleece.

"Did you get a fleece?" asked Courtney.

"A what?"

"One of the red, United Nation fleeces that everyone was given," said Courtney, for clarification, "did you get one? I just notice you're not wearing it."

"I've got one, but it's too small."

"Do you fancy swapping?"

"Well, yes, we could try, what size is yours?" asked Ruan.

"It's a large medium."

"I think I'm a medium medium," said Ruan, patting his stomach.

"I think you're a large medium."

"Thank you very much," said Ruan, sarcastically, "I'll dig it out for you later when my bag gets here."

There was a lull in the conversation, accompanied by some tea gazing, before Ruan broke the silence.

"Are you going?" asked Ruan. "I'm sorry. I hope you don't mind me asking."

"Going?" replied Courtney, who was unsure what she was being asked.

"With Seanne? Are you going?"

"Oh, I'm not sure," replied Courtney, honestly. She wasn't sure. She was surprised to be asked the question though.

How did Ruan know about it? Who did know? Did everyone on board know? Were they all invited to go with Seanne?

Courtney had spent so little time socialising with the UN team that she barely even knew their names, never mind what they had been doing and discussing for the last few days. She decided to ask Alain, next time she saw him, find out what had been happening, use his skills as a social butterfly to find out what was going on. It would have been easier to have asked Ruan, after all, he was sat right in front of her, they were sharing a moment over a cup of tea, the conversation was drying up uncomfortably, but it never even crossed her mind to ask him.

"Do you think Carter is all right down there?" asked Ruan. "What was he doing when you left him?"

"He was trying to start up the computers," said Courtney, "after we finish this, shall we walk down quietly and try to scare him? Did you happen to notice if there were any biscuits in the cupboard to go with this tea?"

Two left thumbs

"Are you sure that's all I can help you with?" asked Alain Govenor.

He leaned back in his doctor's chair, at his doctor's desk in his doctor's surgery, stethoscope slung loosely around his neck, expensive pen in shirt pocket, next to what he mistakenly believed to be an oral thermometer, feeling rather smug at the thought of another satisfied patient.

Alain undid his tie, pulling the noose open just enough so that he could undo the top two buttons of his expensively tailored, long sleeve, pink shirt, unworn before today. Unworn for many, many years. Alain felt that the doctor he was playing was the type of doctor who would wear a pink shirt. He had given a lot of thought to the type of doctor he was going to be. His motivation, his character. In actual fact, the doctor Alain was playing was one who would wear the worst possible clothes to be found at the back of the wardrobe of a disgraced former lecturer at a middling university. Clothes that had not seen the light of day since being purchased. Clothes purchased to spite an ex-wife who no longer cared how he dressed. How dare she?

I can finally wear whatever I want to wear, he told himself when newly single. The problem was that Alain had never cultivated a look, in fact he had never even bought his own clothes before, and it was a steep learning curve. Now that he was Alain, the doctor, he could wear the clothes that Alain, the unemployed lecturer, hadn't the confidence to wear.

Heather and Emily both stood up and thanked Alain politely.

"Are you absolutely sure there's nothing else I can do for you?" asked Alain, trying to be helpful, but the way he said it and the fact that he winked nervously, made it sound a little creepy. Even Alain would have admitted that.

"What a perv," said Emily.

"No, I'm very grateful, Doctor. I'll take these and thank you again for seeing me outside of your normal surgery hours," said Heather.

"Your highly restrictive, barely ever open, fake surgery hours," said Emily.

Alain stood up. Of course he did, there was a lady leaving the room.

"When are you off to the research station?" asked Alain, who experienced a tinge of jealousy as he said it.

"Soon, very soon," replied Heather, "Carter's on his way there now, with Ruan and Courtney, and, as soon as we get the green light, we're off. There's going to be trips back and forth all day, there's so much stuff to move. I probably won't see you for three or four days so take care, Alain."

Just as Heather reached out for the door handle, there was a knock on the door.

The tall figure of Lester Cherry-Stone could be seen outside, distorted through the frosted glass, waiting for a response.

"Would you do the honours?" Alain asked Heather, in a convoluted way.

"Do you mean open the door?" asked Heather, to Emily's amusement.

"If you would be so kind," replied Alain.

Heather pulled the door open and greeted Lester warmly, like an old friend. They hugged for one, two, three seconds.

"I think the doctor will see you now," said Heather, to Lester amusement, as she left with Emily.

Lester waited until Heather had gone and then closed the door. You could never be sure if Emily was still around. Was she still there listening?

"You finished with patients for today?" asked Lester.

"Good morning, Lester," said Alain.

"Good morning to you too. Have you finished?"

"I certainly hope so, it's so draining dealing with the sick. What's put you in such a bad mood?"

"Nothing," replied Lester, although that wasn't strictly true. He hadn't heard from his handler for over a week now, he continued to transmit his reports on Hanad's movements and contacts but without response and he was beginning to worry.

"Hanad wants to fire up the drone and get a look at the killing fields. You in, Doctor?"

"I wouldn't miss it for the world."

"Come on then, I'll take you up to Hanad and we'll watch it from there. I've prepped the drone and done the pre-flight checklist already. Hanad's just setting up the tech so we can watch it on the big screen television."

Alain discarded his medical equipment on the desk and followed Lester through the ship to the elevator. The doors opened with their familiar sound as soon as Lester turned the key. Within seconds, they were stepping out into Hanad's apartment, walking across soft designer rugs, and settling into an all enveloping plump sofa.

Lester picked up what looked like a games console controller from the glass-topped coffee table and, almost instantly, the television screen lit up with an image of the back of the ship. With the press of a button and a move of the joystick, the drone lifted into the air leaving the ship far below.

The vibration of the propellors, two of which could be seen at the top of the screen, was enough to distort the on-screen image and loose the clarity, everything was a blur as the drone flew higher and got further away.

"Are you as excited as I am, Doctor?" asked Hanad.

"I can't wait."

"Well, you'll have to wait a little while, it'll take about quarter of an hour for us to get there, would you like a drink while we wait?"

"Do you have a diet cola?"

"Come on, Doctor, you're not going to let me down, are you? Please don't make me drink alone."

"Well, it's a bit early, but I suppose I could have one. A small one."

"Whisky okay?" asked Hanad. "You too, Lester?"

"It's a bit early for me too," said Lester, laughing at the thought.

Hanad wheeled himself over to a drinks trolley with ease and poured three whiskies, of varying sizes, into heavy glasses. He put them on a tray, balanced the tray on his lap, and carefully wheeled himself back to the table where he handed them out, one by one. Drinks sorted, drone on its way, all they had to do now was wait.

"You see that map on the bottom left of the screen, Doctor?" asked Lester, drink in one hand, controller in the other, operating it with just one thumb.

"Yes, I see."

"That's where we started, the blue dot, and that's where we're going, the red dot. The pointy arrow in between is where we are now. You can see altitude on the left and ground speed on the right, distance to go is there somewhere as well. You want to fly it for a while?"

"I'd better not, I never really got the hang of computer games, wouldn't want to crash your expensive toy," said Alain, directing his last comment to Hanad.

"Expensive? You don't know the half of it. You can't buy these, you know," said Hanad, "this was custom made when we fitted out the ship. This is bespoke, one of a kind. Nothing else can touch it in terms of speed and range, well, maybe some military drones. It wasn't cheap and I certainly wouldn't be happy if you crashed it. That goes for you too, Lester."

"And do you fly it?" asked Alain.

"Me?" asked Hanad, a man who didn't like to do anything, especially when he could pay someone else to do it and have the whip hand. "No, I'm crazy, all over the place, it's like I've got two left thumbs," said Hanad, with a straight face.

"Is that a real thing?" asked Alain.

"Oh yes," replied Hanad, "you're a doctor, you should know."

Alain sipped his whisky. Not his first choice for a mid-morning drink but he had a plan. It involved sipping it slowly and firmly turning down all offers of a refill. His mouth and throat came alive with the taste, the warmth, the memories. Ah, the memories.

"Can you see the line of the coast there, on the left, Doctor?" asked Lester.

He was flying the drone with skill and some ease. It was speeding along at top speed, vibrating silently, but making good progress.

"Are you over the sea right now?" asked Alain, before taking another tiny sip of whisky.

"Yeah," replied Lester without taking his eyes off the screen, "there should still be plenty of sea ice around this time of year but here's no sign of it, not here anyway. Once we're round this headland, can you see? Just in front of us, then we should be close to where the satellite pictures were taken."

Hanad, released the brake on his wheelchair and rolled himself a few feet further forward. He put his glass of whisky down onto the glass coffee table with a clunk.

Do you want a coaster for that? Alain wanted to ask. He was holding his own glass in both hands on his lap, too scared to put it on the table, in case he got told off. Now that

Hanad had made the first move, Alain shuffled himself forward to sit on the edge of the sofa and he put his own glass down.

"Let me get you a coaster for that, before you scratch the table," said Hanad, who then made a big display of wheeling himself to the drinks trolley and returning with a pile of cheap, round, white, paper coasters, the sort you find in a hotel poolside bar, sodden wet and stuck to the tables, not the sort you would expect to find in a multi-millionaire's swanky apartment.

Hanad took one for himself and tossed the remaining stack across the table in the direction of Alain and Lester, where it spread out like a pack of cards. Pick a coaster, any coaster.

"Lester, why are we vibrating so much?" asked Hanad, curtly. "I thought you fixed the problem with the dampers. We're not going to be able to see anything at this rate."

"I did fix it. We flew a test flight two days ago and it was fine."

"We?" asked Hanad, arms outstretched with open palms. It was clear from the gesture that he was absolving himself of any responsibility or blame.

"I flew a test flight. It was fine Hanad, you saw it, there were no problems, I promise you," said Lester, respectfully, "when we get lower and the speed reduces, it'll be a lot better."

This is why I don't like you, thought Alain, about Hanad. Feeling vindicated.

As the drone rounded the headland, Lester skilfully cut some speed and swept the drone in a long arc round to the left and then he flew them lower and lower until the screen in front of them was filled with a juddering picture of absolute bloodshed and carnage. A red martian landscape of bloodstained rocks and ice as far as the eye could see.

Lester piloted them as low as he could safely go and, despite the camera vibration and the occasional glitch in the signal, it was clear what they were looking at. On the bare bloodstained rock and the crimson ice lay the butchered remains of a colony of penguins.

"Oh, man," said Lester, "this is sick."

"And not in a good way," said Alain, by way of clarification. He knew the meaning of sick had changed in his lifetime but he wasn't exactly sure how.

"Your Miss Woodbeard is going to shit herself when she sees this, isn't she, Doctor?" asked Hanad, laughing at the image he had conjured up his mind.

"Oh, come on," snapped Alain, "that's below the belt. She's going to be devastated when she see's this. The last few years have been tough on her. This is the last thing I would want her to see."

"I'm sorry," said Hanad, holding up his hands in apology, "I didn't mean to be insensitive."

They watched on, in silence, as the they flew over a seemingly never-ending scene of slaughter and brutality, death in every direction, continuously repeating, over and over. Wherever Lester chose to point the drone, every available surface had been painted in blood and strewn with body parts, but what stood out on the big screen in front of them was not the sheer scale of the barbarity that had taken place but the tiny patches of unspoilt white ice that dotted the battlefield. Pristine ice, unsullied, shining like a lighthouse, surrounded by a sea of indescribable savagery.

Every now and again, one of them would spot something as they flew past and Lester would manoeuvre back to get a better look. They saw dead penguins standing upright, frozen in place, they saw the occasional polar bear on all fours, picking its way carefully through the body parts, stopping and rising up onto its hind legs to stare at the drone above its head, revealing a dirty red underbelly, stained in blood.

After a while, the shocking scenes became less shocking, they all desensitized remarkably quickly, In their minds, the scrolling scene in front of them was no longer made up of dead penguins, the body parts had become part of the landscape, part of the bloody pattern on the carpet over which they were flying.

Lester continued to steer the drone around, looking for signs of life, but there was little hope, just more of the same, more death, more blood, from left to right, from top to bottom, the screen was filled with endless devastation.

"Can you go higher?" asked Hanad after some time. "Maybe we can get an idea of the scale of the damage."

"Sure thing," replied Lester, pulling back on the joystick but, before he could gain enough height, the battery warning light began to flash and he pulled up a menu on screen and ordered the drone to return on autopilot.

"Wow, that right there is some pretty weird shit," said Lester, slumping back into the sofa and tossing the controller onto the spare seat between himself and Alain.

"I need another one of these," said Alain, pushing his empty glass, sipped dry, towards Hanad.

"Would you mind doing the honours, Doctor."

"Not at all," said Alain as he endeavoured to extricate himself from the embrace of the sofa. His legs felt weak as he stood upright. Under normal circumstances, he would feel lightheaded at the sight of a single drop of blood, but his brain had never had to process quite this much. He was struggling to comprehend the sheer scale of what they had witnessed.

He took all three glasses over to the drinks cabinet and, caught a glimpse of himself in the mirror, he was greeted by a ghost, a pale shadow of the man he was ten minutes ago, changed both physically and emotionally.

Alain returned with the whisky and they watched the drone return to the ship on the big screen television, but then, suddenly, the air was filled with the voice of Sander Alexanderson, the ship's second in command.

"Would Doctor Alain Govenor please come to the bridge as soon as possible. That's Doctor Alain Govenor. Please come to the bridge as soon as possible."

"How did he do that?" asked Alain. "I didn't even know we had a tannoy, why haven't I heard it before?"

"Are you serious?" asked Lester. "They make tannoy announcements every frickin' day."

"I guess if it's not about me then I don't really listen," said Alain, laughing with embarrassment at his own self-centredness.

"I guess this is your first medical emergency then," said Lester, smiling, "good luck, Doctor, you're going to need it. I'll take you down in the elevator with me, I need to check the dampers on that drone again."

"Before you go," interrupted Hanad, "I don't think there's any need to tell people what we've just seen. We don't want to spoil the surprise for them, do we?"

Once in the elevator, Lester turned the key and they began to descend.

"How do you work for someone like that?" asked Alain.

"I guess I'm just better at taking orders from people I don't like than you are," was all Lester would say on the subject.

Lester and Alain parted ways after leaving the elevator. Lester headed out onto the deck while Alain made his way towards the front of the ship to the bridge where he was greeted by a scene of relaxed calm. The squat figure of Sander Alexanderson was there with two other crew members, each had a warm drink in a mug, steam still rising. The ship's captain, Mikaela Larson, was stood at the back of the bridge, hands on hips, observing.

"Can I smell bovril?" asked Alain.

"You look a bit pale, Doctor," said Sander, "are you okay?"

"I've just seen something that no one should ever, ever, have to see."

"That's what being a doctor is all about I guess," said Sander in response.

"Er, yes, well, erm," stammered Alain, "what's going on, what's the emergency?"

"I've got the research station on the radio," said Sander holding up a wireless radio handset that looked, to Alain, very much like his cordless home phone, "there's been an accident and they need your help."

"You do know that I'm not a real doctor don't you, Sander?"

"If it looks like a doctor, walks like a doctor and quacks like a doctor," said Mikaela, rather unhelpfully.

Sander handed the radio handset to a very nervous Alain, the whiskey having done nothing to steady his hands.

"Just press the button when you want to talk."

"Hello," said Alain before pressing the button, "hello, hello."

"Alain, is that you?" asked Courtney, her voice coming clearly through the handset's speaker.

"Yes, it's me, what's the problem?"

"It's Carter. We found him unconscious, he's taken a blow to the head. There's a lump coming up, a big lump. He's sat up and talking now but he's not making much sense. I think he's concussed."

"Er, right," said Alain, thinking on his feet, "so I guess you need to stay with him, get some ice on the bump and don't let him fall asleep. I'm coming over to you, I'll be there soon. Don't worry."

"I don't think we've got any ice," said Courtney, "we've only just got the power back on."

"Try looking outside," said Alain, barely concealing his exasperation. He didn't want to snap at Courtney, it wasn't her he was angry with. He was angry with Carter for getting hurt. He wouldn't be in this situation, this stressful situation, if it wasn't for Carter. How dare he require medical help.

What am I going to do? thought Alain as he handed the radio handset back to Sander. I'm way out of my depth.

"How do I get to him?" Alain asked, unable to think straight, a rising feeling of panic was making him feel nauseous.

"There's a snowcat waiting for you," said Sander, "it's ready to go. Heather left about twenty minutes ago, she's already on her way. Grab what you need and make your way down to the jetty, they're waiting for you there. Is there anything else I can do to help, Alain?"

"No, thank you, Sander."

Alain rushed down the steps to his room and quickly packed a bag and put his Antarctic gear on, well, I say Antarctic gear, Alain was hoping to get by with lots of layers and some twenty-year-old ski wear that he had last worn some, well, twenty years ago. Gaudily coloured with a lightning strike motif, zig zagging across the front and back, he looked ready to travel back in time and hit the slopes but he looked woefully unprepared for the Antarctic weather. Luckily for him, all he had to contend with was some dry, rather mild weather, for this time of year.

With his bulging rucksack thrown across one shoulder, Alain made his way up to the medical bay and grabbed a few supplies. He had been thinking about what to take with him since he left the bridge, he assumed there would be some medical kit at the research station so he threw a few additional supplies and a box of painkillers into his bag.

He sat at his desk and put his head in his hands. Everything is going to be all right, he told himself. It's only a mild concussion, happens every day, bed rest and painkillers. Exude an air of authority, they're counting on me, I just need to give the impression that I know what I'm doing. I can do that. Done it all my life. Confidence not competence.

Doctor Alain's bedside chat with panicking Alain seemed to do the trick.

His new mantra helped to calm him. Confidence not competence. He could fake one but not the other so, just in case, Alain opened the top drawer and loaded the gun, burying it well down in his bag, among his clothes. Just in case.

Confidence not competence, Alain thought to himself as he opened the rear door to the snowcat. He threw his bag onto one seat and himself onto another.

"We were waiting all this time, just for you, were we?" asked Seanne from the window seat on the far side. "What are you doing here, Alain?"

"Medical emergency, anyway, what are you doing here? You're not part of the UN team, what are you going to the research station for?"

"It's a stepping stone," replied Seanne, who exhaled as she centered herself. This was a big moment for her. One step closer.

"I don't know what I'm doing, Seanne," said Alain, in an increasing common moment of self-doubt.

"None of us know what we're doing, Alain, all anyone expects of us is that we try to do the best we can and be the best person we can be. Be best, Alain. Be best."

The size of a satsuma

Alain had expected there to be an air of panic at the research station when he arrived but he was greeted by a scene of quiet efficiency. A chain of people had been formed, to pass boxes and bags between them, as they unloaded supplies, carrying them into the research station and into the surrounding outbuildings.

Alain walked across the icy surface, breathing in the air, it smelt like no other place on earth, the air was crystal clear, pure filtered, fresh. He was so pleased that he had been able to come here, even in the current circumstances, and he smiled a happy, contented smile.

Alain stopped to have a good look round, taking in his surroundings, before he walked to the nearest end of the research station and mounted the steps. After he entered, he put down his bag, took off his sunglasses, and unzipped his ski suit. He slipped his arms out of the sleeves and tied them around his waist.

Alain saw Courtney, Ruan and Heather, deep in conversation, so he picked up his bag, got into character and approached them.

"Thank God you're here, Alain," said Courtney. Her opposition to Alain taking on the role of doctor had all but vanished in this time of need.

"Come on, Alain, he's through here," said Heather, leading the way.

"How's the patient?" asked Alain as he walked though the door. Alain had spent the last hour thinking about what to say when he got here and this seemed as good an opening gambit as any of the others he had come up with.

Carter was sat on a bed in one of the bedrooms that consisted of six beds on three bunks, his head perilously close to the bottom of the bunk above. He clutched a plastic bag full of ice, wrapped in a towel, pressed hard against the back of his head and his face broke into a relieved smile when he saw Alain walk in.

"Am I glad to see you," said Carter.

"Doctor in the house," said Ruan, raising his arms above his head in celebration, "whoop whoop."

Alain took a seat on the bottom bunk, opposite Carter, and turned on the bedside manner.

"How are you feeling?"

"I'm fine now, Doctor, I've just got a bit of a bump."

"Lean forward slightly and let me see."

Carter leaned forward and removed the ice pack so Alain, and the others, could see. He had an angry red swelling on the back of his head, approximately the size of a satsuma, using the official, international, fruit-based, scale system for head injuries.

There was a gasp from Courtney and an audible, "Ooooh," from Ruan.

"It looks sore. How did it happen?" asked Alain.

"I stood up and banged my head on a shelf."

"That was a rather silly thing to do, wasn't it?" asked Alain, while smiling.

"I can't be sure, Doc," said Carter, smiling back at Alain, "but I don't think I did it deliberately."

"Have you got a headache?"

"Yes."

"Any dizziness?"

"A bit but feeling better now."

"Blurred vision?"

"No, I don't think so."

"I just want to check your vision," said Alain, "is that okay?"

Alain put his index finger up in front of Carter's face and asked him to follow the movement of his finger, which he did for a while. That's got to be a good sign, thought Alain, although he wasn't sure what he was looking for.

"Have you taken anything for it?"

"Not yet, we thought we'd better wait until you got here," said Courtney, speaking to Alain as if he was a real doctor.

"Take a couple of painkillers and rest. Someone should stay with you tonight, just to keep an eye on you, but I think you're going to be all right. Stay here, eat something if you can, drink plenty of fluids, keep your strength up and get plenty of rest. You'll live."

Alain pulled a packet of painkillers out of his bag and tossed them in Carter's direction. As his right hand was still holding the ice pack, he tried to catch them with his left but, even with the advantage of unnaturally large hands, his lack of coordination let him down and they landed in his lap.

"Will you stay here overnight, Alain, just in case there's any problems?" asked Heather.

"Of course I will."

That's one in the eye for Hanad, thought Alain. No one tells Doctor Alain Govenor where he can and can't go.

"Erm, Heather," said Alain, "are you aware that Seanne is here? She was with me on the snowcat when I came over."

"I wasn't aware but thank you for letting me know," said Heather, "I assumed she would be here sooner or later, it will be easier if we set out from here rather than from the ship."

"We?" asked Alain, incredulously.

"I meant her, it'll be easier if she sets out from here."

"Are you thinking about going?" asked Alain.

"We are," said Emily who had been reclining on the bunk above Carter this whole time, "we're almost there, aren't we?"

Heather ignored Emily, and Alain.

"Are you going Doctor?" asked Ruan. "It would be amazing if there's something out there, wouldn't it?"

"Like Heather, I'm undecided," was Alain's diplomatic response.

"Ruan," said Heather, "would you mind staying with Carter for a while and then I'll get someone to come in and take over from you in about an hour?"

"Not a problem," said Ruan, "I'll teach him to beatbox to pass the time."

"I'm okay on my own," said Carter, horrified at the thought of listening to Ruan beatboxing for an hour.

"Doctor's orders," said Alain and that was the end of the discussion.

"Look, Courtney, could I have a word in private?" asked Alain.

Emily's ears pricked up. Listening in on a private conversation, what could be better? The other options were following Heather outside to oversee the loading and unloading of equipment or to stay and marvel at Ruan's beatboxing prowess. It was a no-brainer.

Heather made her excuses and left.

"Got to show my face outside, remind them who's boss," she said, only half joking.

"Shall we take a walk outside?" Alain asked Courtney, as he dumped his bag onto one of the spare beds.

Emily followed Courtney, who followed Alain, outside and down the steps. They walked to the far end of the research station, away from the work going on, out of earshot, or so they thought.

"What is it, Alain?" asked Courtney, curious to find out what he had to say.

"When are you going to see the penguin colony?"

"Tomorrow. Carter is the scientist in charge of the research programme and he wants to be there, so Heather said we should wait for him. If he's feeling better tomorrow, then he can come with us, but I don't think we'll put it off any longer than that."

"Don't go."

"Why not?"

"I've seen it. Just now, back on the ship, I saw it. Hanad, Lester and I, we watched it from a drone. You don't want to see it."

"See what?"

"The penguins. They're all dead. We saw it from a drone. You were right to be worried. They're all dead. All of them."

"Spoilers, Alain. Spoilers. Why are you telling me this?" asked Courtney, who's head was spinning.

"Because I don't want to see you hurt. I know you've suffered, you've taken the blame for this and it wasn't your fault. Don't go. You can't see this. If you see it you'll never be able to forget it."

"How did you expect me to react to this, Alain?" asked Courtney, who was struggling to understand why he would have told her.

Emily was stood just behind Alain so she could see Courtney's face. It was difficult to tell if the look on Courtney's face was one of horror or anger. Horror at what Alain had told her, that her brain was still trying to process, or anger at Alain for telling her in the first place.

It was anger, definitely anger, decided Emily. Maybe a touch of horror with a splash of disappointment, a sprinkle of contempt, but mainly anger.

Don't say anything, thought Courtney, you'll only make things worse.

"Give me a minute," she said, as she turned and took a few paces away.

"I'm just trying to protect you," said Alain as Courtney turned her back on him. He said it to reassure Courtney of his motives but also to reassure himself. This didn't seem to be going very well. She had a right to know but did he have the right to tell her, to make the decision on her behalf? He was starting to think that maybe he shouldn't have told her.

I don't need protecting, thought Courtney, as she walked away without looking back.

For months now, Courtney had been clinging to the hope that maybe, just maybe, it hadn't ended in disaster. Maybe they would find an intact penguin colony living peacefully alongside the newly introduced polar bears, maybe she wasn't a penguin murderer, maybe everyone else was wrong and she was right. She wasn't totally naive, she knew there would be some casualties along the way, after all, the polar bears would need to feed on something, but what Alain had described didn't sound like nature working harmoniously in balance.

"Why did you tell her this?" Emily asked Alain. "What were you thinking? Do you really think she wants to hear this from you? Why couldn't you just let her see it for herself, let her deal with it and process it when she's ready?"

Emily circled Alain, as she threw questions at him, her annoyance clearly visible for no one to see. She threw her hands up in the air in frustration and looked over to see where Heather was. She spotted her over by one of the snowcats, helping three others lift a large wooden crate out of one of the box trailers that was towed there earlier.

Courtney had spotted Heather as well. She walked towards her, away from Alain, muttering under her breath.

Emily ran after Courtney but not before calling Alain a stupid twat, her face inches away from his as she shouted at him.

Courtney walked right up to Heather, who had just lowered the crate to the floor with knees straight, back bent.

"I need a drink," said Courtney.

"So do I," said Emily.

Heather looked up at Courtney and Emily from her current position, bent over, catching her breath, and it was obvious to her that they were both upset.

"I've got just the thing," said Heather as she stood upright, "come on, I've been saving a bottle of ouzo for a special occasion but..."

Courtney made a gagging noise at the mention of ouzo.

"Are you insulting my Greek heritage?" asked Heather, only half joking.

"Not at all," replied Courtney, "it's just that it's a, erm, it's an acquired taste and I'm not sure that I've acquired it."

"That's probably because you've been drinking the cheap stuff," said Heather, "wait until you've tried this, they only make a few hundred bottles a year, it's crafted by artisans using water from the same springs that the Gods drank from. You can't not like it."

As they walked the short distance to the research station, Courtney remembered something she wanted to ask Heather.

"Is Emily here?"

"Of course," replied Heather, looking round to check.

"Was she here when I arrived earlier, you know, with Carter?"

"I don't think so. She was on the ship with me."

"Oh," replied Courtney. She was a little disappointed that Emily hadn't been there to see her evil twin, to lip read her, and she was also a little embarrassed that she had been talking to herself, but surely no one would ever know, unless she told them.

"I saw my doppelgänger, my evil twin, when I was opening up the window shutters. She was trying to tell me something, but when I slapped her she got angry and I ran away."

"You slapped her?" squealed Emily with delight. "You bitch."

"Why did you slap her?" asked Heather.

"She was trying to tell me something, but I couldn't read her lips to see what she was saying. I got a bit annoyed with her and so I slapped her and I know I shouldn't have. Then I panicked and ran away and I fell over and hurt my knee and..."

"Did she go for you?" interrupted Heather.

"I don't know. I thought she would, so I ran away. She was trying to tell me something, I just don't know what she was trying to tell me. It must be important."

"Oh my God," said Heather.

"Ask her what Alain just told her," said Emily and Heather did, but not until they had taken off their outer layers and settled themselves at a quiet table in the communal area, situated in the central pod of the research base.

"Ask her what Alain said?" repeated Emily, impatient for Heather to be brought up to speed.

"Tell me what just happened, with Alain, I can see you're upset," said Heather, as she leaned back in her chair to let Courtney talk, and she did talk, with just a little persuasion and the odd prompt now and again. She told Heather about Alain, Lester and Hanad, how they had already flown a drone over the penguin colony, how they had witnessed the destruction of the colony by Courtney's polar bears.

Courtney necked another shot of ouzo, trying hard not to wince, for fear of offending Heather. She then proceeded to complain about Alain for quite a long time, describing in detail the look on his face as he gave her the news. Emily chipped in now and again to reinforce what Courtney was saying.

"I'm so angry with him. I just couldn't talk to him, I had to walk away," said Courtney.

Heather could understand Courtney wanting to shoot the messenger but, on the other hand, she must have known that there was a good chance that they were going to find a lot of dead penguins. The satellite pictures weren't conclusive evidence but they certainly indicated that there was a major problem. All the people who had called Courtney a penguin murderer, well, they can't all be wrong. Heather concluded that Courtney had been in denial for so long that it was, actually, a shock, finding out that it was real, that it had happened as she feared.

"It's all my fault," said Courtney.

"It's not," said Heather, "it's not all your fault, we've all had a part to play in this."

"You don't understand."

"I'm pretty sure I do, we all do," said Heather, bringing Emily into the support group that she was assembling.

"It's not your fault," said Emily.

"Even Emily says it's not your fault," said Heather.

"You don't understand at all. It is my fault," said Courtney, forcing down another ouzo. She didn't attempt to hide her disgust this time, she shivered and grimaced before slamming her empty glass onto the table.

"I wrote the paper that started all this, I theorised about introducing a predator species like the polar bear to a new environment, with new prey. It was my idea. Someone at the UN read my paper, even though it hadn't been published or reviewed, but they saw a copy of it and they contacted me to talk about it. That's how I ended up going on Polar Saviour. It was my idea to relocate the polar bears. I came up with the idea, I described the theory, the process, the problems, the practicalities, the possible outcomes, but I didn't foresee this. I stupidly thought they'd live together in harmony like some technicolour cartoon world where all the animals get on with each other and skip around and sing happy songs. This is way beyond any worst case scenario that I came up with. I knew there would be some teething problems, that it would have some sort of impact on the penguin population, before things calmed down and settled into some sort of equilibrium, but I never imagined this."

"But you told me that you fought to stop Polar Saviour, that you argued against it," said Heather.

"I did, but it was my idea in the first place, I started it, but I couldn't get them to stop it, it got out of control," was all that Courtney could say in her defence. She hung her head in shame and her hair fell around her face, hiding her tears, and her glasses started to slip down. Courtney pushed her glasses back up and wiped her runny nose on her sleeve, all in one swift movement.

Emily sat open-mouthed, looking at Heather to read her reaction.

"It's all my fault," spluttered Courtney, "I've been telling everyone it's all my fault because it is. It was my idea. I am a penguin murderer. Everyone was right."

Heather was rather annoyed at Courtney for lying to her previously but she did her best to console her.

"I know you're not to blame," said Heather, "I know you've not been entirely truthful with me, but it's still not your fault. You might have speculated on the idea in the first place, but they should have researched it properly before acting on it. It's not your fault that the world got in a tizz about a dying polar bear and demanded action and someone in authority decided to act without thinking about the consequences."

"What did you think? You know, when you first heard about what we were planning to do on Polar Saviour," asked Courtney, looking Heather in the eye.

"I know, I know," said Emily, raising her hand, "can I answer that one? You thought it was a fucking stupid idea. I remember you getting really annoyed."

"It didn't seem to me to be a particularly well thought out plan," said Heather, choosing her words carefully at first, "I mean, there must have been other options that didn't involve spending hundreds of millions of pounds to move a few hundred animals twelve thousand miles just to stop them going through some bins."

"Hello, ladies," said Ruan, rubbing his eyes as he approached the table, looking rather tired, "who fancies a spell looking after our patient?"

"How is he?" asked Heather.

"I don't know, he's asleep," replied Ruan,"I think I might have fallen asleep as well, just for a short while."

"Here, Courtney," said Ruan as he held out a scrumpled up, red, United Nations fleece, "try this one on for size."

Red all over

Alain spent a comfortable night in the bunk next to Carter, with the intention of keeping an eye on him but, instead, Alain slept soundly, as did Carter. The next morning, Carter was given the all-clear after a brief physical examination from Alain. The good news spread quickly, although getting the all-clear from someone with absolutely no medical experience isn't quite the ringing endorsement it sounds.

The lump on the back of Carter's head was now officially categorised as plum, on the fruit-based scale system, and also on the fruit-based colour chart. It was still sore to the touch, although the headache had gone, but Carter had experienced no other problems since the original incident. It was decided that he was well enough to travel and could lead the team setting out to discover what had happened to the penguin colony.

Carter's plan had always been to take two snowcats and camp overnight with half a dozen of the least incompetent members of the team. They would take samples, measurements, and observations over a twenty-four hour period and monitor the activities of any polar bears in the area, set up some remote cameras and then pack up and return the next day. The second snowcat was there to take back the day trippers and the gawpers, when they got bored. There didn't seem to be any good reason to change the plan so the two snowcats set off in tandem under grey skies.

Courtney, in the second of the snowcats, reserved for the day trippers, silently gazed out of the window, straining to see the horizon, to get her first look at the grotesque scene that Alain had described to her yesterday. She barely took any notice of Heather and Seanne, sat across the aisle from her, and she certainly didn't see Emily sat up front with the driver, a blonde viking with piercing blue eyes and a twenty-year-old beard. Emily had already nicknamed him Beardy Blue Eyes, as she didn't know his real name.

The snowcat could easily seat twelve passengers, in three rows of seats, the front two rows of seats were full of camping equipment and Courtney, Seanne and Heather were seated in the back row. Heather was sat by the window on the right-hand side, earphones in, blue parka coat, zipped almost to the top. Whatever she was listening to, through the earphones, was amusing her and every now and again she would stifle a laugh and look across to see if she was annoying Seanne or Courtney.

Seanne, who was sat next to Heather, was wearing the same golden, curly hair as before, tumbling artificially around her face, her light brown skin glowing with youth, shiny and shimmery, as Brian had described it. She was calm and still, with a composure that defied her age, deep in her own thoughts, possibly meditating, her lips moving slightly, mouthing a silent mantra.

Courtney had taken off her gloves and was nervously fiddling with anything she could touch while looking down at her lap. She examined her fingers, turning her hands over, she looked over at Seanne and Heather but neither met her gaze. She was suffering the same anxiety she had felt on the way to board the ship, the same anxiety she had felt, almost constantly, for the last few years. She played with the zip and the buttons on her parka, she put her gloves on, took them off again, she checked the contents of each pocket of her jacket, trying to avoid thinking about where they were heading and what they might find there.

Gradually, the slaughterhouse came into view, as they descended towards the ocean, the colour change being the most obvious sign, but there was also the smell, not the smell of rotten meat, or offal, or blood but excrement and death, a smell that said something isn't right here, turn back, danger! A smell that generated saliva in the mouth and a feeling of nausea.

"I can see it and smell it," said Emily who had the best vantage point. Even she could catch the faint aroma coming through the air vents into the cabin. "We're almost there," she added.

Courtney tucked her blonde hair behind her left ear and pressed the side of her face against the window, to get a better view, her ear and cheek were tingling from contact with the cold glass. She could see it now, spreading out in front of them, growing larger and larger as they approached. This was it, the fruits of her labour, she was finally going to see for herself what Operation Polar Saviour had achieved, what the public had demanded, before they performed a u-turn and washed their hands of it.

What have I done? Courtney asked herself. Surely I can't be responsible for all this?

She felt sick, really sick, pit of the stomach sick, she wanted to close her eyes to shut it out, she wanted to get into bed and curl up into a ball, pull the duvet over her head and stay there until it was all over. She knew. She had always known. Since the first satellite photographs, she had known. It had all gone horribly wrong and it was all her fault. No more denial, no more hope. It was there in front of her, in black and white and red all over, like a bad joke.

It wasn't the emerging scene in front of her that terrified Courtney though, it was the aftermath, the rest of her life, the finger pointing, the disapproval, the words spoken behind her back. Always being judged on what happened here. One mistake, spotlighted, highlighted, picked apart and put back together again, investigated, examined, judged and always the same conclusion. Guilty as charged. Sentenced to a lifetime of guilt.

You know who that is, don't you? people would ask. That's Courtney Woodbeard. Do you remember her? She's the penguin murderer? Yes, that penguin murderer. Not the other penguin murderer, not a penguin murderer but The Penguin Murderer. The original and the best. For the rest of her life, unless she could do something even more shocking, something that repulsed people even more than being responsible for the deaths of thousands, tens of thousands, hundreds of thousands of penguins. Hundreds of thousands of cute cuddly penguins all slaughtered, all her fault.

The thought of doing something good, something compassionate and heart warming, something charitable, to win hearts and minds, had never even crossed Courtney's mind. Without an experienced hand to guide her, without a soothing voice in her ear, the only way out of this was to do something even worse. A downward spiral of increasingly disgusting, inhumane acts to shake off the last nickname and earn a new one, until she finally found one that she could live with, one that she would be happy to have graffitied across the front window of her house, in perpetuity.

"Are you okay, Courtney?" asked Seanne. "You're very quiet."

"I'm fine," said Courtney, "just a bit tired, that's all."

Courtney wasn't fine and she wasn't tired. She just didn't want to talk about it. Well, she did, but it's difficult to open up to someone to tell them your private doubts and worries.

She envied Heather for having Emily to talk to. If only I could talk to my sister, my evil twin, she thought. I must stop calling her that, I must stop thinking of her as inherently evil. Maybe I should name her, humanise her. What should I call her? I'll try to think of her as Courtney Two, or Courtney Too, until I find the right name for her.

Shaggy, who was driving the first snowcat, pulled to a stop about twenty metres from the outskirts of the bloodshed. In the other snowcat, Beardy Blue Eyes slowed to a crawl and parked alongside the first snowcat, making sure that they were parallel, the front and rear lined up, as he slowly inched into place, backwards and forward, forwards and backwards, until he was satisfied they were exactly in line.

Carter was first out, pulling up the hood of his red parka and zipping it up as he stepped down onto the ice, rifle in hand. He was followed out of the first snowcat by a mixture of young students and even younger gap year students, with barely two weeks training and assessment between them and certainly no real Antarctic experience. As they tumbled out of the snowcat, the conditions seemed to catch them by surprise as they scrambled to pull scarves across mouths and put goggles or sunglasses on.

Carter seemed pleased with the location they had stopped at, it was upwind and slightly sheltered and seemed, to him, to be an ideal place to spend the night. Carter took charge, as he usually did, and dished out orders to make camp, keep watch and stay alert. Once they had done the necessary basics, they could then start the real work.

Tents were unloaded from the snowcats along with cooking equipment, chairs, food, water, camera equipment, sleeping bags and rucksacks of warm clothes, and most of it was just dumped on the ground in a haphazard way and lay there untouched, while the students attempted to assemble the tents and secure them to the ice.

The two drivers walked over to each other and Shaggy pulled out a packet of cigarettes and a lighter. He offered one to Beardy Blue Eyes which was dismissed with a wave of the hand. Shaggy knew his colleague didn't smoke but offered one every time, just to be polite.

Courtney, Heather, Seanne and Emily had gathered in a little group and were all staring out towards the scene in front of them, trying to take it in, trying to comprehend what had taken place here.

Courtney was the first to break the silence, the first to process what they were looking at, and snap back to reality. She had less trouble comprehending it than the others, as she had been preparing herself for this moment, visualising it, dreaming of it, night and day, imagining how she would react when she finally saw it. She was numb to it, to the death, she had already processed it, dealt with it, buried it, moved on. It wasn't about the death any more, or the mistakes that had been made, it was about her, about her coping with it, dealing with it, dealing with the consequences of it, if she could.

"What's the plan then?" asked Courtney.

"I don't think I was prepared for the scale of this," said Heather, ignoring the question, "this is indiscriminate slaughter, this isn't animals killing for food, this is killing for sport. I've never seen this in polar bears before, I mean, they'll play with their food, they'll toss a seal around for fun, but this is something else."

"I'm guessing that this isn't normal then?" asked Seanne.

"They've never had this much food put in front of them before," said Heather, "once they started killing, I should imagine panic set in among the penguins and they probably started running in all direction. We need to bear in mind that the polar bears won't have seen penguins before, except in a zoo."

"So what are we doing then?" asked Courtney. "We can't stand here staring for the rest of the day."

"I'm going to get a better look, see if I can find a whole one," said Emily as she walked off, almost skipped off, away from the others.

"So, what are we doing?" asked Courtney, impatiently.

"Carter will get the camp set up and then we'll go out and collect some penguin parts and polar bear shit and bag them up for analysis," said Heather, rather crudely.

"Do we really need to collect stool samples to tell what the polar bears have been eating?" asked Courtney. "We can all see what they've been eating, all we're going to find is BFF."

"BFF?" asked Heather, slightly confused.

"Beaks, feet and feathers," replied Courtney, "all the bits that they couldn't digest, the bits they put in sausages and burgers."

"I think you know, as a scientist yourself, that we can't just make assumptions about these things."

"And what are we going to do with all the pieces of penguin we collect?" asked Courtney.

"Well, we'll try to get a whole one, if we can," said Heather, "although collecting all the right pieces might be more difficult than I'd originally thought. They're scattered everywhere. It's like someone got dozens of jigsaws of bloodstained penguins and then took all the pieces, mixed them up and then scattered them all over the place. I think we'll be lucky if we can find a whole penguin to do an autopsy on. I'm going to walk down and help them set up camp, they look like they're struggling. What are you going to do? You coming, or are you going to sit here and cry about it?"

"I'm going to sit here and cry," said Courtney, after briefly considering the two options.

"Shall I grab us a couple of chairs?" asked Seanne, spotting a number of fold-out camping chairs in the pile of equipment next to the empty snowcat.

Uncomfortably seated, Courtney took off her glasses and put on a pair of prescription sunglasses to shield her eyes from the glare of the sun.

"The sun's bright, isn't it?" asked Seanne, by way of small talk, as she put on her own, more fashionable, sun goggles.

"This is incredible, isn't it?" said Seanne, when she didn't get a response. "I didn't really know what to expect but this is nature at its wildest, don't you agree?"

"It's wild all right," replied Courtney.

"How are you feeling? Are you okay?"

"I'm fine," replied Courtney, "it's what we were expecting, it matches the data from the satellite pictures."

"But how are you feeling, talk to me about it, this isn't fine. You need to talk to someone, open up about what you're feeling, you can't bottle up this kind of thing, it won't do any good in the long term."

"I don't feel anything," said Courtney, "I dealt with it before we got here. I don't feel anything, just empty, cold, emotionless. It is what it is."

"If you need to talk, I'm here for you."

"Thank you, Seanne. You're on my list of people I can talk to if I need to. You, Alain, Heather and plenty more, you're all on the list. There's no shortage of people who want to know how I'm feeling, what I'm thinking, so you can all talk about me behind my back."

"It's not like that. We all care about you, we all want what's best for you. We worry about you. I heard you had a run in with your sister, at the research station yesterday morning."

"More gossip?" asked Courtney.

"People talk. They're cooped up in confined spaces and they talk. We all want to help you and support you."

"Maybe I don't want help and support, maybe I just want to be left alone."

"Your sister isn't going to leave you alone. It's going to keep happening, you know that," said Seanne, "I can help you find out what she wants, what she's trying to tell you. You're damned to repeat this, over and over, your whole life, until you get an answer and if you come with me you can get an answer. He knows the answer. We can go there and find out."

"Why would I go with you?" asked Courtney.

"Why did you come here?" asked Seanne. "You knew what was here and yet you still came."

"It's not quite the same thing," replied Courtney.

"You knew what was here, and yet you still put yourself through this, you still came."

"I did, but why would I go with you?" asked Courtney. "You don't know what's out there, you don't even know if there's anything out there."

"There's answers out there. Answers for all of us and you're looking for answers. Join us. Come with us."

"Who is us? You and Brian?"

"You'd be surprised."

"You're asking me to put aside any common sense or logic and just to believe you. To have faith. To trust what some old shaman has told you, probably in an attempt to get rid of you and shut you up."

"That would be one way of looking at it, a cynical, world-weary way of looking at it. Maybe you need to start looking at things differently. Maybe you need to let some good into your life. You can't keep beating yourself up and shutting people out. I'm passionate about this. I've been searching for this my whole life and now, finally, I'm almost there. I've almost got the answers I need. In the next few days, I'm going to find out what my name is. And you could find out what your evil twin sister is trying to tell you."

"Courtney Two," interrupted Courtney.

"Courtney Too. Is that what you've called her?" asked Seanne. "It's a good name for now, but you can find out who she really is, find out what she wants to tell you. You can help her. She can help you. You just need to loosen up, let go of the things that are stopping you, the things that are holding you back. Put a little trust in someone else. You need to believe in something."

Seanne reached out an arm and placed her hand on Courtney's shoulder. Their eyes met, through tinted glass and neither could tell what the other was thinking. Seanne removed her goggles and pleaded with Courtney.

"You need to do this for yourself. Step out of your comfort zone and stop punishing yourself. We all want to help you, just let us in."

"Look, I can see how passionate you are about this," said Courtney, "but you don't win an argument with passion. All you do is let someone know how much you care. I know you care, I even believe that you care about me, that you think you're trying to help me, but..."

Seanne interrupted Courtney by laughing and she pointed way off into the distance.

"Carter just fell over," said Seanne, "did you see that? He tripped over a penguin."

Carter struggled to his feet and looked around to see if anyone had been watching. Courtney and Seanne both waved as he looked across at them.

"Who else is going?" asked Courtney.

"Does it matter? Would it change your mind if you found out someone else was going, someone who's opinion you trusted, someone you had known for a long time?"

"Alain?"

"Alain, Heather, Emily, Carter, Lester, Ruan, Shaggy. Who would tip the scales? Which one of them would make you change your mind?"

"Shaggy? The snowcat driver? He's not going. I mean, just look at him. You're not telling me that he's going with you."

"Not yet but I'm working on it. It would be nice to be able to drive the first part of the way, wouldn't it?" asked Seanne.

"I suppose it would. It's a long journey then?"

"It's been a long journey getting here. What's left is the easy part. He'll guide us, he knows the way and he'll guide us."

"I'll think about it," said Courtney, not really meaning it, but already thinking about it. I must find out who else is going, she thought.

"That's all I've ever asked of you, to have an open mind. We want to help you, if you'll let us," said Seanne, who couldn't disguise how happy she was with the progress she was making with Courtney. From, no, to, I'll think about it. A giant leap.

Carter walked over to Courtney and Seanne and threw a large, transparent, plastic bag onto the ground in front of them. The bag contained about a dozen frozen penguin heads.

"What are they?" asked Courtney.

"I think they're penguin heads," said Seanne, clearly disgusted.

"No, I mean what breed are they?" asked Courtney.

"They're penguins," said Seanne.

"You get different types of penguin," said Courtney, "king, emperor, rockhopper..."

"Really?" asked Seanne. "I thought they were just penguins."

"I'm not sure what these are," said Carter, "they're smaller than a king but, to be honest, they are such a mess I'm not sure if they're all the same breed. Could you help me set up some of the cameras please, Courtney, unless you're too busy? It's easier if there's two people doing it."

The two of them left Seanne alone and walked up to the top of the slope where there was a good view and an ideal site to locate one of the cameras. Carter placed his rifle on the ground as he set up the stand, a four legged tripod, a tetrapod? A quadrupedalpod? Once the stand had been assembled and secured, Carter fixed the camera on top and handed a computer tablet to Courtney.

"I'll adjust the camera and you tell me what you can see on the tablet," said Carter, "let me know when I've got it pointing in the right direction. It'll be streaming live from here and I don't want to have to come back and adjust it at a later date."

"What do you want in frame, just the edge of the sea in the background?" asked Courtney.

"That should do it, tell me when it's level."

After only a couple of minutes, the camera was in position and both of them were happy with what they had done and they began to walk back down the slope towards Seanne.

"Good job," said Carter, "you and Seanne getting on?" he asked as they walked back.

"She's trying to persuade me to go and see her shaman."

"And?"

"Like I said," replied Courtney, "she's trying to persuade me. You're not going, are you?"

"I don't have any, erm," said Carter, trying to think of the right words, "any issues, that need resolving. No questions to ask. Nothing to find out about myself. I'm a pretty simple guy. What you see is what you get. No secrets, no worries."

"None at all? Nothing you would want to ask?"

"Not that I can think of."

"No secrets we need to know about?" asked Courtney.

"Nope."

"Well, you could always go and ask why you keep getting drunk and running around with your cock out?"

They both laughed and turned to look at each other. Carter blushed, his normally pasty face reddened dramatically until it matched the colour of his jacket.

"Maybe I'll do that," he said, "maybe I will."

He's a big fan of genocide

Courtney sat with Seanne for several hours, waiting for Heather to finish whatever it was she was doing. They sat like an old couple at the beach, staring at a sea of body parts that lapped at their feet, occasionally reading a book or taking out an item of food from a pocket, unwrapping it, offering a piece to the other and then eating. But mainly staring into the distance. Nothing much was said.

The sheer scale of what was staring them in the face was incomprehensible. They were consciously aware of what they were seeing, Courtney especially, but it still didn't seem possible, it didn't seem real. It was only on closer inspection that the monstrousness of what they were looking at became clear. Only when they got close enough to make out the individual parts, that made up the whole scene, did they really feel the revulsion, the sickness, the horror, at the inhumanity of it all. Like a beautiful painting that, on closer inspection, glasses off, from inches away, you realise has been made up of thousands of tiny painted swastikas. For that reason, they stayed where they were and viewed it from a distance.

"So, when are you planning on going?" asked Courtney, while taking her sunglasses off. She didn't want to ask but had been unable to resist. She tried, she did, but she didn't try hard enough.

Seanne turned slowly to look at Courtney but without speaking. It would have been easy to say the wrong thing. Courtney was agitated, angry and irritable, constantly fidgeting, it was clear to Seanne that she was going through some internal turmoil. Seanne's mere presence seemed to be getting on Courtney's nerves, so she watched without replying, but that just seemed to annoy Courtney even more.

"So?" asked Courtney again, more aggressively.

"Is Thursday good for you?" asked Seanne, calmly, not wanting to scare Courtney off, now she had expressed an interest.

"I don't know. What day it is today?" said Courtney.

"It's Monday today," said Seanne, "Tuesday tomorrow, Wednesday after that and then we leave."

"We? Getting ahead of ourselves aren't we?"

"Well, we all leave on Thursday, whether you come with me or go back to the ship, you're leaving on Thursday, whether you like it or not. Party's over."

"I didn't realise," said Courtney, "I've lost track of time and I haven't had a chance to read the logistics schedule that we were given. We're going Thursday then?"

"That's right," replied Seanne, "I really would love for you to come with us."

"How will we get back after we've found the shaman, you know, after we've got our answers?" asked Courtney.

"Do you want me to print you out a logistics schedule? Would you read it if I did?"

"Probably not. Can't you just tell me?"

"Just trust me. I've got it all worked out. Are you coming with us then?" asked Seanne, but she didn't get a response. Courtney just put her sunglasses back on and they continued to watch Carter in the hope that he would fall over again. They watched polar bears in the distance, turning over pieces of penguin, looking for what? Who knows? Probably not even the polar bears. They watched Heather trying to show some students how to set up camp. They closed their eyes and faced the sun, the faint heat just enough to warm the skin. They each got up and took a walk to stretch their legs but they avoided walking too close to the frozen body parts, as it required too much effort to avoid treading on beaks, feet, or feathers.

Seanne sat relaxed, focused, serene, quite pleased with herself. Had she had a breakthrough with Courtney?

Heather finally walked over to them and asked if they were ready to go back to the research station. As they gathered their things ready to leave, a polar bear approached, still several hundred metres away, but Carter strode towards it and readied his gun to fire a warning shot. As it turned out, a bit of noise from Carter was enough to scare it away, for now.

"Snowcat's ready," said Heather, "you got everything?"

"Yes, Mum," said Courtney, sarcastically, as she walked past Heather, towards the snowcat, "can we go home now?"

"Glad you came?" Heather asked Seanne.

"Oh yes," replied Seanne, "thank you for inviting me. It's a horrific sight, but I wouldn't have missed this for the world. It's incredible out here."

"No problem," replied Heather.

"I hope when the time is right you'll come with me and let me return the favour."

"That would be nice," replied Heather, in her most non-committal tone of voice.

"Can we? Can we?" asked Emily.

"Hurry up," shouted Courtney, from beside the snowcat, where she was already waiting.

As the first one there, Courtney felt obliged to bagsy the front passenger seat, alongside Mr Beardy Blue Eyes. She waited impatiently for the others to arrive before they clambered into the back. Heather sat directly behind the driver and she put Carter's transparent, plastic bag of penguin heads on the seat next to her. Seanne and Emily sat in the two seats behind Courtney.

As soon as they were all on board and the doors were closed, they reversed back and headed uphill towards the research station.

"Can you put the radio on?" asked Courtney.

"What do you want to listen to?" asked Beardy Blue Eyes.

"Music, anything, what have you got?" asked Courtney. "Put Antarctic FM on or South Pole radio, anything will do."

Beardy Blue Eyes leaned forward and turned the radio on but there was just static noise. After trying to tune it for a few seconds he gave up and turned it off.

"No signal, we're too far away."

"Well, thanks for trying," said Courtney, not really meaning it.

"So, Mr Beardy Blue Eyes," said Courtney, mischievously, as she addressed their driver for the day, "Seanne wants to know what your real name is. She loves to find out what people's real names are, don't you, Seanne? You can't imagine what lengths she goes to find out people's real names. What's yours?"

"Gustaf."

"Gustaf what?"

"Gustaf Hylianson."

Courtney turned in her seat, as far as the seatbelt would allow, so she could see Seanne, who was sat behind her.

"Is that his real name, Seanne? Or is he just called that because he's the son of Mr and Mrs Hylian?"

"No," said Gustaf, before Seanne could respond, "my father's name is Hylianson. We don't put an extra 'son' at the end with every new generation, otherwise I would be called Gustaf Hyliansonsonson and so on."

"Is that right?" asked Courtney. "Every day's a school day. What does Gustaf mean?"

"It doesn't mean anything. It was my grandfather's name."

"It must mean something, all names mean something. Like king of the Staffs or windy stick."

"It's Polish isn't it?" asked Heather. "With a V?"

"No, Swedish, Gustaf with an F," said Gustaf, in clarification, and that was the end of the lesson.

Courtney was in a foul mood. She was, at least, grateful that Heather and Seanne seemed to recognised the fact and they kept quiet. Unbeknown to Courtney, Emily was very keen to poke the bear, to make it more grizzly. She kept up a running commentary of things she wanted Heather to ask Courtney.

"Ask her who killed all the penguins?"

"Ask her if she's coming with us to see the shaman?"

"Ask her what the name Courtney means?"

"Ask her if she's okay?"

"Go on, ask her. Go on."

Courtney could sense something was going on behind her but she couldn't tell what it was, which annoyed her even more.

"Ask her where she's going to move the polar bears to next," said Emily, "why don't you suggest that she moves them to Australia so they can kill all the kangaroos?"

Emily and Heather collapsed into a fit of giggles that Heather tried, unsuccessfully, to hide from Courtney.

Courtney bit her tongue.

As the snowcat pulled up to the research station, Courtney undid her seatbelt, opened the door and jumped down. She walked straight up the steps into the research station without looking back.

"What's up with her?" Heather asked Seanne.

"You tell me," replied Seanne.

"You were sat with her at the killing fields, what did she say?"

"Nothing, we talked earlier, but she's barely said anything for the last few hours."

"Is she always like this?" asked Gustaf, turning to look for an answer.

"Most of the time," said Emily.

"Not always," said Heather, "she's just upset. She blames herself for what happened."

"Aaah, she's The Penguin Murderer," said Gustaf, having a lightbulb moment, "I get it now, that makes sense. Is she going to be okay?"

"It's nothing a few drinks and a good night's sleep won't cure," said Heather, reaching forward to pat Gustaf on the shoulder.

"Thanks for the lift, Gustaf with an F, where are you off to now?"

"I'm going to the wharf where your ship is moored but I'll be back tomorrow morning to help when they've packed up camp."

"I better get this bag of penguin heads inside before they start to defrost," said Heather, for probably the only time in her life. I mean, she might say it again, she's still young, there's plenty of time left, but I think it's highly unlikely.

Seanne, Heather and Emily stepped down from the snowcat and made their way to the steps by the research station entrance, the ice cracked and crunched beneath their feet as they walked. Once inside, Heather cleaned her steamed-up glasses with a tissue and made her way to one of the laboratories, where she casually threw the bag of heads into the bottom of one of the freezers, quickly shutting the door to stop it falling out. Next, she dumped her jacket and bag on her bunk and removed some outer layers of clothing before making her way to the central communal area to get something to eat.

The food at the research station was barely adequate. Nowhere near as satisfying as the food they ate on board ship. There was no fresh food, just the basic supplies they had brought with them to restock the research station. There was also no chef, so they took it in turns to cook. Today it was the turn of two of the younger members of the expedition team, Midna and Tetra, and it tasted exactly how you would expect food to taste, if it had been rehydrated and warmed through by two Antarctic studies PhD students and then left on a serving counter under a heat lamp for several hours.

Courtney had chosen to sit alone at the middle table, slap bang in the centre of the room, which was quiet, save for a few others either eating, or working, or just passing through.

"The food here is fucking shit," said Courtney, loud enough for everyone to hear.

"I agree," said Heather, as she joined Courtney at the table, "let's ask Brian to come over and cook us something nice before we leave. I'll get Seanne to speak to him, she seems to have him house trained."

"I don't care," said Courtney, "it's not going to change anything."

"It'll make the food nicer."

"It won't bring back all those penguins."

"Nothing will bring back the penguins, Courtney," said Heather, "even if you had a time machine and went back to before this happened, you wouldn't be able to stop it. It would have happened anyway, whatever you tried to do."

"I still feel guilty, like it's my fault."

Before Heather could respond, Ruan joined them at the table holding a tray with both hands. On the tray was a plate and cutlery, and on the plate was something grey and unpalatable.

"Did someone say the food was shit?" asked Ruan.

Ruan was closely followed by Alain Govenor, who hovered near the table, wary of Courtney, waiting for an invitation to join them. None came.

"What are you still doing here, Doctor?" asked Ruan.

It was the closest Alain was going to get to an invite so he sat down next to Ruan, across the table from Courtney.

"Well, to be totally honest, I'm a bit scared to go back actually."

"Hanad?" asked Ruan.

"How did you guess?" asked Alain. "I'm not physically scared of him, he just, well, he's just a bit unpredictable. I'm never sure where I stand with him and he didn't really want me to come over here in the first place. Once I'm back on the ship, I'm not sure if I'll be able to leave again."

"He seemed all right to me," said Ruan, "I've not really spoken to him much though."

"I'm also worried about you," said Alain, addressing his comments toward Courtney.

"Don't waste your time," was Courtney's response.

"But I do worry, I have a duty of care, not just for your physical health but also your mental wellbeing."

"You've got no duty of care, Alain," snapped Courtney, "you're not a real, fucking doctor. You never were and you never will be. I'm going for a lie down," she said, pushing her tray away from her and standing up to leave.

Courtney walked out of the communal area and into the corridor leading to the accommodation pods. It brought back memories of when she was opening the shutters and trying to speak to Courtney Two. Memories of fear and frustration, but she had other things to worry about right now.

Courtney opened the door to her room and, after throwing some clothes off her bunk and onto the floor, she threw herself onto the bed and lay staring at the bottom of the bunk above her. Her attention was drawn to a stand of cotton hanging down between the wooden slats so she reached out and pulled it and it began to unravel, getting longer and longer until she pulled so hard it broke off and wrapped itself around her fingers. She flicked her hand several times before the cotton detached itself and it fell off onto the floor, next to the bed.

Why am I such a horrid person? Courtney asked herself. I'm being horrible to people and they haven't done anything wrong, I mean, Alain is an idiot sometimes but he does care about me, he tracked me down after all these years. He came all this way to support me and I'm just really rude to him. And Heather, I could have a friend for life there but I keep pushing her away. I'm never going to be able to forget what I saw today. Those poor penguins. What must it have been like in the middle of it all? I'm responsible for that, for all the suffering. When the world finds out what happened, when they get confirmation, when they see the photographs, the videos, the death, they're going to blame it on me. I feel sick at the thought of it.

I need to count to ten before I react, before I say anything. I get too angry, too quickly, and it stops me thinking things through and coming up with the right words to describe my feelings. I need to convince everyone here that I'm a better person that the one they've witnessed over the last few days.

Those poor penguins.

What is Courtney Two trying to tell me? To be a better person? Surely she has something more important to say than some advice about my personal growth. If only I knew what she wanted to tell me. It must be important, for her to have haunted me all this time, but she seems so much more determined to communicate with me now than she ever did before.

Lost in her thoughts, worries repeated, over and over, muddled and confused, her mind darting from one worry to the next, Courtney closed her eyes and lost track of time.

How long have I been here, thought Courtney. Did I fall asleep? I need to go back into the communal area and apologise to them all, as a group and then individually, she decided. What am I going to say to make this right? I need to apologise to Alain first. I've treated him terribly, I've been rude to him in front of everyone. I need to tell him that I know how much he cares about me, and how we all appreciate him stepping up to be the ship's doctor. I need to tell him that I feel safer knowing that he's looking out for me and I feel proud that he still takes an interest in me and my career, even after all these years.

I need to tell Heather that I like her, that she's a good friend, hopefully a friend for life, and that I'm an idiot. I need to apologise for being rude to her all day. The same with Seanne, although not so much the friend for life. I need to let her know that I support her in her search and, if there's anything I can do to help her, then I will.

I need to apologise to Ruan and everyone else in the room for creating an uncomfortable atmosphere, where people were too afraid to say anything for fear of me snapping at them. I'm not going to apologise for thinking the food is shit, although I might need to apologise for saying it.

I need to do this now while it's still fresh in my mind. I'll do it in this order, general apology, Alain, Seanne and then Heather. General, Alain, Seanne, Heather, repeated over and over until she couldn't forget.

Courtney was unsure how long she had been lying on the bed. She hoped that everyone would still be together at the table, so she could apologise to them all at once, rather than having to track them down individually. She was already feeling better just thinking about apologising. It will be heart warming, just don't cry and get upset, she thought. If they won't accept an apology, then I'll keep trying. I will make things right.

Courtney swing her legs round and sat on the edge of the bed, careful to avoid banging her head on the top bunk. She stood up and tried to make her hair and her clothes look like she hadn't just been lying in bed but without much success. She walked back into the communal area and found Heather,

Seanne, Alain, Ruan and a young man, who's name Courtney didn't know, sat at the table deep in conversation.

"It doesn't matter what we try to do to save the planet," said Alain, "if the global population keeps on growing then we're screwed anyway."

"It's not population growth that's the problem, Alain," said Ruan, "it's consumption. We're using more and more resources to make more and more stuff that we don't need. If the richest countries stopped mining fossil fuels and producing so much waste and pollution then the relatively low levels of population growth wouldn't be an issue."

Courtney approached the table and sat on the chair she had vacated just twenty minutes ago. Her uneaten food was still on the plate, on the table in front of her. She interrupted the flow of the conversation, but not in the way that she had planned. Any thought of apologising, or trying to be a nicer person, went out of the window as soon as she heard Alain talking about population control. It brought back memories that she just had to share.

"Would you like to know Alain's views on population control?" asked Courtney, eagerly, while looking at the surprised faces around the table.

"No, no, no, I know what you're going to say, but no, Courtney, don't," said Alain, who was now sat bolt upright and giving Courtney the hardest of stares.

"He's a big fan of genocide is our Alain."

"Oh, come on, Courtney," he protested.

"A big fan. He did a lecture once where he got a bit sidetracked. He was so easy to sidetrack, but this time he got onto the subject of population control. And it all came out. Tell them what you said, Alain, go on, tell them."

"It's a long time ago, Courtney. A long time ago. Do you still hold the same views as you did twenty years ago?"

"I do on things like genocide. And it's not like it was just the once that we got you onto the subject. A big fan of genocide, weren't you? Big fan of popping something in the water supply, sterilising the working classes. Big fan of the holocaust."

"Bloody hell, Courtney," protested Alain, "I never said holocaust."

"You wanted some sort of enforced death date didn't you, if I remember correctly, like that film where everyone dies when they get to thirty. Not so keen on that now, are you? Do you want to change it from thirty to sixty? Or seventy?"

"No," said Alain, just to be contrary, "thirty sounds like a good age to me. No one over the age of thirty has ever done anything worthwhile. All the great art, music and literature was created by young people. Name me one opera, one album, or painting, or novel, worthy of my time, created by someone over the age of thirty. You can't, can you? Anyway, I'm not the only person here who's over thirty."

"No, but you're the only one who loves genocide. I bet you loved seeing all those dead penguins, keeps down the population, doesn't it? The odd cull now and again. Stops them breeding out of control, doesn't it?"

"I know why you're saying this, Courtney. You're angry with me."

"Spoilers, Alain."

"Actually, that's not why you're angry is it? I don't even think you're angry with me."

"Don't you?"

"No, I think you're angry with yourself. You're disappointed in yourself. You've let yourself down. You're just taking it out on me because you think I'll sit here and take it and then we'll both apologise tomorrow and everyone will forget what a little shit you were. Well, I'm not going to sit here and take it, I'm going to go outside for a smoke. If anyone would like to join me then, please, feel free."

Alain stood up quickly, his legs pushed back on his chair but it didn't fall over onto the floor in the dramatic way that

Alain had intended, it just made a scraping noise on the floor as it slid backwards. With nothing in his hand to throw on the table in disgust, Alain just turned and walked away without making too much of a scene.

No one followed.

"I'm sorry," said Courtney, in a barely audible whisper, "I came back in here to apologise but I've just made it worse."

"Maybe you should go after him if you want to apologise," said Ruan, who had avoided Courtney's wrath so far and hadn't witnessed the worst of her foul mood earlier.

"Leave him for now, Courtney, let him calm down," said Heather, "he ain't worth it."

"He ain't worth it," said Emily, in a generic cockney accent.

"He is worth it. You're all worth it. I'm sorry. I just spend so much time managing my own worries, my own anxiety that I don't have time to worry about other people and their feelings. It's a full time job just getting through the day and I struggle with it. Seeing the penguins today really affected me."

"It affected us all," said Seanne, "we're all suffering. You're not alone."

"Come with me," said Heather, who put an arm around Courtney and led her away from the table, just as tears started to run down Courtney's face and into the corners of her mouth. Her shoulders shook as she sobbed and she could taste the saltiness of her tears as the others at the table approached and enveloped her, and Heather, in a large sympathetic hug.

"It's going to be all right," someone said from the edge of the huddle, "it's all going to be all right."

It didn't mean anything

The next morning, Alain stood outside the research station in his lightning-embossed skiwear, hands shivering, trying to have his first smoke of the day. The wind had picked up considerably overnight, blowing down towards the sea, so Alain positioned himself with his back to the wind and cupped his hands around the lighter but, no matter how many times he tried, he still couldn't get a flame.

Some people would take it as a sign, but not Alain. He raced up the steps to the research station and went in, closing the door behind him to shut out the wind. He lit the joint, that he had rolled in bed first thing this morning, and he went back outside to smoke it.

He knew his skiwear might be insufficient for the Antarctic weather, but he hadn't expected to spend so much time outdoors, certainly not in these conditions. He had a woollen hat that he wore pulled down over the hood of the ski suit and many layers on underneath, but the wind didn't seem to respect his fashion choices and it buffeted and chilled him intensely.

Alain was relieved to see two snowcats approaching the research station, stirring up a great trail behind them, like the vapour trail of an aeroplane. He already knew that Shaggy would allow him to sit in the heated cabin of the snowcat while he smoked and he took this as a sign from above that he was meant to be a smoker. In his time of need, his prayers had been answered, although his prayers had been vague and more expletive-ridden than a celebrity, social media meltdown.

Shaggy slammed on the brakes and swung the steering wheel at the last minute, leaving the snowcat parked at an odd angle. Gustaf, in the second snowcat, pulled up alongside, inching the snowcat into place before turning the wheel to leave the two vehicles parallel with the wheels pointing in the same direction.

Carter bounded out of the first snowcat and bellowed instructions to those behind him. Even though he was only a short distance away from Alain, his voice was lost in the wind.

Alain approached the first snowcat, hoping to jump in the cab with Shaggy to finish his smoke in peace, but he stopped in his tracks when he saw the tall figure of Lester Cherry-Stone and the even more imposing bulk of Brian Unsafe, clumsily exiting the second snowcat behind Gustaf.

"What are you doing here?" he shouted towards them, although they didn't hear him.

Brian approached and gave Alain a hug, briefly lifting him off the ground while shouting greetings into his ear. He put Alain back down and walking on towards the research station. Lester approached Alain more cautiously and, once he was close enough, Lester leaned in and shouted to be heard.

"I need to talk to you, Alain."

"Follow me," shouted Alain in response, as he led Lester through the stream of people and equipment making its way from the snowcats to the research station. They jumped up into Shaggy's snowcat and closed the door behind them. It was as if someone had pressed mute and turned the sound off.

Alain relit what was left of his joint and turned to make eye contact with Lester. He saw a troubled look in Lester's eyes, his tired but beautiful eyes. He stared into his eyes for too long, far too long, now it was uncomfortable, but he couldn't look away.

"I need a favour from you, Doctor," said Lester, who was impressively dressed, compared to Alain. He wore a very expensive looking, dark coloured, Arctic parka and matching trousers. Circular goggles hung around his neck over a scarf that he had pulled up to cover the lower part of his face. He stamped his boots to shake off some ice and pulled down the scarf before he spoke again.

"I need to borrow something from you."

"Whatever it is, you're welcome to have it," said Alain, without a second thought.

"I need your gun," said Lester, with a straight face, no joking around, straight to the point.

"My gun?"

"Your gun."

"What do you need it for?"

"I've been compromised. Hanad knows I'm a spy."

"A spy? Who are you spying for?"

"I told you all this."

"Did you?"

"Don't you remember?"

"Well, no not really, you dropped some hints about something secret but I didn't read too much into it. I thought you were joking around or drunk."

"No joke, Doctor," said Lester, "I think he's going to kill me and I need to kill him first."

"But why would he want to kill you?"

"Because I've been spying on him."

"But you work for him."

"I know but I've been spying on Hanad and reporting back to someone else about Hanad's movements and who he meets with and now he's found out about it."

"Well, how did he do that? Have you got a mole?"

"A mole? What are you talking about?"

"I don't really know," said Alain, "I'm not really au fait with this spying malarkey. How did he find out?"

"He overheard me on the radio, sending a status update to my handler. I'm sure it was him. I heard someone outside the door and when I went to look there was no one there but his elevator had just gone up, so it must have been him listening to me."

"Are you sure? It seems like very little to go on."

"I'm sure, Doc."

"Well, I mean, I'd love to, but I'm sorry, Lester, old chap. I brought the gun here for my own protection, from the polar bears, you know, not for you to shoot someone in cold blood."

"You brought it for self defence and I'm asking you if I can use it for self defence. You don't know Hanad like I know Hanad. It's a race now, Doctor, the clock is counting down, either I kill him or he kills me."

"I think you might be getting a bit carried away, have you been drinking?"

"You know I've been drinking and you know I can still function and make decisions. I'm not delusional, my judgement hasn't been impaired. You know that."

"Sorry," said Alain, sheepishly.

"Can I please have the gun?"

"Sorry, Lester. I brought it for self defence but I think I might need to use it to protect someone else. Protect them from themselves. Stop them doing something stupid, like I'm stopping you from doing something stupid. Do you realise what would happen if you shot someone?"

"Well, hopefully I'll kill him and no one will find out. One clean shot and then toss the body and the wheelchair overboard."

"Well, if you're lucky, but what will probably happen is that someone will hear the gunshot and find the body before you dump it in the sea and then they'll radio over here and ask for a doctor. I'll have to go back to the ship and try to save his life. Well, I'm not a bloody doctor, I don't know how to treat a gunshot wound."

"That's a good thing."

"Not if he dies it isn't. I'll end up facing a medical negligence suit. I'll be struck off."

"You're not a real doctor. What does it matter?"

"No, Lester, no, I can't."

"I thought we were friends, Doctor."

"We are."

"Where's Courtney?" asked Lester, to Alain's surprise. "Is she here?"

"I'm not sure," replied Alain cautiously, "we had a bit of a barney yesterday and we haven't spoken since."

"A barney?" asked Lester. "What's a barney?"

"An argument," replied Alain, "about genocide. Only it wasn't really about genocide. It was, well, it's complicated."

"If you won't help me, Doctor, I'm sure she will."

"What makes you think Courtney can help?" asked Alain.

"You're not the only person I've confided in, Doctor. Is she inside?"

"I think so."

"Well, I'm going to look for Courtney," said Lester, reaching for the door handle, "think about what I'm asking you to do, Alain," he added, as menacingly as he could.

Alain sat alone in the snowcat for a few minutes more, mindfully smoking, enjoying every lungful before inhaling a loose scrag of tobacco. The resulting coughing fit put an end to his pleasure.

Lester took very little time locating Courtney. The research station was effectively one long corridor with rooms coming off it and he soon found Courtney in one of the accommodation pods, where she was sharing a room with Heather, Seanne and three other female members of the research team.

Courtney was sat on her bunk, dressed in navy blue, thermal trousers and a matching top, and a particularly thick pair of grey socks. She was running her fingers through her hair to try to calm it down.

"Hello, Penguin Lady," said Lester, by way of a cheeky greeting, "I bet you didn't expect to see me here, did you?"

"Lester, it's so nice to see you after all this time. How long has it been? All of two days? Have you missed me that much?" asked Courtney, while laughing.

"May I sit down?" asked Lester. "There's something I need your help with."

"Please do."

Lester sat on the bunk opposite Courtney's and began to strip off some of his outer layers to make himself more comfortable. Courtney watched as he peeled away layer upon layer until she could see the definition of his muscular arms and chest through the last thin layers of clothing.

"I'm in trouble," said Lester, jumping straight to the point, "you know I told you that I was spying on Hanad?"

"Did you?"

"Your first night on the ship, I told you I had a secret, that I was a spy."

"Did you? I remember something about you having a secret but that could have meant anything. I assumed you were drunk."

"What is wrong with you people? Don't you ever listen to anything I say?" snapped Lester, in frustration.

"You people?" asked Courtney, not knowing if she should be offended or not. "You people? What's that supposed to mean?"

"Alain. You and Alain, you don't listen when people talk to you."

"Sorry, but don't lump me in with Alain. What's he done now? No, don't tell me. I don't want to know. I upset him last night you know. We're not talking, well, we've not spoken since. I owe him an apology."

"Well, when you get to apologise to him, could you ask him for a favour?"

"I'm not sure he'll be that receptive to me asking him for anything, but what do you need?"

"I need his gun," replied Lester with a straight face.

"What for?"

"To protect myself from Hanad. He's found out I've been spying on him and I think he's going to have me killed."

"No way."

"Yes way."

"But Hanad? I mean, really? Why would he do that?" asked Courtney.

"Just trust me. I need you to ask Alain to lend me his gun, just for a little while."

"Okay, okay, I'll ask him when I speak to him but what do I get in return?"

"What do you want?" asked Lester, who was willing to agree to anything to get his hands on Alain's gun. As far as Lester was concerned the threat from Hanad was real, a clear and present danger. He didn't want to take the gun from Alain by force, but he was a desperate man and desperate men do desperate things.

"I've been horrible to everyone since I got here," said Courtney, sheepishly, "there's so many people I need to apologise to. I got really upset yesterday when I went to see the penguin colony. You saw it too, didn't you?"

Lester nodded in the affirmative.

"And the day before, when we arrived here, I was chased by my evil twin, have I told you about her?"

"I've heard about her. What happened exactly?"

"I slapped her."

"Wow. You're full of surprises aren't you?"

"And then she chased me and I fell over but I got away. She's trying to tell me something, trying to communicate with me."

"Where did you see her?"

"Everywhere. Once the shutters are down and the lights are on, she's there in the reflection, in every room, wherever I go, she's there. I couldn't understand what she was trying to say. We tried on the ship, to communicate with her, but that didn't end very well."

"I heard about that. I wish I'd been there to see it."

"How did you hear about it?"

"People have got nothing better to do than gossip. You must know that."

"I didn't realise so much of my private life was public knowledge."

"Look, everyone knows about Heather's imaginary friend Emily. Everyone knows that Seanne is going to head on out to look for a shaman. Everyone knows that Alain's not a real doctor. Everyone knows everything about The Penguin Lady and in a couple of hours everyone will know that Hanad is trying to kill me. You want to talk to your evil reflection?"

"Yes."

"Well, I'm your man. Communication is what I do. It's my job. It's what I'm trained to do. If there's a way to communicate with her then I'll think of it."

You didn't do a very good job in communicating to me that you were a spy, was what Courtney wanted to say, but she held her tongue. Lesson learnt.

"You need to apologise to pretty much everyone, right?" said Lester, enthusiastically, an idea forming in his mind. "And you want to find out what she's trying to tell you, right?"

Courtney nodded, curious to find out what Lester was thinking.

"I've spent a long time in places like this, on ships, in barracks, locked down and people need something that brings them together, a shared experience. And it doesn't always have to involve drinking, I mean, it usually does but it doesn't have to."

"Okay," said Courtney, still waiting to hear what Lester's plan was.

"Let's invite everyone to a seance."

"A seance?" asked Courtney. "But why?"

"We invite everyone to come and we try to communicate with her, like a seance. I know she's not dead but she interacts with you doesn't she? Like a spirit?"

"Sort of," admitted Courtney.

"Well, we get everyone together, strength in numbers. You can apologise to them all, if you need to, clear the air, then we summon her. Nice and calm, we close the shutters, gather round, hold hands, sing kumbaya, whatever. She's in the reflection in the window right? So we give her a way to communicate with us. If we steam up the window then she could write on the glass. Maybe that would work. She's touched things before, hasn't she?"

"You've seen seances in films though, haven't you?" asked Courtney "You know how they usually end, don't you?"

"You said yourself, it's not a seance, we're not trying to summon the dead, we're not going to accidentally raise an army of dead penguins. All we're trying to do is create a situation where she can communicate with you. She tells you what you want to hear, or whatever, then you persuade Alain to lend me his gun. It's a slam dunk."

"Job's a good'un," said Courtney.

"Yeah, that as well."

"How will you persuade everyone to come?" asked Courtney.

"Hell, that's the easy part. I'm pretty persuasive when I want to be, but there's no need. I guarantee, that by the time word gets out, you won't be able to stop people from coming. They'll be walking all the way from the ship and banging on the door to get in. If I radio that Russian research station, that's hundreds of miles way, they'll find a way to get here. The problem is not, how do we get people to come, it's, how to organise crowd control when they all turn up."

You weren't very persuasive when you asked Alain to give you his gun, thought Courtney.

"We need to start spreading the word," said Lester, "let me go and tell people. This afternoon? Is that good for you?"

"That's fine," said Courtney, "mind your head when you stand up, I've already banged mine on the top bunk once this morning."

"Thank you for the advice. I'd better start to rile up a mob. Do you think I'll get more people to come by telling them we're having a seance or by telling them you're going embarrass yourself by making a public apology?"

Courtney smiled but she didn't feel like laughing.

Lester's plan didn't really involve Courtney at all, she was just a distraction, to get everyone in one place while he searched for Alain's gun.

Making the apology didn't bother Courtney, after all, it was just an apology, it didn't mean anything. What concerned her was that everyone would be there when she tried to contact Courtney Two. That's not how she had envisioned it, she was meant to be alone, just the two of them, in private, in secret, but Courtney had been unable to summon up the courage to confront Courtney Two again. She avoided looking towards the windows in the evening, when the light changed, in case she caught a glimpse of something, or someone, but now the decision had been made for her, she had been carried along by Lester's plan and now it was too late to back out.

Within minutes of Lester leaving, Heather and Emily burst through the door, well, Heather burst through the door, Emily just arrived somehow.

"Tell me it's not a joke," said Heather, wary of getting too excited only to be disappointed later.

"It's not a joke."

"So, you're doing it?"

"Do you mean the seance or the apology?" asked Courtney, putting air quotes around seance and then around apology, because Courtney knew it wasn't a real seance, no one was dead, and it wasn't a real apology, no one was sorry.

"Both. Do both," said Heather, "it'll be good for you, cathartic, I can't wait. We'll both be there to hold your hand. What's Lester's involvement in all this?"

"I'm doing him a favour in return."

"Are you now?" asked Heather, suggestively.

"Nothing like that," said Courtney, with more than a hint of disappointment in her voice, "he wants to borrow Alain's gun to shoot Hanad."

She said it as if it was the most normal thing in the world. Borrow a gun to shoot someone. She had never even seen a handgun close up, until last week, when Alain produced one out of his desk drawer and now the idea of someone getting shot was just part of normal conversation.

"I am so going to watch that," said Emily, excitedly.

"Why Alain's gun?" was Heather's puzzled response. "There's other guns here, I mean we've got at least four rifles for our own protection. The snowcat drivers have their own guns, what's so special about Alain's gun?"

"I don't know. Maybe he's going to say that Alain shot Hanad. We know Alain doesn't like him."

"But why would he tell you about it? By the end of the day, everyone will know that Lester wants Alain's gun so he can shoot Hanad."

"Are you calling me a gossip?" asked Courtney.

"Well, if the cap fits."

But, before Courtney could plead not guilty, the door opened and Seanne appeared in the doorway. The sound of voices could be heard along the corridor, above the noise of the wind from outside, the sound of anticipation, of expectation, a buzz was spreading throughout the research station. Lester was right. His plan was working, the circus was coming to town and anyone who was anyone was going to be there. The excitement could also be heard in Seanne's voice.

"No way," she squealed.

"Yes way," replied Courtney and Emily in unison.

Emily couldn't stop clapping her hands. She loved it the last time they summoned Courtney Two, her heart was racing just at the thought of it. She couldn't wait for them to do it again, even though the first time hadn't exactly gone to plan.

"In front of everyone?" asked Seanne. "Oh, my Lord, this is going to be awesome. Tell me again, what happened last time?"

"Last time, I ran away and fell over," said Courtney, modestly, in the briefest of summaries, "and the time before that, Heather threw a fleece over my head and wrestled me to the ground."

"Oh, please, can I do it this time?" asked Seanne. "Please let me wrestle you to the ground. Would you mind?" Seanne asked, addressing the question to Heather.

"Be my guest," said Heather, "I did enjoy doing it but I think it would be funnier, this time, to watch someone else have a go."

"Don't I get a say in this?" asked Courtney, who was beginning to enjoying being the centre of attention.

"No," they all replied in unison.

Awooga

Courtney half expected there to be music playing over the tannoy as she walked to the communal area. She had never considered what ring walk song she would choose to accompany her as she approached her destiny, so she just randomly hummed something to herself as she walked.

As she approached, she could smell the food that Brian had been cooking with the fresh produce he had brought over from the ship. No more shit food, thought Courtney. Until Brian goes back. How long is he here for? Is he staying long enough to go with Seanne?

She could hear Lester working the crowd. They let out a huge cheer, it sounded like there were hundreds of people there. How did he get so many people to turn up? Where did they all come from? They surely didn't have time to come all the way from the Russian research station?

The scene, that greeted Courtney as she walked through the door, was a bit of a let down. They were certainly noisy, bar room noisy, and Lester had done a good job working them into a frenzy, if the number of people stood up on the tables was anything to go by, but there can't have been more than twenty people in the room.

Courtney recognised the majority of them, although she still didn't know the names of half the people on the expedition team. Shaggy and Gustaf were both there, waiting for the winds to ease before returning to the dock. There were no Russians. No one else from the ship had come over. If Lester had just told them that Brian was here, doing the cooking, he'd have got a similar sized crowd.

Courtney felt deflated, she had been sold a dud. Promises had been made and they hadn't been kept. Maybe it will be better like this, thought Courtney. After all, if it turns out as bad as the last two times then the fewer people here the better.

Due to the crowd's exuberance, Courtney was forced to high five people she didn't know as she made her way through to the front. She wore Ruan's UN fleece across her shoulders, like a cape, so she could give it to Seanne to bundle over her head, if things got out of hand.

The smell of freshly cooked food reminded Courtney that she was doing this on an empty stomach. Would they all mind waiting while she had something to eat? What is that smell? Melted cheese? Tomatoes? Garlic?

"Here she is," shouted Lester, as he appeared beside her. He grabbed Courtney's wrist and raised her arm above her head. Courtney nodded at the crowd and gave a little courtesy, once Lester had let go of her arm.

"Before we start," said Lester, waiting for the noise to die down, "before we start, there's something that I think Courtney would like to say to you all and something she especially wants to say to our good doctor, Alain Govenor."

There was an audible, "Ooooh," from the crowd, followed by some scattered laughs.

Have they all been drinking? Courtney asked herself.

Lester pulled out a chair and positioned it next to Courtney. He offered his hand to help her up and she accepted. She got up onto the chair, rather wobbly at first, and then she steadied herself ready to address her fans.

"Courtney, everyone," said Lester, who stepped back into the crowd and out of sight.

What am I apologising for? Courtney thought. I should have written something down before I stood up here. What am I going to say?

"Erm, if I don't owe you an apology," said Courtney, pausing for effect, "then I'm sorry, you'll have to wait until next time. If I do owe you an apology, then I'm sorry, please accept my apologies, especially you, Doctor Alain Govenor."

That'll do, thought Courtney as she stepped down from the chair. A few people began to halfheartedly clap her halfhearted apology but not enough for it to become a round of applause. Courtney removed the fleece from around her shoulders and handed it to Seanne.

"If anything happens, and you think I'm in danger, then we need to break the link between her and me," said Courtney, "I'll close my eyes and I'm sure someone will open the shutters but, if you need to, throw this over my head, just in case."

"And wrestle you to the ground?" asked Seanne.

"Only if you think it's absolutely necessary. I'd rather you didn't, I've still got a bruise on my hip from when Heather did it."

"Where's Lester gone?" asked Courtney, looking around the room. "He was meant to be organising this."

"I'll do it," said Heather, "I think I saw him slip out the door."

"Who's closing the shutters?" asked Heather, loudly, looking towards the control panel.

"I'll do it," said Carter, from over by the door, raising a giant hand into the air like a pupil who knows the right answer.

"Okay, everyone," said Heather, taking charge in Lester's absence, "I'm not sure if you've all heard about this but Courtney is being haunted by the ghost of her dead twin sister, or something like that, we're not quite sure. When we close the shutters, we're hoping she'll appear to Courtney in the reflection in the glass and then we can try to communicate with her. This isn't a seance so you don't need to hold hands, unless you want to. I will ask you all to stay quiet though. If anything goes wrong then, Carter, you open the shutters and we'll look after Courtney down this end."

Several of the crowd were holding mobile phones, filming what was happening, including Ruan, who had worked his way to the front and had the best position to film from.

"Are you ready?" asked Heather.

"I'm ready," replied Courtney, although how could she be? How do you prepare to face a lifetime of fear? Courtney had been haunted by this for as long as she could remember. Maybe she was finally due some answers.

"Everyone ready?" asked Heather, raising her voice.

A simple, "Yes," would have done but, instead, they responded with a mix of whoops, claps and clinking of glasses and someone repeatedly shouting, "Awooga," at the top of their voice. Lester had whipped up the crowd before Courtney arrived, but the mood in the room didn't reflect the respectable, scientific background of most of those present. The chance to let off steam had made them all giddy with excitement.

"CARTER," shouted Heather, to be heard above the noise of the crowd, "can you start the shutters, please?"

Everyone's attention was drawn towards the window, they could all see the terrible conditions outside. The wind had really picked up and was buffeting the research station, a blizzard of ice and other debris was passing by and occasionally slamming into the windows. Outside, anything that hadn't been secured down was either lying on its side or being blown along, until it struck something else and came to a rest.

The mechanical sound of the shutters began instantly, as soon as Carter activated the switch. The shutters moved down to cover the windows which started to act like mirrors, to reflect the scene inside the research station. Gradually, the room fell silent and everyone watched to see what was going to happen next.

"Where's Lester?" asked Courtney, looking round towards Heather.

"He's not here," said Heather.

"He said we should try to breathe on the glass, to see if she can communicate with us by writing in the condensation."

"I suppose it's worth a try," said Heather.

"Who is going to do it?" asked Courtney. "I thought Lester was going to do it."

"I think it needs to be you," said Heather, who was reluctant to get any closer.

As the shutters finished descending, the window reflected the performance being staged inside the research station. Seanne stood ready to pounce, the fleece gripped ever so tightly in her hands. Heather tried to take a few steps back, to give Courtney more space, but she was being pressed forward by the crowd, as they shuffled in to get a better look. Ruan was now stood next to Heather, just a short distance away from Courtney, still filming on his mobile phone. Brian had come out of the kitchen and was at the back looking over people's heads. They all waited, all silent, just the sound of the wind, battering the shutters, as a background soundtrack.

Courtney stepped towards the glass and saw, alongside her own reflection, the eerie reflection of someone who looked very similar to her. She took a step to her right and moved closer, her own reflection beginning to merge with that of her twin, the outline of the faces lining up as she got nearer and nearer. She could see that the nose was different, the same green eyes but slightly higher on the face, or was the nose just longer? The lips were fuller, the hair the same length, almost identical but not quite, the outline of the face lined up, almost perfectly, with her own.

Courtney was close enough to the window to see her breath start to form on the glass as she breathed out. She leaned in, getting as close to the reflection as she dared, she wanted to stop, to turn to the room and say something amusing to break the tension. She was aware of everyone watching, she could feel it, feel the anticipation in the room, she could feel her heart beating. She tried to calm her racing heart, but it had gone, it was out of the gates, already bolted.

"Tell her to get closer," said Emily.

"Go on," whispered Heather, "you can do it."

Courtney put her face closer and closer to the window until her nose almost touched the glass. She looked into the reflection of her own eyes, for reassurance, and then she breathed out through her mouth. A roundish patch of condensation formed on the glass, just in front of her. She took a step back and waited.

What if this doesn't work? thought Courtney. What if she doesn't understand what we're trying to do?

The condensation started to fade so Courtney cautiously leaned in again, her nose touching the glass this time, and she breathed on the glass once more. She stepped back, raised her arm and, with one finger, wrote the word, 'hi,' on the window and waited to see if there was any response.

The figure in the reflection didn't move.

Courtney was conscious of all the eyes watching her, all the people holding their breath, silently waiting for something to happen. She was determined not to disappoint them so she leaned in once more and breathed on the glass, a patch of condensation appeared with the word, 'hi,' still faintly visible, just below the mark her nose had made on the window.

Courtney stepped back and looked at her two reflections. She raised her arm to brush her hair back behind her ear and she saw the reflection also raise their arm but, instead of touching their hair, the hand reached out a finger to the condensation on the glass and wrote the word, 'go.'

"Did you see that?" asked Courtney, very quietly.

"I see it," said Heather, from close by.

"Come on," shouted a voice from the crowd, "do something."

"Did you not see?" asked Courtney, turning to address the crowd.

"See what?" asked Ruan, still filming. "There's nowt there, love?"

"Did you not see it?" asked Courtney, but the crowd were impatient and losing interest.

"What happened?" someone asked.

"I didn't see anything."

"Was that it?"

"What a waste of time."

Courtney turned to Heather for reassurance.

"You saw it, didn't you?"

"Yes," said Heather, "go. It said go."

"Did you see it?" Courtney asked Seanne.

"I'm not sure," said Seanne, "I was holding onto the fleece really hard and concentrating on you, in case something happened. I'm not sure what I saw."

Alain stepped out of the crowd, gun clearly visible, tucked into the belt of his trousers, cold against his skin.

"Did it work?" he asked.

"Did you see it?" asked Courtney in response.

"I'm not sure," said Alain, "I don't think so. Did Ruan get anything on camera?"

The disappointment was obvious as the disgruntled crowd began to break up and scatter. Several of them had words with Lester as he came back into the room. Carter, seeing that it was all over, flicked the switch to open the shutters and came to Lester's aid.

"Come on, people," said Carter, authoritatively, "no one got hurt, none of you paid to see it so I don't know why you're all so upset. Summoning the dead isn't a science. What were you expecting? You should think yourselves lucky that nothing did happen, imagine your faces if she'd summoned up the dead. You'd have all shat yourselves fighting to get out of here. You should thank your lucky stars that we're not fighting off an army of zombie penguins right now."

Within a few minutes, most of the people in the room had dispersed. Courtney, Alain, Seanne, Heather, and Lester, all huddled around Ruan, watching the footage on his mobile phone. They could see Courtney, they could see Courtney's reflection, they saw her breathe on the glass but that was it. There was nothing there, no ghost writing, no communication with the spirit world, nothing.

"We could always try again," said Ruan, trying to be helpful.

"You definitely saw something, didn't you?" Courtney asked Heather. "Did Emily see it as well?"

"I did," said Emily, "it said go."

"I thought I saw it but now I'm starting to doubt myself," said Heather, "there's nothing on film but, at the time, I was sure I saw something. Ruan, can you put the video onto a bigger screen so we can get a better look at it?"

"Sure," replied Ruan, "let me do it now and I'll let you know what I find."

"Where were you?" Courtney asked Lester. "You were meant to be helping."

"I had things to take care of," replied Lester, who had rifled through Alain's belongings, searching his bunk, his rucksack and any other hiding places, while the seance had been taking place.

"I thought you were meant to be on my side," said Courtney.

"There are no sides," said Lester, "there's just me and you and I'll worry about what's best for me and you worry about what's best for you. Don't forget that you owe me. You need to speak to Alain."

Ruan went off with Lester to find a computer and Seanne handed the fleece back to Courtney before following Brian into the kitchen. Courtney, Heather and Alain were left trying to work out what just happened.

They sat down at one of the tables, one of the tables without footprints on the top, and they went over what had happened. As it turned out, Alain was next to useless, he hadn't seen anything, he was too far away, he hadn't really been looking. Courtney and Heather were both convinced they had seen something, they had both seen the word, 'go,' written on the glass, but they were both starting to doubt themselves. How could they both have seen it if no one else did?

"What does it mean?" asked Courtney. "Go where? Go from this place, go home, go back to the ship? Go with Seanne? How am I meant to know?"

"Maybe it was just the first two letters of a word," suggested Alain, unhelpfully, "maybe it's a word that begins with go, maybe you didn't breathe on enough of the glass for her to write what she wanted to say."

"What word do you think she was trying to write Alain?" asked Courtney. "Gonads? Goldmine? Maybe she was trying to tell us about an abandoned goldmine hidden somewhere near here."

"I'm just trying to help," pleaded Alain.

"Sorry, Alain," replied Courtney, "I know you are but it isn't actually helping."

Alain got up to leave, just as Brian Unsafe appeared from the kitchen, in his chef's whites, with a bowl of pasta that he put on the table in front of Courtney.

"Here, Seanne said you haven't eaten," said Brian.

"Oh, thank you, Brian," said Courtney, picking up the knife and fork and tucking in.

"You should have asked me," said Brian as he sat down at the table.

"Asked you what, Brian?" Courtney said, between mouthfuls.

"Well, with my showbiz background, you should have got me to host whatever it was you just did. Lester didn't even stay to see what happened. I wouldn't have let it end like that. I would have had the crowd in the palm of my hand, like a proper ringmaster."

"Would you have had to wear blackface to do it?" asked Courtney, cheekily.

"I wouldn't have had to, no, it's not compulsory," replied Brian, laughing. He took Courtney's comment in good spirit, just a bit of fun between friends.

"What did you see?" asked Brian. "From your reaction I could tell that there was something there."

"She, er we, saw the word, 'go,' written on the glass," said Heather, "but it's not clear what it means. It's left more questions than answers."

"And only the two of you saw it?" asked Brian.

"That's right, oh, and Emily as well," said Heather, "she saw it, Ruan filmed it, but there didn't seem to be anything caught on camera."

"Seanne said you both have the sight, that's why only you two could see it. Your minds are already open to the supernatural, you've both had the sight for most of your life. The other people here, their minds are closed, they haven't experienced anything like this before, they don't believe in anything, they're skeptics, they're doubters, they're non-believers. They didn't expect to see anything, they didn't believe they'd see anything, so they didn't."

"Some of them must have expected to see something. Why else would they have come?" asked Courtney.

"To see you fail," replied Brian, bluntly, "oh, and the free drink that Lester promised everyone."

"Does everyone want to see me fail?" asked Courtney.

"Not everyone," replied Brian, leaning back in his chair and removing his chefs hat, revealing another smaller hat underneath, "there are some people here who want to see you succeed, they want you to get answers. Seanne does. I do. When you go, I'll go with you if you want me to."

"Go where?"

"To the shaman of course."

"You really think he exists?"

"After what you've just seen today, what you've seen all your life, are you going to deny his existence?" asked Brian. "You've seen things that most people aren't capable of seeing and you believe in their existence, don't you? You believe that Emily exists, don't you? You believe that there's someone, from beyond this world, trying to communicate with you, don't you? You're a scientist, but you've seen things that defy explanation, there's no evidence they exist, beyond what you've seen with your own eyes, and yet you still believe in them? You still have faith in your ability to judge when something is real or not, don't you?"

"I'm not sure," said Courtney, turning to Heather for support, "we both saw it, but I'm struggling with the fact that I saw it, it was so clear, there was definitely something there, and yet no one else saw it."

"You both have doubts?" asked Brian.

"There was definitely something written on the window," said Emily.

"I don't know what to believe," said Heather, "I saw it but how can we have seen it?"

"You should believe what you see with your own eyes," said Brian, "many people in this world believe in things that have no supporting evidence whatsoever, no science to justify it, things that require a leap of faith. You have more than that, you have the evidence of your own eyes. There's a friend of mine who won't believe in anything, unless he's actually seen it himself, he'll deny the existence of anything he hasn't personally witnessed, he doesn't trust anyone enough to take their word for it, he thinks that photographs can be faked, film footage can be altered, experts can't be trusted, that there's always some conspiracy at work behind the scenes involving lizard aliens. What you have is priceless. You believe in something and you've witnessed it with your own eyes, and yet you still doubt yourselves."

"You're right," said Courtney, "I've seen enough. I know what I saw. I don't need Ruan to come back in here, with footage of it happening, to validate my opinion, because I was there, I saw it."

"You're right," said Heather.

"So," asked Brian, "what are you going to do now?"

One heavily armed lady

"I'm going to get Alain to lend his gun to Lester, that's what I'm going to do now," said Courtney but, before she could do anything, Ruan returned with the news they had all expected. There was nothing on the recording. He had gone through it frame by frame and there was no second reflection in the window and no writing on the glass. Ruan was expecting everyone to be disappointed by the news but they took it better than he thought they would.

"It doesn't matter, Ruan," said Heather, "thank you for checking, but it doesn't matter, we know what we saw and we don't need supporting evidence to back it up."

"That's good," said Ruan, "because there isn't any. Nothing. I've been through every second of the footage and there's nothing there."

"Did you see anything at the time, Ruan?" asked Courtney.

"No, I don't think so," replied Ruan, "but I trust you and, if you tell me you saw it, then that's good enough for me. What did it say again? Go? Go where?"

"What do you think?" asked Heather, returning the question to Ruan, as she had a habit of doing.

"Go with Seanne?" said Ruan cautiously, hoping he had the right answer.

"Could be but we don't know," replied Heather, "it's one possibility."

"We are going though, aren't we?" asked Emily. "Courtney is coming with us now, isn't she?"

"I think so," said Heather, "but I really don't know."

With everyone having drifted back to work, the excitement and anticipation that had spread through the research station, during the seance, had dissipated and everything seemed to have returned to normal.

The sound of the wind, buffeting the research station, was beginning to gradually die down. The size of the objects, hitting the walls and the windows, were decreasing, reducing both the noise and the levels of anxiety inside. It appeared that the worst of it was over, until Alain Govenor burst through the door, almost collapsing to his knees and shouting, in a far higher pitched voice than he had ever intended, or had ever used before.

"We're under attack," he squealed.

Brian, Ruan, Heather and Courtney looked at each other, but only found confused faces staring back.

"Under attack, Doctor?" asked Ruan.

"What are you talking about, Alain?" said Heather as she stood up.

"We're under attack," repeated Alain as he quickly approached their table, half running, half walking, almost skipping towards them.

"Look out of the window," said Alain, pointing his finger, "they've got guns and everything."

Heather calmly walked over to look out of the nearest window and she saw a snowcat parked up near the entrance. Hanad was sat sideways on the front passenger seat, legs swung round, door open, sunglasses on. Alongside the snowcat, either side of Hanad, stood two figures clad all in white, except for black boots and black assault rifles, clutched diagonally across their chests. The wind whipped at the fur on their hoods as they stood stock still, legs apart.

There were two unmarked cardboard boxes on the ground in front of the snowcat, stacked one on top of the other, the flaps of the lid buffeted backwards and forwards by the wind.

"Go out and see what they're saying to each other, would you, Emily," said Heather calmly, "we need to find out what's going on."

"Lester is helping Carter to barricade the door," said Alain, still panicking, "we need to close the shutters right now."

"Are the shutters bulletproof?" asked Heather.

"I don't know," said Alain, finally stopping to think.

"They don't look bulletproof to me," said Courtney as she peered out of the window at the snowcat outside.

"Then why bother closing them?" asked Heather. "It's only going to stop us from seeing what's going on outside."

"What is he doing?" asked Brian. "He's just sat there. Should we send someone out to talk to him?"

"I'm not going," said Alain, "we need to find a place to hide."

"I think there's a priest hole next to the fireplace in the living room, Alain, if you want to hide in there," said Courtney.

"Very funny," replied Alain, "you won't be joking when they're walking through the research station shooting everyone, picking us off one by one. Then you'll want somewhere to hide."

"What makes you think they want to kill us?" asked Courtney.

"Why else would he be here with two goons, armed to the teeth?" asked Alain, ramping up the panic level. "He's come for Lester and me, I know it. "

"Then we just hand the two of you over and no one needs to die," replied Courtney, matter-of-factly.

"But we'll die," wailed Alain.

"Why would he come all this way to find you and then kill you?" asked Heather. "If he wanted to kill you, he'd have sent the two goons on their own. The fact that he's come all this way with them must mean that he wants something else."

"Maybe he wants to torture them first, before he watches them die," said Courtney.

"Thanks, Courtney," said Alain, "thanks a lot. That's exactly what I wanted to hear right now. I'm going back to make sure the door is barricaded. If he came here for one of you, I'd do everything in my power to protect you, but I see which way the wind is blowing. Don't expect me to go quietly. If you cut a deal to save your own lives, don't expect me to just walk out of here and hand myself over."

Alain turned on his heels and raced back to man the barricade.

"Emily's back," said Heather, "what are they saying?"

"Nothing really," replied Emily, "the two with guns are just stood there, looking around. Hanad keeps asking them where everyone is and the driver is sat playing a farming simulator on his mobile phone."

"What's in the boxes?" asked Heather.

"It looks like beer, bottles of beer."

"Right," said Heather, "it sounds like they're waiting for us to go out so, shall we?"

"Are you sure?" asked Brian. "I mean, is it safe? It doesn't look like the most friendly of situations."

"He come to our house and he's brought beer," said Heather.

"Lager or bitter?" asked Ruan.

"Emily," said Heather, "pop back out and find out what beer he's brought."

Heather turned from addressing Emily to look upon Courtney, Ruan and Brian's scared little faces. They were like children, all confused, wanting mummy to tell them what to do. At least, that's how Heather saw it.

"Let's go," said Heather, "I think we've got a parley to attend."

"Like the pirates?" asked Ruan.

"Like the pirates," confirmed Heather.

The four of them headed in the direction that Alain had gone, increasing their strength in numbers as they went. All eyes were staring out of the windows to see what was going on but, as Heather marched past, they joined the tail of the procession and Heather entered the final pod at the head of an army of followers. Well, maybe a small flock.

Carter was armed, rifle in hand, stood at one end of the window, he leaned forwards to peer out without giving away his position. Lester and Alain were in the centre of the room, arguing and wrestling over Alain's handgun. They both had hold of the gun, which was still tucked into the belt of Alain's trousers. As they pulled on the gun, the waistband of his trousers was lifted further and further up, as the gun was now entangled in both Alain's trousers and his boxer shorts.

"What are you two doing?" asked Heather. "Just give him the gun, Alain. Come on. I can't watch any more of your homoerotic grappling. Either get a room or hand it over."

After a few more seconds of tugging, Lester let go of the gun and held his hand out flat, waiting for Alain to hand it over.

"Come on, old man," said Lester, "you put up a good fight."

"Old man?" replied Alain, mock offended. "I really ought to shoot you now, just for that."

"Do you need a hand?" asked Lester. "I think it's caught up in..."

"It's okay, it's okay," replied Alain, "just get me some scissors and I'll cut it free. It's all tangled up in my pants."

The two of them joined forces to look for some scissors, searching desk tops and drawers until they found some. Alain had to undo his belt and unzip his trousers while they struggled to cut the gun loose from where it had become entangled with the cotton and elastic of his boxer shorts. Eventually, it came free.

"What have you done to the door?" asked Heather, on seeing the barricade that Carter and Lester had built. "How am I meant to get outside?"

Boxes, desks, bags, skis, filing cabinets, books, computers, shoes and coats. If it was in the room, and it was near the door, it had been added to the barricade in a frantic, desperate attempt to obstruct Hanad's entry to the building.

"I'll have to go out the other way," said Heather in frustration, "you haven't barricaded the door at the other end as well, have you?"

"No, sorry, not yet," said Carter, sheepishly.

"Would you be able to clear all this stuff away from the door so I can invite our guest inside please, Carter?" asked Heather.

"No, we can't," insisted Alain, "he's here to kill us."

"If you open that door you're sentencing us both to death," said Lester, in his most dramatic tone of voice.

"Why would he want to kill you both?" asked Heather, who was struggling to understand the logic behind their fear.

Alain and Lester both started to speak at once. Then stopped. They waited for each other and then both started to speak at the same time.

"After you," said Lester.

"No, no," said Alain, "I insist that you go first."

"Are you sure?" asked Lester.

"Spit it out," said Courtney, "come on, one of you, Alain, tell us what's going on in your tiny little head."

Alain acted all offended, but he wanted to speak first and this had worked out perfectly.

"Well, if you all want to know, then I shall tell you," said Alain as he took centre stage. It was time for Alain's Doctor to deliver a scene stealing monologue, worthy of the highest of praise but, having given it no thought and having had no time to prepare, he instead delivered an off-the-cuff, childish, ill-thought-out, petulant, borderline-racist. rant including the lines...

...he never wanted me to come ashore in the first place... just look at him, I mean, just look at him...he's had it in for me since the day I got here...he still thinks I'm a real doctor, the idiot...he looks like he's killed before...he'd rather shoot me than let me leave that ship...he's not like us...I'm literally worth more dead to him than I am alive...

Even Lester stood open-mouthed, aghast at Alain's speech. They were supposed to be in this together, brothers in arms, it was the two of them against Hanad, do or die. Lester took a sidewards step to physically distance himself from Alain. He struggled to see how someone he had spent so much time with, someone who seemed like an intelligent, well-educated man, could come across as an incoherent, paranoid, lunatic. His arguments ranged from the bizarre to the irrational and back again.

Alain had the audience's attention, that much was certain, although he struggled to convince them that he was in any danger. The audience wasn't convinced and Alain knew it. He pulled up a chair and slumped into it with his head in his hands, thinking he was going to die.

"Listen," said Lester, who still had Alain's gun in his hand, "I can't tell you why Hanad wants to kill me. I would like to tell you but then I'd have to kill you."

Lester realised that he had better stop now or he would start to sound like Alain. Everyone had taken a small shuffling step backwards when he mentioned killing them, while waving Alain's gun around.

"Hanad's been on the radio all day," confessed Lester, "trying to find out where we were and when we were coming back but I kept cutting him off. That's probably why he's here. He wanted us to go back to the ship, so he could kill us, and now he's come to do the job himself."

"Is that it?" asked Heather. "A man you both work for is trying to find out why neither of you are at work and he turns up here with a couple of boxes of beer, as a peace offering, and your first thought is to barricade the door and wrestle each other for the nearest gun. I'm disappointed in you, Carter, for getting carried along with all this. Get this stuff cleared away from the door. I'm going to walk down the other end. I'll go out that way to speak to him. You can either come with me or watch out the window, I don't care."

The crowd parted to allow Heather a clear route towards the door. Some people followed her and some pressed their faces up against the window to see what was going on outside. Carter began to remove some of the smaller items from the barricade, a pencil case, several notebooks, a woollen hat and scarf, a penguin shaped paperweight and a packet of cotton swabs.

It took forever for Heather to get to the other end of the research station, to get into her outdoor gear, to get down the steps and begin the long walk back towards Hanad. Those that had gone with her were oblivious to the enormous amount of time the whole process was taking, unlike those with noses pressed up against the glass, waiting impatiently.

By the time Heather came into view, the last of the heavy items were being pulled away from the previously barricaded door, allowing Carter to open it and step outside, rifle in hand.

To the people looking out of the research station window, Heather appeared to be striding purposely towards Hanad, although she wasn't actually making much headway. She was leaning backwards, battling a strong tailwind that was threatening to blow her over, and taking tiny, little, shuffling steps towards her destination.

Heather had her own doubts. Who doesn't? Has he really come here to kill someone? I don't believe it. Why would he?

If he was going to shoot me then he'd have done it by now. It isn't meant to end like this, is it?

Her palms were sweating, inside her gloves. It was too cold to take them off and wipe her hands so she just carried on sweating, inside wet gloves.

As she approached the snowcat, Hanad gestured to her to get in before he swung his legs round and closed the front passenger door. Neither of Hanad's associates moved, as she approached. They both stood completely still, braced against the wind, staring into the distance, keeping watch.

Heather opened one of the rear doors and clambered up into the snowcat. She closed the door behind her, shutting out the noise of the wind and then she shuffled across the seats until she was behind the driver and able to see Hanad.

"Hello, Professor," said Hanad, "I was starting to think it was too windy for someone to come out and greet me."

"Oh, Hanad," replied Heather, warmly, "I've told you, it's Heather, please, no one calls me Professor."

"Ah, Heather, yes, a beautiful name. Did you see that I brought you some beers?"

"I saw. That's very kind. Are they all for me?"

"Oh, no no no," spluttered Hanad, "they're for sharing, there's more there, than even you could drink, I should think. I never go to someone's house without bringing them a gift."

"And do you often go to someone's house with two heavily armed men?"

"Sorry to correct you," said Hanad.

He wasn't. He loved correcting people. Who doesn't?

"One heavily armed gentleman and one heavily armed lady," said Hanad, barely unable to conceal his delight. It was almost like he had planned it this way, with the intention of catching someone out.

Hanad waved his hand in a dismissive way and proceeded to talk down the role of his henchpersons.

"They're just here for protection from the polar bears," added Hanad, "one cannot be too careful. You must know this?"

"Is that all?" asked Heather, trying to tease something else out of Hanad, to try to work out why he was really there. "What is it that you've come all this way for?" she asked.

"My Doctor and my Communication Manager. I'm getting lonely without them. I'm worried. I know I don't look like a man who worries about anything but I worry about them and I'd like to have them back. I'm upset that you didn't respond to any of my messages."

"I know. I'm sorry. I've only just found out that we've had a problem with our radio set all day. We've only just managed to fix it," said Heather, who saw no reason to make things worse by dropping Lester in it.

"Are you going to invite me in?" asked Hanad. "I hadn't planned to come all this way but, now that I'm here, it would be a shame not to have a look round."

"Can I ask you a question?" asked Heather. "Without you taking offence?"

"Now I'm intrigued," said Hanad, which Heather took as an invitation to continue.

"Lester and Alain seem to have worked each other into a bit of a frenzy. They both seem to believe that you've come here to kill them. I'd like to be able to reassure them both, before I invite you in."

Hanad paused for thought. It was a lot to take in. Two employees both thinking he was going to kill them. Was he really that terrible a boss that they would think that of him?

"We have different management styles, you and I. You're a scientist and I'm a businessman," said Hanad, thinking carefully about how to put his thoughts into words, "you have a scientific approach to your work, your staff are trained to be professional and to maintain certain standards, They respect you because you set an example, you all work methodically towards the same goal. Whereas, I am a businessman, a lot of what I do is based on people's impressions of me. They don't invest in the business, they don't invest in the numbers on a spreadsheet, they invest in me, in my ability to make them money. Because of this, I have to present a certain image, I am not a man to be messed with, I am a man who gets results, a man who will stop at nothing in the pursuit of financial reward but I have no blood on my hands."

"You promise?" asked Heather.

"The image I present is important to me and to the success of my business. You think I behave like the villain in a spy movie? You think I behave like this by accident? No, but I am not a villain, I am just a man who has worked hard to get where I am and I'm working even harder to keep it that way. I came here because I was concerned for the welfare of two of my employees. My doctor has been here for three days now, without word, and Lester, I have no idea what Lester is doing here."

"Would you like to come inside?" asked Heather, who was convinced that no harm would come to either Alain or Lester.

"I would love to but I think it would be more trouble than it's worth," said Hanad, playing hard to get, "I would have to be helped into my wheelchair and carried up the stairs and that's not really the strongman image I'm looking to project."

"Oh, come on," said Heather, who was determined to show Hanad around the research station, "It'll take two minutes to get you inside and you've come all this way. Come inside and have a beer with us, please."

Hanad couldn't resist any longer. He was so excited about coming here and he couldn't wait to get inside. If he turned down this invitation he might never get another chance.

Hanad opened the door to the snowcat and swung his legs round to face the doorway. A quick wave towards the two henchpersons brought them running over and, within seconds, he was out of the snowcat, into the wheelchair, and being carried up the steps past Carter and into the research station.

This is a dream come true, thought Hanad as they carefully lowered his wheelchair onto the floor.

I'm going to name it after you

No shots were fired and Hanad's visit passed without incident. After helping him into the research station, the henchpersons stayed outside to keep watch for polar bears but neither of them saw any. Hanad spent over an hour looking round the research station, taking a particular interest in the laboratories and asking questions about what kind of research they did there. He repeatedly rejected all offers of a beer and insisted on returning to the ship that evening, despite the poor weather.

Lester and Alain both made, what sounded like, sincere apologies to Hanad and both promised to return to the ship the next morning. Brian attempted to keep out of sight in the kitchen but was eventually spotted by Hanad and was dragged back to the ship that evening as, according to Hanad, the food on the ship that day was shit and now he knew why.

The rest of the evening was uneventful and, although there was plenty of beer, there wasn't enough for Carter to be persuaded to do a naked lap outside. Maybe Courtney's teasing about it had made him think twice. Or maybe there just wasn't enough beer.

Courtney woke from a fitful night's sleep that involved constantly going over the events of the previous day in her head. She was sure, absolutely sure, that she had seen Courtney Two write on the glass. Go. Why couldn't she have been more clear in what she wrote? More explicit. Go where? She weighed up the options. Go with Seanne. Find out who Courtney Two is. End the nightmares, the worries, the anxiety. Freeze to death or go home with no answers? Would her recent experience make her more likely to confront Courtney Two again, to seek answers? Or would she just slip back into the old routine? Avoiding, coping, just about managing, but still alive.

She was going, definitely going. That much was sure. That was decided, but going where?

In the end, it came down to how she felt, how anxious she felt. When she thought of going home, when she thought of a renewed wave of public abuse, once the fate of the penguins was confirmed, when she thought of the nightmares, of Courtney Two pursuing her, she felt fear, clamminess, panic. But when she thought of going with Seanne, it felt exciting, it made her smile, it felt like a new beginning, an adventure, a new morning, the light filling the room when the curtains are flung open.

Heather flung open the curtains and bright sunlight filled the cramped sleeping pod, causing Courtney to cover her eyes with her forearm. Despite the lack of sleep, Courtney felt positive, today was a new day, time to fulfil her destiny. She sat up in bed, leaning on one elbow. Heather was rubbing her eyes as she looked round the room in a state of confusion, trying to work out what to do next, Seanne crawled down into her bed and pulled the covers up over her head. There may have been signs of life on the top bunks, but Courtney couldn't see if they were awake or not, either way, Courtney wanted them all to share her positivity. She didn't want these good vibes to go to waste.

"Good morning, everyone," said Courtney in a loud, cheerful voice, loud enough to wake any heavy sleepers.

"What is wrong with you?" asked Heather, who was still a bit disoriented.

Outside, the wind had died down to almost nothing and there wasn't a cloud in sight, just sun and blue sky, the weather was positively balmy. Melt water was dripping from every overhang and the ground was soft and wet. Even a weak sun, distant and low in the sky, can exert its authority over the ice, if given enough time.

Courtney pulled back the covers and swung herself out of bed. No time to waste. She dressed quickly, simply adding more layers to the ones she had slept in until she finally felt warm enough. Heather took a lot longer, everything needed more thought. She searched for clean socks for an age, before realising that she had already put them on.

Both ended up dressed in an odd combination of indoor and outdoor layers, selected from the few items they had left that were dry and clean. It didn't seem worthwhile doing any laundry when they were leaving tomorrow. Courtney toyed with the idea of tying up her hair as it was now at the stage where she no longer had any influence over it. A shower was definitely on the cards for later, or maybe a hat, just to cover it up.

When Heather was finally ready, they headed to breakfast together. This morning, breakfast was being cooked by Reshma-Jade and Ruan and they did their best with limited resources and limited cooking ability. Despite their best efforts, Courtney pushed her plate away after a few mouthfuls and grimaced before washing away the taste with some coffee.

"Do you not want that?" asked Heather.

"No," said Courtney, pulling a face, "do you want it?"

"Oh, Christ no, it's foul," said Heather, eating another mouthful.

"Have you got time to talk?" asked Heather. "While Emily isn't here."

"Where is she?"

"I don't know. I can't see her at the moment."

"Is everything okay between you two?"

"Yes, sort of. You know she really wants to go with Seanne? She wants people to be able to see her, she wants to be a real girl, like Pinocchio, if you know what I mean. But I don't really want to go. I want to go home to Anna."

"You can't always do what Emily wants," said Courtney.

"We don't. We never do what Emily wants, as she keeps reminding me. We always do what I want. She's never wanted anything this much and she can't go without me. I have to go for her, for her peace of mind, for my own sanity."

"How long will it take us?"

"To find the shaman?" asked Heather.

"Yup."

"I don't know, days, weeks, who knows?" asked Heather. "You know, when I think about it, sometimes it feels like a suicide pact in a religious cult, I mean, Emily and Brian seem to be enchanted by her, they'd follow her anywhere, but I've never heard Seanne talk about coming back, I've only ever heard her talk about going. I don't even know if she plans to come back, I mean, she frames it as a black and white decision between going and getting answers, or not going and having a miserable life in a world of pollution and pandemics, floods and famines, mass graves, imaginary friends, evil twins and having penguin murderer written on the front of your house."

"Heaven or hell," said Courtney.

"You have to die before you get to heaven," said Heather, trying to reinforce her point.

"You have to die before you get to hell, too," said Courtney.

"I suppose so," said Heather.

"I think we ought to make sure it's not a suicide pact before we leave," said Courtney, "we are all going though, aren't we?"

"We are but, even if there's a plan to get back, we could still die out there," said Heather.

"That's a cheery thought," said Courtney.

"I need to go and finish writing my report," said Heather, rejecting what was left of her breakfast. "if we go with her, I can't send Carter back empty-handed."

"What are you going to write?" asked Courtney, who was concerned that the report would blame her. She had been thinking about it for some time now, trying to ignore the thought, pushing it out of sight so she didn't have to worry about it. She assumed her name would feature strongly in the report and she hadn't been able to persuade herself otherwise.

"Basically," said Heather, "we need a team permanently tracking the polar bears and more accurate satellite data showing the location of penguin colonies to stop this happening again. We need a mobile team on the ground to monitor things, we need eyes on the remaining penguin colonies and an action plan to protect all the local wildlife, while also safeguarding the polar bear population. And someone needs to fund it."

"Is that it?"

"Well, I haven't finished writing it yet but that's the gist of it."

"Do I get a mention?"

"Do you want a mention?" asked Heather.

"I just thought…"

"What would you like me to write? That you were a valuable member of the team? That I couldn't have done it without you?"

"You don't blame me then?"

"Of course not."

"After everything I've told you, about it being my idea, you still don't blame me?"

"Stop being The Penguin Murderer and start being Courtney Woodbeard."

"Whatever that means," said Courtney as she stood up.

A smile lit up Courtney's face causing Heather to smile back. We're definitely going, thought Courtney. Maybe it's time to find out who else is going with us.

Courtney walked over to another table, where Alain and Lester were eating together. There was a lull in the conversation so she sat at the empty chair between them and waited for them to acknowledge her presence.

"My two favourite boys," she said to tease them, "I thought you were meant to be back at the ship first thing this morning?"

"I don't think anyone would begrudge us a leisurely breakfast, even Hanad, do you?" asked Alain, resplendent in an olive coloured tailored suit. Tweed, or moleskin? Courtney couldn't tell. It had a matching waistcoat and today's doctor look was completed by a cravat and a pocket handkerchief. Alain looked even more dapper sat next to Lester, who was dressed in a tight, black t shirt and cargo pants.

"Leisurely breakfast or last meal?" teased Courtney.

"A bit of both," said Lester.

"You should have got up early and had breakfast on the ship," suggested Courtney.

"I realise that now," said Lester, who was absent-mindedly pushing his food around the plate with a fork.

"Where's your ski suit, Alain?" asked Courtney.

Alain looked round to see who was listening before he replied.

"Don't tell anyone, it's a bit embarrassing really, I only noticed this morning. There's a hole in the groin where the fabric has rotted through. I could get my fist through it. I hope no one noticed."

Courtney stifled a laugh and chose not to comment on Alain's wardrobe malfunction.

"I've a favour to ask you, Alain," said Courtney, turning to wink at Lester.

"Can Lester please borrow your gun?"

"Oh, you're so funny," said Lester, pretending to be annoyed, although he was actually rather annoyed that Courtney hadn't kept her side of the bargain.

"Are we quits now?" Courtney asked Lester. "You wanted me to ask him, didn't you? Did you two enjoy your wrestle yesterday?"

"It's all resolved now," said Lester, "no thanks to you," he added as an afterthought.

"So who's got the gun now then?" asked Courtney, unwilling to let it go.

"I've got it, just in case," said Lester.

"He's promised to give it back though," said Alain, "once we know that Hanad isn't going to kill us both."

"He doesn't want to kill you, Alain," said Lester, for the umpteenth time, "he just wants the ship's doctor to be on the ship. It's me he wants to kill, that's why I've got the gun, for my own protection."

"Are you coming with us?" asked Courtney.

"On your crazy trip?" asked Lester. "With Seanne?"

"Is it crazy?" asked Courtney. "To walk out into Antarctica to search for something that might not even be there? Is that crazy? Do you think it's a suicide pact? Like a religious cult?"

"What makes you say that?" asked Alain.

"Because I've never heard Seanne talk about what happen's afterwards. Is there a plan to come back? Has she mentioned it to either of you?"

"She hasn't," said Alain, "but she's so obsessed with finding this shaman and finding out her real name. He's the destination, the end of the journey. She probably hasn't even thought about how to get back."

"That's what worries me. Well, it worries Heather, and me, I suppose," said Courtney.

"Do you actually want answers, Courtney?" asked Alain. "I mean, I like to think that I know you quite well, at least I did, and I sort of got the impression that you like things the way they are. You sort of enjoy being unhappy. It's part of you, part of your personality, and if you found your answers, if you got your cure, then you wouldn't be the same person anymore."

"Do you like me the way I am?" asked Courtney. "With all my faults? All my worries?"

"I do," said Alain, "I mean, you're hard work, you are, I'm sorry, but that's the truth. But, if you go with Seanne, will I like the Courtney that comes back? Will you like her?"

"I'd like the opportunity to meet her and make up my own mind," said Courtney.

"Well, I hope it works out for you," said Alain.

"You want to know my opinion?" asked Lester, sitting upright, stretching his arms, shoulders back, chest out, making himself as imposing as possible. "I think you still love her, Alain, and that you hate your life back home so much that you're going to come back here tomorrow and go with Courtney."

"Oh, come on," said Alain, blushing.

"I tell you what," said Lester, "I'll make a deal with you both right now. If Hanad has found out about me and I end up killing him using Alain's gun, in self defence of course, then I'll come with you both."

"Let's all shake on it," said Alain.

"Three people can't shake hands together," said Lester, "there's too many left hands and not enough right hands."

"We can try, can't we," asked Alain, who was the first to stand up, "come on then, a three way handshake."

Lester and Courtney joined him and they formed a tight circle, crossed arms, and attempted to shake hands, all together at the same time but they couldn't make it work so they sealed the deal with a fist bump.

"See you tomorrow, hopefully," said Courtney, although that would mean wishing harm on Hanad, something Courtney only realised as the words left her lips.

Courtney was getting very excited about tomorrow but the decision to go had only raised more questions, more concerns. Will I find out who Courtney Two is? Is Lester coming with us? What should I pack? Who else is going? Is Alain still in love with me? Are we coming back? Should I have a shower today or tomorrow morning?

After a brief hug with Alain, and a slightly longer one with Lester, that she didn't want to end, Courtney went to get more coffee. There, she found Ruan on his knees, tidying up around the coffee machine, picking up the tiny milk cartons and the wooden sticks from around the bin. She stared down at his bald head, waiting for him to notice her.

"You get to cook breakfast and clean up?" asked Courtney, who hadn't cooked or cleaned since she arrived. She wasn't even aware that a rota existed or that other people had to cover for her.

"So, Ruan, what have you heard? Who else is going? Are you going?" asked Courtney, enthusiastically.

Ruan struggled to get up off the floor, brushing the dirt from his knees and his palms as he stood up.

"I can't believe you're going to do it," said Ruan.

"You think I'm crazy as well?" asked Courtney.

"I know you saw that thing in the window. I believe you, honestly, I do, and I know you've taken it as some sort of sign, but there's no way I'm going. I want to go home and see my wife and kids. Whatever state the world is in right now, and whatever state my marriage is in, it's still a better option than freezing to death looking for something that doesn't exist."

"And when I say it doesn't exist," added Ruan, "I mean it doesn't exist. It. Does. Not. Exist."

"When we find the place that the shaman lives and we have to give it a name," said Courtney, "I'm going to name it after you."

Ruan laughed at the thought of something finally being named after him. He had started to think it was never going to happen. Just a childhood dream. It should have been a skyscraper he designed and built, or a hospital wing he tirelessly raised money for, or a sports stadium, named in honour of his sporting prowess, not a yurt in the middle of Antarctica, but it would have to do.

"That would be very kind," said Ruan, taking Courtney at her word, "but, seriously, Seanne has her own thing going on and you shouldn't get involved. She can't help you. You're just there to hold her hand when she dies, when she freezes to death in a tent, assuming that she dies before you. What you're looking for isn't out there."

"Have you ever heard her talk about coming back?"

"Alain asked me the same question," said Ruan.

"And what did you tell him?"

"I told him that Seanne is obsessed with the shaman and he's the destination, the end of the line. You'll just be collateral damage. We all are."

"Heather thinks it might be a religious cult, suicide pact type thing," said Courtney, just to see Ruan's response.

"Does that make you one of her disciples?"

"Can't I be a cheerleader instead?" asked Courtney.

"Have you spoken to her about it? To Seanne? Have you asked her what the plan is?"

"No, not really," replied Courtney, "do you think I should? You do, don't you? How do I ask her? What do I say?"

"Don't ask her anything," said Ruan, "just tell her your concerns but, if she isn't coming back, are you still going?"

Courtney carefully considered her response. What would she do? Would she still go?

She didn't need to decide now, though, as Ruan wasn't waiting around for an answer. He proceeded to carry out his kitchen duties by clearing the empty tables and taking the plates and bowls into the kitchen to scrape a considerable amount of food waste into the bin.

I need to speak to Seanne, thought Courtney, as she walked back towards their sleeping accommodation. I wonder if she's awake yet?

Courtney tapped quietly on the door. No reply. She turned the handle and pushed gently, hoping to open the door silently, presumably so she didn't wake Seanne, even though she was hoping that Seanne was already awake.

The curtains had been redrawn and, although they didn't keep out all the light, they made things more difficult for Courtney. She picked her way through the rucksacks, clothes and shoes, discarded on the floor, taking care over where she put her feet, testing the ground tentatively on each step. It felt like she was creeping around someone else's bedroom in the dark, which I suppose she was.

There was no movement from Seanne's bunk, just a lump buried under the covers. It looked too small to be a grown woman. How did she take up so little space? thought Courtney. Is it even her?

There was only one pillow on the bed when all the other beds had two. Where was the other pillow? Courtney looked round the room but she couldn't see it. That didn't mean it wasn't there. It wasn't the tidiest of rooms and the missing pillow could have been concealed under any number of discarded items or been folded up and put in one of the small storage cupboards.

Courtney moved a little closer to listen for signs of breathing. She watched the surface of the duvet cover closely for any movement. If she was breathing, the duvet would be moving, wouldn't it? Rising and falling, expanding and contracting, but there was nothing, no movement, no sound of breathing.

Courtney placed her hand on the duvet cover where she thought Seanne's shoulder might be. She intended to give her a shake to try to wake her, just a loose grip on the shoulder and small movements, rocking back and forth, probably accompanied by a light voice saying, Seanne, love, are you awake?

But, when Courtney's hand touched the bed, it wasn't a hard shoulder she touched, it was soft and forgiving, not like a shoulder at all. Was this the missing pillow? Where was Seanne? Courtney started to panic. If she's not here, then where is she? What if she's done a bunk, left already, hidden a pillow in her bed to fool us all and set off for the shaman on her own? She wouldn't, would she? Oh God, she has, hasn't she? She's gone without me!

Without hesitation, Courtney grabbed the corner of the duvet and pulled hard. She hoped to reveal the missing pillow and expose Seanne's duplicity, but it didn't quite work out that way. Instead, Seanne screamed as her comfortable, warm, slumber was cruelly interrupted. Courtney staggered backwards, ears ringing, heart racing, she panicked and turned to run towards the door but her foot landed on a sock ball, almost twisting her ankle, and she fell sideways onto her own bed, narrowly missing the top bunk with her head as she fell.

"What the hell are you doing?" asked Seanne.

Happy days

Carter heard the scream and came running. His big frame filled the doorway as he burst in and turned the light on. Seanne and Courtney both put their hands up to shield their eyes.

"Everything okay?" asked Carter, in a warm, comforting voice. So warm and comforting that it sounded like he was telling them that everything was okay rather than asking if it was.

"Yes," said Courtney, "I just came in to talk to Seanne and I think I startled her."

"I've got some early results on the penguin survey that we did, if you want to see the results later," said Carter.

"I will, I would. I'd like to," said Courtney, "I'll be along in a bit."

Carter left without another word, leaving the two of them alone. He left the light on and the door ajar.

"You have to stop creeping up on people," said Seanne, "you'll give yourself a heart attack. You nearly gave me a heart attack. What were you thinking?"

"I thought you'd gone," said Courtney, "I mean, I thought you might have gone without me."

"Well, I'm still here."

"I'm really glad. I'm sorry I woke you but I've got a few questions I need to ask you," said Courtney, "for my own peace of mind."

"Can it wait until later?" asked Seanne. "I need to get dressed, meditate, exercise and then have breakfast."

"Breakfast was awful."

"Was it? How bad was it?"

"Really bad," said Courtney.

Seanne rearranged herself so she was sat up on the bed facing Courtney. She moved a pillow to support her back and turned the duvet round so it covered her body and legs before it spilled over onto the floor. She pulled the duvet cover up, almost to her chin, and she tucked her arms over it before clasping her hands together on her lap. Her shoulders and arms were covered by the black, long sleeved, thermal vest she wore to bed and her hair was covered by a red, green and yellow, silk headscarf, tightly knotted round her head.

"Okay, tell me what is it you want to know," said Seanne, now she was comfortable, "and I'll try my best to help."

"Well, I know we're going to leave here, that's obvious. And I know we're going to arrive at your shaman, hopefully, but I just need to know what happens in between, you know, in between leaving here and arriving there. Oh, and after, what happens afterwards? How do we get back? We are coming back, aren't we?"

"Are you having doubts about coming with me?"

"Oh, I've got doubts about everything," explained Courtney, "is the shaman real? Can you even find him? Will he want to help us? Will he be able to? Are we coming back? Will we get lost? Will we freeze to death or starve to death first? Will we get so hungry that we have to kill someone and eat them? Who will it be? Who is going? Who's the weakest among us? What will they taste like?"

"Chicken," interrupted Seanne, "they'll taste like chicken. You'll close your eyes and imagine that it's chicken and that's what you'll taste. But you don't have to worry about that because you're the weakest, Courtney."

"I'm what?" asked Courtney, rather surprised by where the conversation had ended up, even though she was the one leading it.

"You're the weakest, so, we'll eat you first, does that makes you feel any better?"

"Well, I suppose that's a good thing isn't it?" asked Courtney, unsure if she was being made fun of. "Look, I know it's a lot of questions, and it's easy to make a joke out of it but I am worried. I do worry but they're genuine concerns, in that I am genuinely concerned about all these things. I'm just telling you so you understand my thought process. I've got doubts about everything, you shouldn't read too much into me having doubts about going."

"How do you find the time to worry about so many things?" asked Seanne. "How do you fit it all in to your day? Have you tried meditating or mindfulness? It could help you."

"No, I haven't, but I control it. I do a lot of my worrying at night to ease the pressure during the day."

"Now you're the one making jokes."

"I'm not joking. I literally don't have enough time in the day to worry about everything that flits through my head so I put some of the worries aside and save them for later."

"What's your biggest concern right now?" asked Seanne. "Tell me, and we'll deal with that one first?"

"Biggest?"

"Yes, what's troubling you the most right now."

Do I tell her? thought Courtney. It's going to sound stupid when I say it, she's going to make me feel foolish and then she's obviously going to deny it. Should I ask her something else first? Build up to it? Should I save the big worry until last? Find out who is going and then ask if we are all going to die?

"Two things," said Seanne.

"I'm sorry," said Courtney.

"Two things. If it's too hard to think of your biggest concern then tell me two things that are troubling you. Or three. Can you narrow it down to three things. I'll be like a genie, I'll grant you three questions. That's all you get, three questions, no follow ups. Clear your mind and then go. Ask me. First question that pops into your head. Ask me. Go."

Courtney hesitated, then asked, "Is any of this real?"

"All of it is real, Courtney, unless you're dreaming. You're not dreaming, are you?"

"I thought I was asking the questions," said Courtney, "you can't answer my questions with questions of your own."

"Of course it's real," said Seanne, to reassure Courtney, "when did it stop feeling real?"

"When I got the call to go on Operation Polar Saviour. At that point, everything started to tumble out of control and I've been swept along, with no say in any of it, and I've ended up here having to make a decision about whether to live or die."

"No one is going to die, Courtney. It's perfectly safe. We're borrowing the clothing and equipment that's already here. We'll return it before the Chileans arrive to reclaim the research station and they'll never know about it. Brian's got the food sorted, he's been commandeering supplies from the ship's larder for the past week. It's all been worked out."

"Did you get one of the drivers to agree to go?"

"Is that your second question?"

"If you like," replied Courtney.

"Shaggy is coming, for the adventure. He's stoked, apparently, whatever that means. We'll take his snowcat as far as we can and then walk from there. We'll take extra fuel for the snowcat so we can pick it up on the way back. No one is going to freeze to death, I mean, it's going to be fourteen degrees outside today, this is beautiful weather, this weather doesn't cause death, it creates life. And no one is going to starve to death. I can promise you now that we're not going to have to eat each other."

"How can you be so sure?"

"I know I'm not going to be able to convince you, am I?" asked Seanne. "You're pre-programmed to say no, to reject anything new or anything good in your life. You're trapped. You need to set yourself free, I can't do it for you. Spread your wings. Break out of your cage and come fly with us. Close your eyes and imagine yourself soaring above the ground."

Courtney didn't recognise herself in the picture Seanne was painting so she chose to ignore what sounded like new-age claptrap and plough on ahead.

"Who else is going?" she asked.

"Brian, Heather, Emily, you. Alain wants to but only if you're going. There's a few undecideds, like you. They can come with us if they want or they can stay here and go back to the ship. No one is being forced to go, Courtney."

"Is the whole thing part of a suicide cult?"

"I'm afraid you've had your three questions. Now, I really have to get up and get dressed."

Courtney pleaded for one more question, just one more, but Seanne was adamant.

Seanne shuffled Courtney back towards the door and out of the room, so she could have some privacy. As she left, Courtney took great care not to look at the uncovered mirror on the wall. She had papered over it and taped the edges, when she first occupied the room but someone had torn the paper off to use the mirror.

Courtney walked towards the main entrance to the research station, where she thought Carter would be working at one of the computers. Since recovering from concussion, he had divided his time between analysing the samples they took, monitoring the cameras they had set up, and messaging the UN scientific support team with updates of their progress.

Courtney entered the room where Carter had concussed himself, just three days ago, and where Lester and Alain had fought over the gun in Alain's underpants. It was a large open space with the main entrance at one end and the door to the accommodation pods at the other. It was effectively a large corridor with some desks and computers. It was also used as a dumping ground for anything coming in or out of the research station. The equipment was beginning to pile up in preparation for their departure tomorrow.

Carter was sat at one of the computers with his back to the door, he either didn't hear Courtney enter or he chose to ignore her. Even with the small number of people currently occupying the research base, there was a near constant trickle of people passing through, from door to door, and Carter had trained himself not to look up, not to interrupt his work but, if they greeted him and engaged him in conversation, then he would turn in his chair and give them his full attention, charming and funny, he would entertain them with stories and jokes and they would leave feeling better about themselves, better about the world.

Courtney walked up behind Carter and waited for him to turn round but he didn't.

"Where's the shelf you banged your head on?" she asked, making him jump.

Carter quickly span round in his chair when he heard Courtney's voice. His feet would have caught Courtney on the shins if she hadn't taken a small step back.

"There's no shelves in here," said Courtney, turning her head to look round the room, "what really happened?"

"It's always you, isn't it?" asked Carter, who hadn't appreciated the surprise. "Creeping up on people, accusing people, making them jump, and now you're what? Investigating my concussion?"

"It's just funny isn't it? Don't you think?" asked Courtney. "You said you banged your head on a shelf but there's no shelves in here and yet we found you here on the floor."

"It was a desk, not a shelf. The underside of this desk. I was plugging something in and they've got those bloody two pin plugs here. I couldn't get it to go in and I was raging.

When I finally got the plug in, I went to stand up and whack. Out cold."

"Ouch," said Courtney.

"I don't know how long I was out for. I woke up on my knees, face down with my arms outstretched. It probably looked like I was praying. Like I was prostrating myself under the desk."

"Ooh er," said Courtney, never one to miss a euphemism, "and did your life flash before your eyes, in a blur of tartan?"

"Aye, it was exactly like that," said Carter, laughing, "all Scottish people see tartan flash before their eyes when they die, everyone knows that."

Carter's initial irritation, at being rudely interrupted by Courtney, was subsiding as his heart rate came down.

"When I came round, I sort of rolled out from under the desk onto the floor here and I think that's where you found me," added Carter, gesturing towards the floor next to the desk.

"You know there's computers in the labs where you don't have people walking past and opening the door every five minutes," said Courtney.

"I know but I like it in here. I've slept under this desk. I feel some sort of connection to this room."

"That's just weird," said Courtney as she sat down on a spare chair, "do you feel a connection to me because I saved your life? Do you have to save my life now to return the favour? Am I your guardian angel?"

"I was never going to die," said Carter, confidently, "you found me on the floor and you called a doctor and I am really grateful. I'm so glad the two of you found me when you did, and got help, but I'd have survived even if you hadn't found me."

"You still owe me," said Courtney.

"You want to know how many penguins you killed?" asked Carter, making Courtney blush, "I've gone over the data the Chileans had on their computers, from when they were last here monitoring the penguin colony, and the size of the colony has reduced dramatically since then. There were about eighty percent less penguins here, this year, compared to the last survey they did, three years ago. That's from the aerial photos, the satellite images and the survey data we took at the site. And do you know what else? We only found two different species of penguins from all the samples we took. There used to be five in this colony."

"So, what you're trying to say is that I didn't kill as many penguins as you hoped?" asked Courtney, looking on the bright side.

"Erm," said Carter as he chose his words carefully, "that's not quite how I would have put it."

"But that's good news isn't it?" asked Courtney. "I thought I'd killed millions of penguins but it might only be a few hundred thousand. Is that what you're saying?"

"It's still a lot of penguins," said Carter.

"And there's only two different types of penguin blood on my hands, isn't that what you said?"

"It's a lot of penguins," said Carter, sadly.

"But it could have been a lot worse, couldn't it?" asked Courtney, using the power of positive thinking that so often deserted her. "This is good news."

"It's not good news for the penguins," said Carter, astonished at Courtney's reaction, her self-centredness, "whether you killed them, or climate change killed them, it doesn't matter, they're still dead."

"But habitat erosion and depleted food stocks must have killed far more penguins than I ever have," said Courtney.

"I thought you'd be upset," said Carter.

"So did I," said Courtney, "I mean, I am a bit but I thought it would be much worse than this. I thought I'd killed millions of penguins, millions and millions. I kept thinking about the worst case scenario, but this has turned out so much better than I imagined. When I saw it with my own eyes, when we stood there, looking at it, smelling it, it confirmed all my worst fears, but this is such good news. I couldn't be happier. Thank you."

Courtney stood up and leaned in towards Carter to give him a hug. He didn't reciprocate, he just sat there, being hugged, with Courtney's chest pushed up against his shoulder and her forehead pressed against the side of his face. Her arms didn't quite reach all the way round his body and the back of the chair. He could tell she was smiling without even seeing her face, she exuded joy.

"You don't get it," said Carter, once he was free from her embrace, "this isn't something to be happy about. This is horrific, for the colony to be reduced by such a scale and then wiped out, it's horrific. People have spend their whole lives, their whole careers, trying to protect colonies like this."

"But it could have been so much worse," said Courtney, "I thought I'd killed millions of them. Oh, thank you, Lord," she said, hypocritically, raising her arms and face to the ceiling as she paced round the room.

"Do you want to know exactly how many you killed?" asked Carter, who was getting increasingly irritated by Courtney.

"No," said Courtney, "no, I don't. I've made my peace with it now. Hundreds of thousands, I can live with that. I thought it was millions. Millions. Oh, I'm so pleased."

But it wasn't even hundreds of thousands. In the data Carter collated, in regard to the density and size of the colony, there were estimated to be only forty thousand breeding pairs this year, but he wasn't going to tell Courtney that. If she found out it was tens of thousands, she would be doing cartwheels outside, uncorking the champagne, and setting off fireworks. She had exasperated Carter so much that he was currently trying to work out whether he should search all the outbuildings for a tin of red paint and then paint the words, 'penguin murderer,' across the doorway to her room. That would teach her. He hadn't entirely ruled it out.

Courtney was in too good a mood to let Carter's obvious disapproval ruin her day. It didn't happen too often but, when the sun did break through the dark clouds, she had to make the most of it. Today was turning out to be one of the sunniest days ever. The genocide she felt responsible for had turned out not to be a genocide, it was only a massacre. Happy days. And Courtney seemed to have accepted that she was going with Seanne. She was going to see the shaman. She was going to get answers, to find out who Courtney Two was and what she wanted.

It's all going to turn out okay. What could go wrong?

Today, I don't care

Courtney spread joy throughout the research station. With the weight of the world off her shoulders, she seemed like a new woman. She left Carter and went to help Ruan and Reshma-Jade clean the floor in the communal area and wipe down the tables after breakfast. Every person she interacted with thought the same thing.

Who are you?

Courtney appeared worry free, happiness personified, she was talkative, friendly, and relaxed, unrecognisable from the Courtney that had reluctantly dragged herself up the gangplank onto the ship in Argentina. She wasn't worry free though, or relaxed, or any of those things, just high on adrenaline, excited about tomorrow, about taking the next step, about joining Seanne on her journey and reaching the end.

"Are you on drugs?" asked Ruan, at one point, when she was helping to wipe down the tables.

While they worked, Heather sat alone at her laptop, drinking a coffee. She was seated at one of the comfortable, padded bench seats, curved to fit around a low table in the corner of the communal area. She watched Courtney clean the tables, chatting and laughing with Ruan and Reshma-Jade. She hadn't seen this side of Courtney before, not for any length of time, just glimpses, a smile, a joke, an irreverent comment. Courtney seemed happiest when teasing others, making fun at their expense, but now she seemed to be finding pleasure in just taking part, joining in, helping out.

Between wiping down two tables, Courtney trotted over towards Heather and bent down to speak quietly.

"What's her name?" she whispered. "The girl over there, cleaning the tables with me?"

"Reshma-Jade," said Heather.

"Thank you," she replied before returning to work.

After leaving the tables spotless and putting out some yellow, slip hazard warning signs on the wet floor, Courtney spent the afternoon helping to load equipment into the snowcats so it could be transported back to the ship. Everywhere she went, people looked at each other and shared confused looks.

Who is this person?

"Why are you so happy?" asked Gustaf at one point, as he helped her lift a large canvas holdall onto the back seat of the snowcat. "You pleased to be going home?"

"I'm not going home," said Courtney.

"Aah, you're one of those, aren't you? You're going with Seanne?"

"That's right," replied Courtney, beaming with joy.

"You think it's a good idea?" asked Gustaf.

"I think it's a great idea," replied Courtney.

"It's a terrible idea," said Gustaf, "do you know how many people die in Antarctica every year? One or two. That's how many. And the reason for that is that we're not reckless, we don't just walk off into the middle of nowhere with no thought for our own safety."

"Shaggy's going, isn't he? So, not everyone shares your opinion."

"Shaggy is one of those people who must have fallen out of a tree as a child. Banged his head or something. You speak to him for long enough, you'll see that something's not quite right, I wouldn't use him as a reason for going."

"You should have told me this yesterday," said Courtney, "because today, I don't care. Nothing's going to spoil today for me."

The sound of a snowcat could be heard faintly in the distance, getting louder and louder as it approached. They were making several trips back and forth to the ship today, so it was no surprise to see another snowcat approaching, but all eyes were drawn by the noise, the engine straining at maximum revs as it raced towards them at high speed. Just as people were starting to take a few steps back and to ask themselves if it was ever going to stop, it pulled up abruptly, to a halt.

Shaggy exited quickly through the driver's door, he jumped down and landed in a puddle of melted ice, the surface water appearing to jump out of the way as he landed.

"Hey," shouted Shaggy, in Courtney's direction, as he swaggered towards her, "got a surprise for you hiding in the back."

Shaggy offered a cigarette to Gustaf, that was politely declined, before Shaggy took one himself, lighting it at the first attempt.

"Go on, have a gander," said Shaggy, encouraging Courtney to investigate.

Courtney walked over to the snowcat but slowed and looked back towards Shaggy for reassurance.

"The back doors," he called out, "under the tarp."

Courtney opened the double rear doors to the snowcat and found a large, black tarpaulin across the luggage area that was writhing and being tossed about as someone struggled to release themselves from under its embrace. Courtney used both hands to grab a corner and pull it back. Underneath, looking rather sheepish, was Lester Cherry-Stone. He laughed long and hard when he saw the look on Courtney's face.

"I bet you weren't expecting to see me again," said Lester as he wriggled free and swung his legs over the tailgate of the snowcat.

"Oh, Lester, no," said Courtney, "what have you done?"

"Don't worry, don't worry," said Lester.

"What's happened to Hanad?" asked Courtney. "Have you killed him?"

"Nothing happened. There's nothing to worry about."

"Where's Alain?" asked Courtney. "Is he at the ship treating him now?"

"Alain's fine, he'll be here tomorrow morning. Nothing happened to Hanad. I just made a choice, that's all. Alain was right. Why did I let Hanad speak to me like that?"

"But why are you hiding in the back of a snowcat like a fugitive? It can't have been just to see my reaction. What's going on? Where's Alain's gun?"

"Alain has Alain's gun. Calm down. This was just to get me out of there without causing a scene, without me having to go through a long, emotional goodbye."

"You mean you haven't told Hanad?" asked Courtney. "Does Alain know? Is he in danger?"

"No, no, you've got Hanad all wrong."

"Do you think he'll come looking for you again?"

"Look, the guy is a bit of an ass but I don't think he overheard me, he doesn't know anything about me spying on him."

"You're a spy?" asked Courtney, in mock astonishment. She staggered back and put her hand to her mouth, eyes wide open in shock.

"You're kidding me right?" asked Lester, ready to fly off the handle.

"Come on, Mr Bond, let's get you inside," said Courtney, "we'll find you somewhere to hide."

Lester reached under the tarpaulin to feel for the handle of his bag and he pulled out a large, green, canvas holdall, stuffed to the brim.

"You got everything?" asked Courtney.

"Got everything I need."

They walked up the steps together to the research station and all the way through to the communal area. On route, Lester dropped his bag off beside the bunk he slept in, last time he stayed the night. As they walked, Courtney stopped and introduced Lester to everyone they met, even though they already knew who he was.

"Look who's here," she said, "look who it is, look who's come to visit us."

"What are you so happy about?" asked Lester, as they approached Heather, who was still sat working on her laptop at one of the tables.

"I had some good news today," said Courtney, heartlessly, "I found out that I didn't kill millions of penguins. It wasn't that many. It was only hundreds of thousands."

"Tens of thousands," said Heather, on overhearing the conversation as they approached.

"Tens of thousands?" asked Courtney. "What do you mean?"

"It was less than a hundred thousand," said Heather, "it's still pretty terrible."

"Oh, you're shitting me," said Courtney, "could this day get any better?"

"Great to see you again, Heather," said Lester as he lowered himself onto the seat next to hers.

"You up to no good?" asked Heather.

"Not this time. I just decided to come along for the ride."

Courtney was stood next to the table, bouncing up and down on tiptoes, rubbing her hands, wiping them on her hips, unable to keep still.

"Do you want to sit down?" asked Lester.

"I don't know if I can," she said, dizzily, "tens of thousands. Oh, my God. Carter asked me if I wanted to know how many had died but I said no, I thought it was going to be bad news."

"Courtney," said Heather, "if you don't want to sit down, would you be kind enough to look in the kitchen and see if there's any cooking sherry or anything. It's not too early for you, is it, Lester?"

Courtney left them alone while she searched for alcohol. Cooking sherry? Really? It sounded like anything would do so Courtney enthusiastically searched every cupboard, every storage area, anywhere big enough to hide a bottle. She found two bottles of scotch whisky, one of which was unopened, six bottles of Prosecco in a sealed cardboard box, eight cans of cider and four bottles of something called Pisco, that appeared to be alcoholic. She put all the bottles and cans together on a table in the kitchen, it was quite a collection she was curating.

"Will this do?" asked Courtney, returning to the table and presenting a bottle of Pisco as if she was a waiter in a restaurant. She had one hand underneath the bottle and one on the neck, displaying the label for them both to read.

"Forty percent, that'll do me," said Lester.

"Are we going to have to drink it out of the bottle?" asked Heather, but sarcasm couldn't dent Courtney's mood. She immediately went back to the kitchen in search of glasses. I saw them in here somewhere, she thought. Now where were they?

Courtney returned with three glasses and put them on the table. Lester opened the bottle and poured out three measures, keeping the bottle close at hand. Courtney finally calmed down enough to sit still and she joined them at the table and they drank, they talked, they laughed, and they drank some more. Afternoon turned to evening, although the light didn't change. They began to attract a crowd and the crowd drank heartily from Courtney collection of liquor.

Carter was late to the party and wasn't best pleased by Heather's inebriated state.

"What's going on here?" asked Carter. "We're meant to be cooking dinner, you and me, it's a last night tradition. You know the expedition leads always cook the food on the last night."

"I rather think I'm a bit too drunk at the moment, Carter, love," said Heather, "would you be so kind as to take care of it without me? I'm not sure I'll be much help to you."

Carter was visibly annoyed, but enough offers of help were made that he accepted the situation.

Carter came out of the kitchen an hour later to tell them that the food was ready, only to find even more drunk people feasting on snacks, tables laden with crisps, sweets and chocolate, plundered from private supplies and offered to one and all.

"Carter, have you tried these?" asked Heather, laughing uncontrollably. "They look like pigs faces."

Carter was not amused. The chicken and pasta that he cooked was well received and got high praise, although he could have presented them with almost anything and they would have eaten it.

As they interrupted their drinking to eat, Emily spotted movement outside. She moved quickly to see what was happening. A snowcat had arrived carrying Hanad's henchpersons, Hilda and Juan.

Emily watched as they exited the snowcat and Hilda instructed the driver to stay where he was. This time, they didn't wait outside to be welcomed, they made their way straight into the research station before leaning their guns up against the wall by the door. They were dressed appropriately for the mild weather, exactly how you would expect goons to dress. Military style. Military lite. Hilda was six foot tall, her long dark hair shaved on one side above the ear. Juan was slightly shorter, head fully shaved with a neatly trimmed beard and moustache.

"Shall we?" said Hilda, after they left their guns leaning against the wall, before they went looking for their prey.

Emily rushed ahead of them to warn Heather about their presence, but Heather was just getting to her feet to deliver a drunken speech to the room.

"I just want to, I wanted to just, to, erm, to say a few words, while I can still stand up," she slurred, as she slid herself upright, leaning against the wall for support, "I wanted to thank you all for your hard work, especially you, Carter. I couldn't have done it without you, but the one thing I really, really want to say to you all…"

At that precise moment the door opened and in walked Hanad's henchpersons.

First to spot them, as he was seated facing the doorway, Lester felt an urge to flee. Surely everyone would protect him this time?

"What are you two doing here?" asked Lester, in the silence that followed their entrance.

"You know why we're here?" asked Hilda.

Lester nodded.

"Hand wants to know where his drone and pilot have gone."

"No guns?" asked Lester.

"We left them by the door, we're not here to shoot anyone, mate," said Juan, "Hanad wants you back and he wants his drone back."

"What happened to the drone?" asked Courtney.

"I needed an excuse to get off the ship so I crashed it," said Lester, "it seemed like a good idea at the time."

"Did you retrieve the drone before you came here?"

"You know," said Lester, "I'm not. I don't. I'm not really. I don't think so, no. I just needed an excuse to get off the ship. I was going to get the drone but then I saw Shaggy about to leave and he hid me in the back of his snowcat. I did mean to get the drone, honestly, I did."

Lester stood up and walked away from the crowded table and beckoned Hilda and Juan to follow him.

"Look, guys," said Lester, "and dolls," he added, in respect to Hilda. Ladies present. "I appreciate you coming all this way for me but I can't go back with you. You can tell Hanad whatever you like. Tell him there was a firefight and we fought you off, or tell him you couldn't find me, or tell him I chained myself to one of the legs of the research station but, whatever you choose to tell him, I ain't going with you folks."

"You got a message for him, Lester?" asked Hilda. "Anything you'd want us to pass on?"

"Tell him I'll always be grateful for the opportunity."

"Are you two going to join us for a drink?" asked Ruan, on his way to the kitchen, but Hilda and Juan seemed to have the answer they wanted, so they made their excuses and left.

People got up to watch out of the window as Hilda and Juan left and a big cheer went up as they drove away.

"Let's drink to Hanad," someone called out and they raised their glasses and drank.

Then they toasted Hilda and Juan. Then Carter. Then Heather. When they ran out of people to toast, they just carried on drinking anyway.

After a while, Carter had seen enough.

"I'd like to say a few words, if that's all right," said a still sober Carter. His disapproval of their drinking revealed his Presbyterian roots, although he normally had no hesitation in putting those to one side and caning it with he best of them. Right now he had something to say and getting drunk wasn't going to help him to say it.

"I'd like to thank everyone who has put the hours in and done the hard work," he said, looking round the group, "to those of you who have worked extra hours or extra shifts to make up for others shortcomings, thank you. Everyone who has helped out, Midna, Reshma-Jade, Tetra, Ralph, Masha, all of you and everyone else I've forgotten to mention, thank you for your hard work. Some of the work you've done here has been heroic. Thank you Ruan, for getting this place working and keeping the lights on, the water running. Fantastic job. We're going home tomorrow and I think we can count this as a success. We came here at short notice, under-equipped and understaffed and most of you had never experienced Antarctic conditions before. We had no doctor and very little time, but we've done what we set out to do. We didn't come here to save the penguins, it was too late for that, but we came here to learn lessons for the future and that's what we've done. We found out what happened, we've documented it, we've taken samples for further analysis and, hopefully, all your hard work will stop this happening again. You're going home as heroes, to me at least."

"But, I'd like to ask you all a question," he continued, "will history judge this a success? We're so close to the end, so close to home. Will it be judged a success if we don't all make it back? If some of us choose to die rather than return? How will history judge us, the survivors? Will it praise us for putting together this expedition at short notice, or will it damn us for not doing more to stop you? Don't ruin this. I don't want your blood on my hands so I'm imploring you now. Please don't go."

"Heather," said Carter as he looked towards her, "I love working with you. You've been fantastic towards me and I understand why you might want to go tomorrow. Er, is she okay?"

All eyes turned to Heather. Her head had nodded forward, her eyes were closed and her chin was resting on her chest, while her hair fell around her face. Someone reached out and held her shoulder and shook her. Her head wobbled as her body moved, she groaned and dribbled slightly but she didn't wake up.

Unable to tell Heather what he was thinking, Carter turned his attention to Courtney.

"Look, Courtney. I've never met anyone so self-centred that they celebrate the deaths of hundreds of thousands of penguins like it's a good thing."

"It wasn't hundreds of penguins, it was thousands," said Courtney, belligerently.

"Tens of thousands," corrected Carter, "it was tens of thousands. Your selfishness knows no bounds."

"Thank you," slurred Courtney, who bowed her head in thanks and then she had to snap it back, to stop her head from spinning.

"You asked me, earlier today, if I had to save your life in return for you having saved mine. Well, that's what I'm trying to do right now. I'm asking you not to go. Not for my sake but for yours. Don't be so stupid, please. You'll die out there, from exposure, or starvation, or frostbite, or any number of things. Please reconsider what you're doing."

"And you," he said, looking straight at Seanne, "you're the worst of them all. You're a charlatan, a fraud, you're making promises to these people that you can't keep. I'm appalled that anyone would be foolish enough to follow you tomorrow. You're going to kill these people. Good people. They'll die and you'll be the one responsible."

Silence followed and then Seanne started to clap slowly, sarcastically.

"Come on, Carter, mate, sit down, have a drink with us," said Ruan.

"Fuck you. Fuck the lot of you."

Let's do this

Sometimes, it is difficult to know when you are dreaming. Courtney didn't know. She looked round to try to work out where she was. The room looked vaguely familiar, old fashioned, a bedroom. Not a child's bedroom but a grown-up room. A self-assembled, chipboard bedroom, white furniture and floral walls. A bulky portable television on a chest of drawers. Polyester curtains, crowned by a pleated pelmet. Bedside tables, three drawers, the tops cluttered with lamps, books and digital alarm clocks, red zeroes flashing. And a mirror, three mirrors in one, mounted above a dressing table. She knew she had been here before. But when?

Her thoughts were foggy. The room, she recognised it but her mind was moving too slowly to remember. She tried to recall the memory she was searching for but, before she found it, a door opened and a fourteen year old Courtney walked in and sat at the dressing table. Teenage Courtney picked up a large hairbrush and was about to run it through her hair when she stopped, she noticed something in the mirror. Someone in the corner of the room, watching her.

At first, Courtney thought she had been spotted. A cold clamminess came over her, spreading from the stomach outwards, all the way to the palms of her hands. Had she been seen? Was she caught, lurking where she shouldn't be? In her parents old bedroom, watching her teenage self, but no, it wasn't Courtney who was spotted, she was merely an observer, a dreamer, it was Courtney Two, approaching the dressing table. This was the moment. First contact. She was seeing the episode, from over twenty years ago, when her evil twin first appeared, first reached out to her, first touched her, causing her to faint and collapse to the floor.

Should she intervene? Could she even move, reach out, stop this happening? She was there, in the room, her mind was there watching, but it seemed like her body wasn't. She could see and feel her arms and legs but she couldn't move them, she couldn't control them. She couldn't reach out, she was paralysed, unable to stop the scene playing out, as it did all those years ago.

Courtney Two approached, getting closer and closer to the dressing table. Young Courtney turned her head to look but there was no one there, no one else in the room but, when she returned her gaze to the mirror, there she was, in the reflection, a doppelgänger, a teenage girl reaching out her arm as she walked closer and closer.

Courtney, still frozen in the corner, didn't see a teenage Courtney Two in the room, she saw herself, a grown woman. She had never asked herself how, or why, Courtney Two had grown along with her. How she had aged as Courtney had aged, how she was dressed as Courtney was dressed. It was the least of her worries. She was always more concerned with who she was, what she wanted, or, if you want to boil it down to the basics, whether she was good or evil. Had she seen Courtney Two like this before, whole, physically in the room, not just in a reflection? She couldn't recall. Not in real life. In a dream, maybe.

Courtney Two reached out to touch young Courtney on the shoulder and, at the first sign of any contact between them, young Courtney went limp and collapsed to the floor, her upper body falling backwards, her head landing on the edge of the soft bed before her torso slid to the ground, the weight of her body pulled her legs up and over the cushioned stool, bringing it down on top of her. She lay still, eyes closed, tucked awkwardly between the end of the bed and the upturned stool.

Courtney Two bent down to check that young Courtney was all right before she turned her attention to Courtney, still watching, still petrified, in the corner of the room. Courtney Two stepped carefully over the body, crumpled on the floor, and looked Courtney in the eye. Can she see me? thought Courtney. Can she touch me? Can she talk to me?

She was the length of the bed away from Courtney. A step closer, then another, until Courtney could feel her breath against her skin. So close. Courtney Two looked at her carefully, scrutinising her, her eyes scanning her face, her hair, her clothes.

"What are you doing?" asked Courtney Two.

"What are you doing?"

"What are you doing, Courtney?" asked Heather. You can't lie around in bed all day. Come on, wake up, Brian's here. I think he's brought bacon with him.

"Where am I?" asked Courtney, her voice a whisper, her throat parched, eyes squinting against the light.

"Come on, get up, lazy bones."

"I saw her," said Courtney, "she was here. I mean, she wasn't here but I saw her. She spoke to me."

"What are you talking about?"

"In my dream, I saw her. Courtney Two. I saw her, she spoke to me."

"What did she say?"

Courtney rubbed her eyes and sat up in bed. The curtains were open and the room was flooded with light. What time was it? Heather was already dressed and Seanne's bed was empty. How long have I been asleep? thought Courtney. She couldn't even remember going to bed, the last thing she could remember was Hilda and Juan arriving. Were they still here? Was Lester still here?

"Is Lester still here?" asked Courtney.

"Of course he is," said Heather, who showed no signs of having drunk herself into a coma last night, she was as fresh faced, clear headed and raring to go as she had ever been.

"What did she say?" asked Heather.

"Who?"

"Courtney Two. In your dream. You said she spoke to you, what did she say?"

"I...I...don't remember. I can't remember what she said, but I remember her face. The look on her face. She was worried about me. I can't remember what she said but I remember what her face said."

"And what did her face say?" asked Heather, reluctantly. She didn't need this today. The plan was to get up, breakfast and then go. The plan didn't involve her nursemaiding Courtney, the plan didn't involve spending the morning persuading Courtney that she was doing the right thing.

"She seemed disappointed in me, like I was doing the wrong thing. Like your parents face when you get dressed for a night out. Disapproving. What does it mean?"

"Tell her to suck it up," said Emily, "if she doesn't get up soon, we're going to be late."

"It means it's time to get up," said Heather, "you'll find out what it means when we get to the shaman. Stop fretting and get some clothes on and pack."

"That told her," said Emily, "high five?"

"High five," said Heather as she high-fived Emily.

"What?" asked Courtney. "Oh, Emily, hi Emily, sorry, I didn't realise the you were here."

"I'm always here," said Emily.

Courtney dragged her reluctant body out of bed and stretched her arms high above her head, up on tiptoes, then a yawn and that was her daily exercise done. She had to sit down on the edge of the bed to get dressed as she soon realised that she was unsteady on her feet. Her head was still throbbing from last night, her eyes were dry and sore, her lips cracked. She struggled into some loose fitting jogging bottoms and decided to start the day with a long overdue shower. She found a towel hanging on the back of a chair that felt dry enough to use. It wan't hers, did that matter?

Then she walked a short distance along the corridor to one of the bathrooms and she showered.

The water woke her up and focused her mind, but she was still parched, still thirsty, so she licked the water from her lips and lifted her face up to drink the warm shower water. Bad idea. She spat it out but it did the trick, it took away the worst of the dryness, moisturised her gums and tongue. Legionnaire's disease was the least of her worries at the moment.

She dried and wrapped herself in someone else's towel and returned to her bunk to get properly dressed. Courtney knew that she would have to carry any clothes she didn't wear so she wore plenty and packed the rest away in her rucksack. She gathered up the remainder of her belongings and put them on the bed to pack later. Some items she still needed to use, like her toothbrush after breakfast, so she left it next to her rucksack. Should she make the bed? Not now. I'm sure someone else will do it. She wanted to lie down, have another five or ten minutes sleep. The invigorating effect of the shower had worn off very quickly. Still half asleep, she left the bedroom and walked the wrong way along the corridor, she opened the door at the end and walked into the entrance pod where Carter was sat at a computer.

Courtney looked round, this wasn't where she was meant to be, she was meant to be going to breakfast. How did she end up here?

"What are you doing?" asked Carter.

"Why did you say that?" asked Courtney.

"Well, you look lost," said Carter, "are you all right? Do you remember much from last night?"

"I was meant to be going for breakfast," said Courtney, who was not quite sure how she had ended up stood where she was, "I must have gone the wrong way, I'm feeling a bit delicate."

"Breakfast is that way," said Carter, pointing towards the door that Courtney had just come in through.

She turned and walked through the pods, following the smell of cooked bacon and eggs, until she got to the communal pod. She must have been the last one to get out of bed and, looking around, no one else looked as bad as she felt.

She walked over to the coffee machine, picked up a cup and put it in the machine. She pressed the button but nothing happened. She pressed it again, still nothing. She took the cup out and looked round for help, but there was none. Was it really worth walking over to a table of people and asking if someone could help her. It wasn't worth the loss of self respect. She would just have orange juice instead.

"What are you doing?" asked Brian as he loomed up behind her. "Do you need a hand?"

"What did you say?" asked Courtney, turning to address Brian.

"Do you need a hand?" asked Brian. "I heard about last night. Have one too many did you?"

"Before that. What did you say?"

"I asked you what you were doing?"

"Why did you ask me that?"

"Erm...well, because you looked like you were struggling. I was just trying to help."

"Could you make me a coffee, please?" asked Courtney. "I can't get it to work."

"How do you like it?" asked Brian, taking the cup out of Courtney's hand.

"I like my coffee like my men, milk with one sugar," said Courtney. She blushed with embarrassment when she realised it made no sense, but at least it brought some colour to her deathly white face.

Team Seanne were all sat together at one table, with Seanne holding court. Courtney went to sit next to Heather but was told that she couldn't.

"Sorry, but Emily is sat there," said Heather so Courtney sat next to Emily instead.

"How are you feeling?" asked a concerned Lester.

"Worse than I look," said Courtney.

"You made it then?" she asked Alain, who was no longer dressed like a doctor. He had cast off his doctor persona and was back to being Alain, boring old Alain. He missed it already, the dressing up, the paraphernalia, the power, he felt naked without it. Struck off in his prime.

Brian walked up to the table and placed a plate in front of Courtney containing a full English breakfast.

"For you, my lady," said Brian, "kitchen's closing, you want anything else?" he asked, looking around the table. He was greeted by a succession of people saying, "No, thank you," and, "Sorry, I couldn't eat any more." Courtney pushed the plate away from her, blowing out her cheeks and making a retching noise.

Forks descended on her plate stripping it before her eyes until all that was left was some unhappy looking scrambled egg and a few forkfuls of baked beans. Brian went round the table clearing away the empty plates, stacking them as he went, before taking them back into the kitchen.

"Shall we meet back here in half an hour?" asked Seanne, smiling from ear to ear as she stood up. She was so close. So close to her goal. Her whole life had been building to this moment. She had thought she would have to face it alone but here she was, with friends. She never thought she would find anyone foolish enough to go with her. Anyone brave enough to go with her. It was a rare combination that was required and she had found it here.

The people at the table began to wander off, bags to pack, goodbyes to say. Shaggy went outside to check over the snowcat, Heather, Emily, Masha and Reshma-Jade all got up to leave. Lester got up to get himself another Irish coffee, to see him through the morning.

"What are you doing?" asked Alain, once the two of them were left alone.

"What am I doing?" asked Courtney. "What am I doing Alain?"

"I'm not sure what you mean," said Alain.

"She asked me, what am I doing?"

"Who did?"

"Courtney Two," said Courtney, "and Heather, and Carter, and Brian and now you. Tell me, Alain, please, I can trust you, what am I doing?"

"Feeling sorry for yourself, by the sound of it. How much did you have to drink last night?"

"I'm serious, Alain, Tell me what I'm doing."

"You're about to join us all on the experience of a lifetime, a hike out into the Antarctic wilderness to find the site of a shaman that has been hidden for years. Do you want answers or not?"

"It doesn't make any sense," said Courtney.

"Does anything ever make any sense?"

"Yes, things usually make sense, but this? Does this? I feel like I'm trapped in my own indecision. It's a nightmare."

"You've already decided to go though, haven't you?" asked Alain.

"I have, but..."

"No buts. If evil Courtney is trying to tell you something then you have to go, to find out what she's trying to say."

"But what if it's all in my imagination?"

"Then where's the harm?" asked Alain.

"But what if we die?"

"We're all going to die, Courtney, you can't put it off forever."

"But what if it's not my time yet?"

"Come here," said Alain, standing up and approaching Courtney with his arms outstretched.

She reluctantly stood up and let herself be hugged by Alain. It'll make him feel better, she thought, but the close physical contact, the warmth of another body was reassuringly comfortable so she wrapped her arms around Alain and hugged him back.

"You want answers, don't you?" asked Alain, as he released her from his grasp.

"Yes," said Courtney, with some caution.

"Then let's go. Pack your bags and meet back here," said Alain, "we're going to do this."

"Whether it kills us or not?" asked Courtney.

"That's right. Whether it kills us or not," replied Alain, nodding in agreement and smiling broadly, "after all, what have we got to live for, eh?"

It wasn't long before they were all gathered back at the table ready to go. Seanne checked that everyone was ready and then she led the way towards the main entrance to the research station, ahead of a train of people, rucksacks, excitement, anticipation, enthusiasm, anxiety and fear.

Ruan and a number of the others formed a loose guard of honour to see them out, patting them on the back and wishing them well.

When they got to the door, Carter was waiting for them. Heather walked up to him and kissed him goodbye, on the cheek.

"Carter," said Heather.

"Yes, Boss."

"Don't forget to lock up when you leave and put the key under the mat, otherwise no one will be able to get back in."

"I'll try to remember."

"Carter," said Courtney.

"Could you make my bed for me before you leave, I didn't have time this morning."

"And mine," said Seanne.

"And mine."

"And mine."

"And mine."

"Leave the place nice and tidy for the Chileans," said Heather, "otherwise it reflects badly on me. And write a note to them apologising for drinking all the alcohol. Do it in my name and sign it for me will you?"

They all gathered by the door to the research station, lightly clothed, sunglasses ready, bags packed.

Heather looked out of the window to find Emily. She was stood next to the snowcat waving up at the window. Shaggy was sat down on one of the snowcat tracks taking a long drag on a cigarette.

"Where's Emily? Is she here?" asked Seanne.

"She's too excited to wait in here, she can't stand still," said Heather, "she's outside waiting for us to follow her, I can see her out the window."

"Okay then, everyone ready?" asked Brian.

The response was mostly in the affirmative, and mainly enthusiastic, but not enthusiastic enough for Brian, who used his pantomime training to gee up the crowd.

"I said, is everyone ready?" he asked again, only louder, as that's what they teach you in pantomime training school, well, that and the behind-you thing.

"Let's do this," said Brian, at the top of his voice, banging his fist several times against the wall by the door, eliciting whoops and cheers from the assembled group.

Then, Seanne opened the door and they left, single file, down the stairs.

Epilogue

Nothing is known of what happened to Courtney, Heather, Seanne, or their companions. Repeated searches failed to uncover their fate. Some people believe that Seanne found her shaman and he provided answers to all their questions and then, suitably enlightened, they choose not to return to their previous lives and they lived out their days, content and worldly-wise. Others say that they perished on the ice and were eaten by polar bears, or they were picked apart by penguins, or they turned on each other when things became desperate.

I fear that we'll never find out the truth, although they have only been missing for ten days...

Printed in Great Britain
by Amazon